Should duty come before love?

The windswept islands of the Outer Hebrides
are a close-knit community, where the local laird
lives to serve his people, and outsiders aren't
always welcome. But as the MacDonald family
moves between London and the isles,
all that could be about to change...

Book 1

A Laird for the Governess

The Laird of Ardmore has sworn never
to remarry...until he meets his feisty
new governess!

Available now

And look for books 2 and 3 coming soon!

Author Note

On Wednesday, January 24, 1810, three women desperately seeking work as governesses presented themselves at Mrs. Gray's hiring agency in London. Marianne, on the run from her predatory stepbrother, was sent to the residence of the Earl of Kingswood (*The Earl's Runaway Governess*). Mary, desperate to clear her imprisoned father's name, made her way to Sir Nicholas Denny in Norfolk (*A Waltz with the Outspoken Governess*). This book tells the story of Lydia, who travels far, far away to the Outer Hebrides, to a lonely laird and a sickly child. Each book can be read as a stand-alone tale.

This book is the first in a new series set between London and the Hebrides. In book two, Angus and his sister, Eilidh, will travel to London with the aim of persuading an English lord to sell land back to the Hebridean people. Little do they know that, while there, they will each meet their match.

I have really enjoyed researching the Hebrides for this series. I do hope you enjoy reading it!

CATHERINE TINLEY

—

A Laird for
the Governess

HARLEQUIN®
HISTORICAL™

Recycling programs
for this product may
not exist in your area.

ISBN-13: 978-1-335-40769-6

A Laird for the Governess

This edition published by arrangement with Harlequin Books S.A.

For questions and comments about the quality of this book,
please contact us at CustomerService@Harlequin.com.

Harlequin Enterprises ULC
22 Adelaide St. West, 41st Floor
Toronto, Ontario M5H 4E3, Canada
www.Harlequin.com

Printed in U.S.A.

Catherine Tinley has loved reading and writing since childhood, and has a particular fondness for love, romance and happy endings. She lives in Ireland with her husband, children, dog and kitten, and can be reached at catherinetinley.com, as well as through Facebook and on Twitter, @catherinetinley.

Books by Catherine Tinley

Harlequin Historical

Christmas Cinderellas
"A Midnight Mistletoe Kiss"
A Waltz with the Outspoken Governess

Lairds of the Isles

A Laird for the Governess

The Ladies of Ledbury House

The Earl's Runaway Governess
Rags-to-Riches Wife
Captivating the Cynical Earl

The Chadcombe Marriages

Waltzing with the Earl
The Captain's Disgraced Lady
The Makings of a Lady

Visit the Author Profile page
at Harlequin.com.

For my Hebridean friend

Tapadh leat, a Charaid

Chapter One

Ardmore Castle, Hebrides, Scotland—January 1810

'I must speak with you, sir.'

Alasdair looked up, his brows knitting with frustration. 'Mrs MacLeod, there is nothing so urgent that it cannot wait until later, when I have finished reading.'

Mrs MacLeod drew herself up to her full height, outrage evident in the line of her body and the expression on her face. Since she was at least a foot smaller than Alasdair, the impact was perhaps rather less than she had intended. 'Sir, I must insist! It is about your daughter.'

Now he was alert. 'Something ails Mairead? What is the matter?'

'Well, yes and no. We both know she is a sickly, weak child—'

He winced at the description, his right hand silently gripping his precious copy of Dante's *Inferno* until the knuckles turned white.

'—and has been since her sickness, but she is six now, though she may look like four.'

'Your point, Mrs MacLeod?'

'Now then, no need to take that tone with me, Alasdair MacDonald. You may be the Laird and I the housekeeper, but I skelped your backside many a time when you were a child yourself. Usually for stealing cakes from the castle kitchens.'

Alasdair could not help it. Despite himself, he grinned. Setting down his book, he leaned back in his comfortable armchair. 'Very well. You have something to say about Mairead and I might as well hear it.'

Mrs MacLeod's eyes narrowed, then she nodded, as if satisfying herself that he was in earnest. 'I am no teacher. Nor am I a nursemaid. She needs more now than what I and the others can do for her.'

Alasdair shrugged. 'I have tried many times to find a governess for her. You know how difficult it is to attract strangers to the islands. Is there no-one in the castle fit to take over teaching her? What of looking in Stornoway, or over in Skye?'

Mrs MacLeod was shaking her head. 'There is no-one befitting her. She is daughter to the Laird and she needs a proper education. Despite being sickly, there is nothing wrong with her mind. I declare she has my head turned with questions I cannot answer, "But *why* is the sky blue, Mrs MacLeod?" "Why do the flowers go away in winter?" "Why am I six now?"'

A pang of guilt went through him. Six years. Six years since Mairead had arrived in their lives, mewling like a cat and sucking her fists. More than five years then, since Hester…

'Sir?'

I cannot teach her myself. It pains me to be in conflict with her.

'I shall write again to the agency in Edinburgh. Perhaps they will find someone suitable this time.'

'And if they do not?'

He shrugged. 'You must do the best you can. She is only six. How hard can it be?'

The half-growl, half-exclamation that emerged from Mrs MacLeod at this gave him to understand that his answer was unsatisfactory. Having no other reply to give her, he simply waited until she turned on her heel and stomped off.

Turning to his book again, he was vexed to discover his attention for reading was gone, like mist off the loch. Picking up a pen, he began drafting yet another letter to the employment agency in Edinburgh. Maybe this time they would find someone willing to take on a stubborn, sickly child on a remote island on the very edge of the world.

London

Yet again, Miss Lydia Farnham, governess, was in trouble. Despite taking a post with a quiet family with—she had specifically checked—*no* young gentlemen, vexation had found her once more. It had found her in the form of the Honourable Geoffrey Barnstable, who was much less honourable than his title suggested. An uncle to her charges, and unmarried, he had taken to visiting at odd hours, demanding to see his young nephews to 'check how they were doing with their book-learning'.

In reality, Lydia knew he had come to discompose
her once again and she was becoming increasingly tired
of it. 'Good day, Mr Barnstable. How may we assist
you?'

'My dear Miss Farnham! As always, it is a delight to
see you—and in such looks!' He bent over her glove-
less hand, smearing it with a wet kiss. Shuddering, she
crossed the room to ring the bell for tea, surreptitiously
wiping her hand in a fold of her printed muslin dress.
The sooner she could get a housemaid into the room
with her, the better.

The Honourable Geoffrey had, thankfully, moved
to the table where the young Barnstable twins were
bent over their slates, working diligently through their
arithmetic. 'Good boys. Well done,' he said generally,
then turned back to Lydia, rubbing his hands together.
'I declare you are a marvel, Miss Farnham. Brains as
well as beauty!' He gave a sickly smile, revealing snuff-
stained brown teeth.

'Please be seated, Mr Barnstable.' She indicated a
straight chair a good three feet from her own armchair.
He would hopefully find it difficult to molest her from
there. 'The boys are good students and a credit to their
family.'

*Unlike you, who bring shame to them with your odi-
ous behaviour.*

'Yes, yes, I do not doubt it.' He sat, but leaned forward, his eyes sweeping across her, lingering on her
chest. 'And how are *you*, Miss Farnham. Are you happy
here?'

'I am content, sir.' Resisting the temptation to ad-
just the lace fichu she had tucked into the neckline of

her dress for modesty, she reflected briefly on her own answer. Apart from his visits, she generally was content here. The boys were easy students, Lord and Lady Barnstable sensible employers—although Lady Barnstable could be rather demanding—and her wages were decent. Her retirement fund remained small, but this was the longest period of paid employment she had had since her father's death, five years before.

When she had first become a governess, she had not anticipated that the greatest challenge to her ongoing employment would be the unwanted advances of dishonourable men. She had managed to fend Mr Barnstable off for nearly a year already and, if the housemaid would but hurry, she might escape his clutches for another day. Lady Barnstable, the Honourable Geoffrey's sister-in-law, had not yet descended and would no doubt still be enjoying her morning dish of chocolate in her bedchamber. Which was exactly the reason Geoffrey was here so early.

'It pains me that so beautiful a lady should be hiding away as a governess.' Reaching across the gap between them, he took her hand.

Instantly, she snapped it away. 'Sir, please do not—'

It was too late. Leaping from his chair, he was beside her, bending over her threateningly. 'Lydia! My dear! You must know that I am mad with love for you!' Hauling her to her feet, he enveloped her in a tight and entirely unwelcome embrace. He smelled of onions, snuff and old sweat.

'Stop! Sir! Do not!' Conscious that the children would also be distressed by what was happening, she pushed at him as hard as she could and stamped on his foot for good measure.

'Ow! I say, no need for that, my girl!'

'The children!' she managed to say. She was trembling from head to toe.

Why does this keep happening to me?

It worked—to some extent. Looking a little shamefaced, he adjusted his cravat, sending a sickly smile towards the boys. 'Miss Farnham and I were just having a little wrestle.'

A little wrestle!

Lydia closed her eyes briefly. Oh, where was Sally? Or Rose? Or any of the housemaids? It seemed like an age since she had rung the bell, although it was probably only a few minutes.

He stepped towards her again and she took a step back, feeling the edge of the chair behind her. 'Lydia! Your modesty does you credit, but I should have made myself clearer. I want no mere dalliance. I am devoted to you. You must know it!'

Was he actually planning to make her an offer of marriage? Surely he would think a mere governess beneath him?

I could not marry him—no, not even for the financial security it would bring. He is abhorrent to me.

'Sir, I appreciate the sentiment, but I cannot return it. I—'

'But only listen, my darling Lydia!' He took both of her hands in his own. His were small, puffed with fat and slick with sweat. 'I have found the most perfect apartment in Mayfair. You can live there and want for nothing. You will have jewels and furs, and servants to command!'

As it dawned on her that his offer was insulting in every way to her character, her morals and her respectability, he pressed on, oblivious. 'My dear! Say yes and come with me this very day, for I can wait no longer to have you in my bed!' Closing the space between them, he embraced her once again and this time she was not quick enough to turn her head to avoid him. His hot mouth pressed on hers, his teeth banging painfully on her lips and his arms closing around her like a vice. Overcome by fear, she whimpered, bringing her hands up to push ineffectually against his paunch.

Dimly, she heard the door open.

Thank goodness!

He would surely have to stop once the housemaid made herself known. They all knew of the Honourable Geoffrey's fixation with the governess and had helped her defuse his ardour on many previous occasions. Never had he tried to kiss her before, though.

'What on earth is going on? Miss Farnham! Geoffrey!'

Instantly, Geoffrey released her and Lydia sagged in relief. Her head was spinning and her senses entirely disordered. He stepped away from her and she collapsed in a heap on the armchair, trembling.

Lady Barnstable marched into the room, clearly outraged. 'Boys, go and find your nurse. You are excused from lessons for the day.'

Needing no second invitation, the twins scampered out of the room without looking back. Lydia had the presence of mind to take one last look at them. She would never see them again, she knew.

'Geoffrey, I thank you for your visit. We shall see you tomorrow, perhaps.' Lady Barnstable was all icy disdain. Geoffrey adjusted his cravat once again, muttered a word of farewell to his sister-in-law and took flight, closing the door behind him. *Like the coward you are*, Lydia thought bitterly.

There was a silence. Gathering herself, Lydia stood to face her employer. Despite her trembling, she lifted her chin.

'Well? Have you anything to say?' Lady Barnstable's tone was harsh.

'There is little point in my saying anything, my lady.' Lydia spoke quietly. 'In such cases the woman is usually blamed, although I have done nothing to encourage Mr Barnstable's attentions.'

Lady Barnstable snorted in disbelief. 'You are a liar, Miss Farnham. To think that I have had such a Jezebel in my own house, teaching my precious children... You are to leave this house immediately and without any further salary. Do you understand me?'

Lydia eyed her defiantly. 'I understand you well enough, my lady. I should not wish to remain in a household where a young lady cannot go unmolested by a dishonourable gentleman such as Mr Barnstable.'

'How dare you tell such falsehoods!' She leaned closer. 'I promise you, Miss Farnham, if you dare to besmirch the reputation of my brother-in-law, I shall ensure that you never have work again with any decent family.'

Lydia had heard enough. Without another word she spun on her heel and swept out of the drawing room, leaving the door wide open.

An hour later, she signed her name in the registry at Mrs Gray's employment agency, a place she had had occasion to visit before. Praying that Mrs Gray would have a suitable position for her, she took a seat in the waiting room, noting that there were two other young ladies already there before her, both of whom could potentially be seeking governess positions. Her heart sank. Amid the cooks and footmen, grooms and serving maids, she had hoped to find an opportunity suited to her skills and position.

Miss Anne Bolton was called in to see Mrs Gray and emerged a half-hour later, giving a small smile of what looked like encouragement. By this stage Lydia had moved to sit next to the other young lady, a Miss Smith, and they were conversing politely. After Miss Smith was called in, Lydia sat as quietly as she could, trying to keep her mind focused. Her small savings would not last long. London lodgings were so expensive! If she could find a cheap place, she had perhaps four months, maybe five, in which to find a post without having to seriously compromise her savings.

The door to Mrs Gray's inner sanctum opened and Miss Smith walked out. Hurrying across to Lydia, she bent to share the news that Mrs Gray had offered her a temporary position in Norfolk, which was exactly where she wanted to be. Her eyes shining, she wished Lydia similar good fortune, then hurried on.

Three more prospects—grooms or footmen, per-haps—were called in, emerging with expressions re-lieved or disappointed, and then, finally, it was Lydia's turn. 'Miss Farnham.'

Her heart pounding, Lydia followed Mrs Gray into her office. The agency owner took her place behind the now familiar rosewood desk and Lydia took her seat, awaiting the inevitable question.

'Well, Miss Farnham? Can you explain how it is that, less than a year since I placed you with the Barnstables, you are returned to me?'

Lydia eyed her helplessly. 'I tried really hard this time, Mrs Gray. I tied my hair in the severest of styles. I wore a fichu every day and only the plainest and loosest of gowns. I barely engaged in conversation with gentle-men and avoided them as much as I could…'

'And yet, here you are.' Mrs Gray's eyes softened briefly. 'Your beauty, Miss Farnham, cannot be hid-den with such tricks and, unfortunately, we both know what some men are.'

'Then you believe me?' She laughed sourly. 'For ev-eryone else seems to instantly think of me as the worst of temptresses.'

'Who was it this time?' Mrs Gray frowned. 'Never say it was Lord Barnstable? I thought it safe to place you there, for it is said he is devoted to his wife.'

'Well, he is,' Lydia replied shortly. 'His brother, how-ever, has taken to visiting their home with increasing frequency.'

Mrs Gray's eyes widened. 'The dishonourable Geof-frey! I might have known!' She shook her head. 'I apol-ogise, Miss Farnham. I should have anticipated this.'

She sighed. 'The difficulty is, no matter where I place you, there will be some heedless man who may eventually start pawing you.'

Lydia shuddered. 'But what am I to do? I cannot change my face, nor my figure. How I wish I were ugly, or a wizened old hag!'

Mrs Gray laughed and patted her hand. 'We both understand the propensity of the world to judge by appearances. I, too, have suffered—although not for any beauty!'

'I can only imagine!' Mrs Gray's skin was dark, her family clearly originating from somewhere in Africa, and yet she had succeeded in building this, one of the busiest hiring agencies in London.

There was a pause, as the two women silently acknowledged each other's struggles.

Mrs Gray nodded firmly. 'I know your character, Miss Farnham. And I know you are a skilled teacher. Now, where can I place you...?'

She closed her dark eyes for a moment and placed both sets of fingertips on her temples. Lydia held her breath, sending up a silent prayer.

Finally, Mrs Gray opened her eyes again. 'You should understand, Miss Farnham, that I have already placed two governesses today.'

Lydia nodded. 'I made Miss Smith's acquaintance. She told me of her posting to Norfolk.'

'A temporary post, but it suited her. The other young lady I have sent to a family in Bedfordshire. That leaves me with only two options for you, Miss Farnham.'

I have options? 'Yes?' Lydia breathed.

'I frequently get requests for temporary governesses

and nursemaids for the duration of the Season. Such posts begin around March and last until June. You might come back in March and see if I have any possibilities.'

Lydia's heart sank, although temporary work was better than nothing, she supposed. 'And the other option?'

Rising, Mrs Gray walked to the table on Lydia's left and lifted a pile of letters. Finding the one she wanted, she brought it back to the desk. 'As I recall, Miss Farnham, you were governess and nurse to young Master Pickering for a time, is that correct?'

'It is.' John Pickering had been thrown from his pony and been paralysed from the waist down at the age of nine. He had been a difficult challenge, Lydia recalled, as his moods would swing towards darkness on many occasions.

'And you were able to manage his care?'

'I was—although I will admit I found it challenging at times.'

'Was that why you left?'

'No! I loved looking after John. It was not that. It was…'

Mrs Gray eyed her steadily.

'John's older brother developed a—a partiality for me. His mama, naturally, did not approve.'

And I was blamed on that occasion as well.

'Ah, yes. I remember now.' Mrs Gray opened the letter and Lydia's gaze dropped to it. Might this be the answer to her prayers? 'I have here an appeal from a friend who owns a similar employment agency. In Edinburgh.'

'Edinburgh. *Scotland?*'

'Yes. Would you have any objection to Scotland?'

'Well, no, of course not. It is just—I have never even been to the north of England. I—'

Mrs Gray set the letter down. 'It is of no matter. Perhaps we should focus on getting you a posting here in London, for the Season.'

'But no, I—can you tell me more about the family in Scotland?'

'Very well. They live on Benbecula, a remote island, I understand—in a place called Ardmore. No, I have not heard of it either. The Laird is widowed and his only child is sickly and does not walk. Her name is Margaret, although she is known as—' she consulted the letter '—Mairead. I am not sure I have pronounced that correctly. The child is six years old.'

'Margaret.' Despite herself, Lydia's heart went out to the unknown child. She knew well how hard little John had found his affliction and she had developed a good understanding of how to help him with his black moods. But the Laird...

'A widower?'

Mrs Gray sighed. 'I understand you. He may be just as challenging as some of the other men you have encountered, but I have always found the Scots to be less tolerant of bad behaviour in their men. There are good people and bad people everywhere, but—and I shall be frank with you, Miss Farnham—I find the young men of the *ton* to be among the most self-indulgent, the most *arrogant* I have encountered. There is something in the manner of their raising—the larks they kick up at University, the gaming hells and places of dubious reputation they frequent here... I believe it encourages some of them to believe they are entitled to behave in whatever manner they wish. My understanding of rural Scotland—and rural England, to be fair—is that they adhere to stricter standards of moral behaviour. In that sense I believe you will have a better chance of being safe from unwanted advances outside the city.'

'I see.' Lydia thought about it for a moment. It made a certain kind of sense. 'What would the salary be? And are there any allowances?'

Mrs Gray smiled. 'I admire a woman who has a good head for the important questions.'

She named a salary that was three times what Lydia had been earning in London, making her gasp. 'Why so generous?'

'They live so remotely that they have struggled to attract prospects to their island. The child has never been properly taught and has physical challenges as well. The Laird's generosity makes sense.' Mrs Gray went on to detail the other benefits—a tea allowance, days off and even an allowance for books.

Lydia, herself a great reader, breathed in amazement. 'A book allowance? How wonderful!'

'Yes, well, it will be difficult to call into Hookham's Lending Library when you are living in Ardmore,' Mrs Gray pointed out drily. 'So, shall I write to Edinburgh to confirm you accept the post?'

Lydia nodded firmly. 'Please do.'

Chapter Two

A little over four weeks later, Lydia set off from Glasgow on what would be the last part of her protracted journey. Her new employer had behaved with reassuring generosity so far, paying for a private carriage and good-quality accommodation to ease the pain of the longest journey she had ever taken. Three days in a rattling coach along the full length of the Great North Road had brought her to Edinburgh—or Dùn Èideann, as some of the locals called it. The schedule had even allowed for two nights in the Scottish capital and she had spent the day in between visiting the new town, glimpsing the glowering castle up above and allowing her body to settle after days and days of uncomfortable travel. The accents were strangely pleasing and she had been treated with respect everywhere she had gone.

The journey westwards took a full day, until finally, one morning in early March, the Broomielaw docks were before her. The Laird, Alexander MacDonald, had written to thank Lydia for accepting the post and had introduced her in writing to his steward, Mr Crawford.

The steward had followed up by letter to explain that she was to end her travels with a journey by ship— a *ship*, for goodness sake!—from Glasgow to a place called Lochboisdale, where someone would meet her. It all sounded extremely daunting and, as she stood on the bustling docks in the pre-dawn chill, a shiver went through her.

Lydia was ashamed to admit that her familiarity with the geography of Greece and Rome, gleaned during her studies of the antiquities, was better than her knowledge of Scotland. She had, naturally, never left England before, although she had twice visited the seaside town of Brighton, there to appreciate the salty air and impressive mass of water. Nothing, however, had prepared her for the prospect of boarding an actual ship and crossing the sea.

The *Mercury* was a pretty sloop with a tall mast and wide mainsail. Lydia eyed it warily, knowing in her head there was no reason why *this* ship should sink on *this* day, just because she was aboard, and yet her stomach was tight with nervousness. When the time came she moved slowly and carefully up the bouncing gangway with what she hoped was an air of calm, and was pleased that the Captain himself came forward to welcome her and lead her to a small cabin which was, he said, to be hers for the duration of the journey. The *Mercury*, he assured her, was perfectly sound and was only five years old, having been constructed in Kelton by master craftsmen. She thanked him for the information, reflecting ruefully that her nervousness must have been plainly apparent.

Her trunks were brought to her cabin shortly afterwards, but rather than hide there, she emerged with great daring to stand on the deck and drink in the sights and sounds that were so strange and new—the bustling pier, the creak and roll of the ship under her feet, the calling of the enormous and decidedly intimidating gulls. When they set sail at sunrise she made the acquaintance of the cabin boy, who laughed at her unsteadiness, but provided her with the names of the beautiful places they would pass—Dunoon and Rothesay on the mighty Clyde, then Kintyre and Arran, Islay and Mull…the names to her seemed fantastical, like something out of a Gothic romance or ancient tale. Gradually her nervousness gave way to calm and then eventually to a dreamy tedium, as if she was destined to stand on this deck for ever, eyeing the magnificent landscapes and adjusting her footing to the pitch and roll of the creaking vessel.

After dark she read by candlelight in her cabin, dined with the Captain and three other gently-born passengers, then tried to sleep in her narrow cot. Tried and failed. Lying awake in the darkness, she reflected on the strangeness that her decision had brought. She was not even going to Scotland, it seemed. She had left mainland Scotland and was now sailing to some tiny islands on the very edge of the old world, to an employer she knew little about.

Laird, not Lord. She frowned. What was the difference? Mr Crawford had referred to her employer as 'The Much Honoured Alexander MacDonald, Laird of Ardmore'. It was not a style of address she had come across before. And despite his name being Alexander,

the Laird had signed himself Alasdair. It was all too
confusing. Would the differences from everything she
knew be too much? After tossing and turning for an age,
she eventually fell into a fitful and unsatisfying sleep.

    She awoke in darkness, momentarily confused, then
recognising that the sound she had just heard was a
gentle tapping on her door. 'Time to rise, miss!' It was
the cabin boy. 'South Uist ahead!'

    South Uist? The name was unfamiliar. She rose,
washed and dressed quickly, then made her way to the
deck, surprised to find she was having to relearn the
steadiness of gait she had developed the day before. She
clutched her cloak tightly around her, reassured to see
the faintest hint of dawn behind and to the right of the
ship. *That means we are going north-west*, she told herself, absurdly pleased at her own deduction. Perhaps her
book-learning might give her an anchor of familiarity in
this world of unknowns. Making her way to the front—
the bow, she reminded herself—she spotted the cabin
boy. 'What was the name of the place you mentioned?'

    'South Uist, miss. We are to dock there soon. That's
where you will leave us.'

    'But am I not to leave at Lochboisdale?'

    'Lochboisdale? Aye.' He corrected her pronunciation,
making the 'bois' sound like 'boys'. 'That's the place
in South Uist where we shall leave you.'

    Realisation dawned. 'So South Uist is the name of
the island?'

    'That's it, aye.' He was looking at her as if she were
to be pitied. 'You do not know where you are going?'

'No.' She shook her head. 'I have no idea where I am going.'

No idea where, nor why, nor what will become of me. This, surely, is the greatest act of idiocy I have ever committed. She gripped the rail on the side of the ship with both hands, conscious of an overwhelming sense of fear. *Lord, what am I doing?* Her stomach churned, her mouth was dry and her palms were suddenly slick with sweat. Oh, why had she been so foolish? If she were turned off in these remote islands, it would be almost impossible to make her way even to Edinburgh, never mind London.

She was used to being alone since Mama and Papa had died, but she still missed them. Papa had been a lawyer and had paid for her to have a good education, but after his sudden death it was clear that Lydia would have to work, as his savings had been limited. Working—and working hard—was not something which bothered Lydia.

What did bother her, and it bothered her very deeply, was the feeling of being completely alone in the world. She had no anchor, no confidant, no-one to advise her or offer wise counsel. She had to be entirely reliant on her own wits and the echoes of her parents' voices in her memory.

Briefly, she allowed herself to recall the grief and despair she had faced after Papa's death. By the time she had begun to recover, his meagre savings had diminished to the point where she had had no option but to seek employment. He had intended to help her find a good husband, she knew, and those savings were to have been her dowry. Instead, he had been taken by a

sudden heart attack, just a year after Mama had perished from a fever, and Lydia's dowry had paid for her
rent and food in those dark days when she had barely
been able to look after herself.

The cabin boy was still talking. 'You can see South
Uist on the port side.' He pointed left. 'Or you *will* see
it, leastways, once the sun rises.'

Her head swung round immediately, her eyes picking out the thin arc of land that was to be her destination. As if in a trance she made her way to that side, the
faintest trace of her own shadow ahead of her. There she
stood, her eyes fixed on the grey curves of land amid the
grey sea and the grey sky, barely seen in the pre-dawn
gloom. Gradually, the sun rose behind her, painting the
scene with colour—first, the palest of hints, then gradually deepening and strengthening as if the world was
being warmed into beauty. The sky—grey, white, pale
blue, then a deep azure. The sea, mirroring itself into
a blue-grey restless froth. And the land, a gentle line
of blue-tinted hills. The line of land thickened as they
approached the bay, revealing itself in a slow uncov-
ering of colour and shape, tint and form. The vegetation looked brown, not green, which was disconcerting.
Where were the fields?

Shouts from the sailors alerted her to the fact they
were making anchor offshore and the cabin boy ad-
vised her to make ready. Lydia took a breath, retied her
bonnet, checked she had her reticule, then waited. Two
sailors brought her trunks and called for her to follow.
She made for the place where she had entered the day
before, curious about what would happen next. They
waited, while a small, brightly-painted boat approached

from the nearby shore. The pier was clearly too small for a ship to dock. As well as her trunks, there were three crates of what must be provisions and she eyed the small boat nervously.

'Is it really safe for all of that to go in that small boat?'

The sailors laughed and one replied in a kindly manner. 'Aye, that's a coble. They fish for salmon in it and it's wide and flat as you see. It is very safe in these waters.' He held her gaze for a little too long, admiration clearly evident in his expression, so she looked away, gathering her cloak more tightly about her.

Ten minutes later she found herself seated in the boat—the *coble*—watching while they loaded the trunks and crates. Reassuringly, it all fitted easily and the men all seemed to know their work. At the last minute, as they began rowing to shore, she turned to lift a hand to the cabin boy. He saluted in response, then turned away. The ship was bound for the Hudson Bay and Rupertsland, a journey of many weeks. This would be the last land the boy would see for a while. And Lydia would likely never see him again.

Her life so far had been a series of farewells. The death of her mother followed by her father a year later. Then, the life of a governess. Never feeling settled, or secure. Never having a permanent home. Developing affection for the children in her care, then being forced by circumstance to leave them. Briefly, she wondered how the Barnstable twins were doing, then shook off the sadness that washed over her. This post was her new start, and these islands, her new home. She would make the best of it.

* * *

'*Fàilte!* Welcome to Ardmore Castle, Miss Farnham! My, you are a pretty one!'

It was late afternoon, the sun was setting and Lydia had finally reached her destination. She alighted from the horse-drawn cart that had been used for the final part of her journey, having truly believed at one point earlier that she would never actually arrive. They had had to wait for low tide in order to cross from South Uist to Benbecula, a delay of almost two hours. As if it had not been enough, crossing the sea in a ship to get to an island, she had then had to wait until it was safe to ford the gap between it and the current island! The notion simply reinforced her sense of utter separation from everything she had ever known. Thanking the driver, and with more than a little relief, she stepped towards the smiling woman who was greeting her.

'Thank you! I am very glad to have arrived.' She ignored the comment about her looks. People often said such things; as long as she was unmolested she would not concern herself with it.

The woman introduced herself as Mrs MacLeod, the housekeeper, and Lydia felt a strange sense of relief at her manner. Here was real warmth, a role and title she understood and a genuinely welcoming smile. Even the fact that Mrs MacLeod had called her by her name was reassuring. The housekeeper was plump and short, with a wide smile and a no-nonsense air. She looked to be in her middle years and carried herself with an air of brisk kindliness. She invited Lydia to accompany her inside the castle, leaving behind the bustling courtyard. The building was impressive—a solid structure of grey stone, with a square keep, a lower, wider section and a roughly rectangular courtyard, complete with lean-to cottages against every wall. The massive doors were solid wood and the Great Hall inside was surprisingly warm, given the cold March winds. Twin fireplaces on either side held blazing fires and a delicious smell— not of woodsmoke, but something else—reached Lydia's nostrils.

'Eilidh, come and take Miss Farnham's cloak and bonnet!' Mrs MacLeod called a young maid who was, it seemed, passing through. 'Since you are here just now, you can have the special job of looking after our new friend, Miss Farnham.'

Eilidh's brown eyes widened. 'Me? *Tapadh leibh*— thank you, Mrs MacLeod!' She curtsied to Lydia, eyeing her a little warily. 'Just tell me what you need. I am happy to serve you, miss.' She looked to be about seventeen.

'I—thank you, Eilidh,' Lydia stammered, unused to having a servant to assist her at all. 'I am sure I shall be just fine.' She handed her cloak to the girl and untied her bonnet, glad to be free of both after another long, long day.

'Once I've put these away I can show you to your room, miss, if you like?'

'That would be lovely, thank you. Unless—should I meet the Laird first? Or Miss Margaret?'

No, no!' Mrs MacLeod dismissed this with a wave of her hand. 'Go and rest a while. Dinner is at six and Eilidh can call you down ten minutes early to meet the Laird and wee Mairead. Do not fret, you will soon find your way about!'

Since Lydia had been fretting over no such thing, this was somewhat cryptic. However, after Eilidh had taken her upstairs, through rooms, down another set of stairs and around corners, she soon began to appreciate the labyrinthine layout of the castle.

I do not believe I shall ever find my way!

Finally, Eilidh opened a heavy wooden door, the last in a short corridor. 'Here is your chamber, miss. Let me just check all is ready for you.'

'What a beautiful room!' Lydia looked about her. A merry fire burned in the grate, the bed looked comfortable and there was a thick carpet under her feet. The stone walls had clearly been recently whitewashed, she realised, and hung with large tapestries rich with colour. The furniture looked solid and well crafted. No rococo clocks or flimsy French sidetables here!

The window was set in a deep alcove and a small door led to the next room. Curious, Lydia opened it, to find the adjoining chamber was laid out as a schoolroom, with a child-sized desk, as well as a larger table for her own use. There were slates and writing materials, as well as a globe, some books and even a small pianoforte. The view was to the west and the sun setting over the horizon. It was breathtakingly beautiful.

Returning to the bedchamber, she complimented Eilidh on both rooms and the maid beamed with pleasure.

'We shall get your trunks brought up directly, miss.' Eilidh bent to poke the fire, then added more strange-looking fuel.

'What is that?'

'This? It's peat, miss. Not many trees around here, so we burn peat.'

'I see.' *Not many trees?* Everything was different, although the burning peat had a wonderful aroma, Lydia had to admit.

Once Eilidh was gone, Lydia freshened up, then checked her hems for mud. Her skirts were relatively clean, thank goodness, so she let down her overdress and brushed and re-pinned her hair. She could do nothing about her features, which unfortunately had brought more than her share of unwanted attention, but she could at least keep her hair and gowns plain and unadorned, and ensure she had a *fichu* to hide her bosom at all times.

Eilidh arrived to fetch her then and butterflies immediately began to flutter in Lydia's innards. Finally, she would meet the Laird.

Alasdair paced the floor in the small salon next to the dining room, feeling unaccountably nervous about meeting Mairead's new governess. Having paid a substantial sum to ensure Miss Farnham a safe and comfortable passage all the way from London, he was now seriously doubting his decision to hire her. What would a soft London woman know of life in the Islands? Of caring for a sickly child?

There was a balance in place in the castle. Everyone knew their role, everyone knew everyone else and their history, and who was related to whom, and—crucially—they all shared a common set of beliefs. Beliefs that would be anathema to many outside Scotland—and particularly those supportive of the Hanoverians. Miss Farnham had already worked as governess to a number of noble families, he knew, and would doubtless never have questioned Elector George's right to the throne. The current king was mad, everyone knew. There was even talk of them making his son Regent in his place. If the rightful king had won at Culloden, things might have been different...

Shaking himself with a reminder that he could not change history, Alasdair returned to the issue at hand. This woman would need to be an excellent governess and he would need to be convinced that she was suitable.

The door opened and he turned. For a moment he paused, as the world around him seemed to shift momentarily. There before him, standing in the doorway, was quite the most beautiful woman he had ever seen.

Chapter Three

Alasdair stood dumbstruck for a moment, then gathered himself and walked forward to greet her, a hand outstretched.

'Miss Farnham? You are welcome to Ardmore. I do hope your long journey was uneventful?' Even as he spoke, his eyes were drinking in her perfection. Deep blue eyes, perfectly framed with thick lashes under delicately arched brows, a pure, creamy complexion, sweetly curved lips. His eyes roved on. A perfect little nose, high cheekbones and a delicate jaw. Her fair hair was drawn back in a tight constraint, yet it served only to enhance the perfect architecture of her face. Briefly, his eyes swept southwards. It was hard to tell beneath Miss Farnham's shapeless gown, but he suspected her form to be as perfect as her features.

As his mind and body took in her beauty, his heart was sinking. It had never occurred to him that the governess might be attractive. If he had stopped to think about it, he might have assumed her to be a woman of middle years, with significant experience in working with children and no threat to the equilibrium of the castle community.

As it was…grimly, he foresaw myriad problems. Every man within a five-mile radius was likely to be smitten with her, their women jealous or fearful. And as for himself… His jaw tightened. He had vowed never to let beauty blind him to a woman's true nature again. If Miss Farnham thought she could charm people into doing her wishes, or avoiding her own responsibilities, then she would soon learn differently!

She took his hand, saying something. Her voice was calm, her speech unaffected. The accent jarred, but then, he had at least anticipated that aspect of what now was increasingly looking like a rash decision.

Briefly, his mind caught up with her words. She had thanked him for the private carriage and the high-quality accommodation she had had during her journey. 'That was all Iain Crawford's doing,' he said shortly. 'Is your chamber to your liking?'

His duty to be hospitable and welcoming was carrying him through the conversation, but inwardly his mind was screaming a warning. This woman was dangerous. Bad enough to be knowingly employing a Sassenach to educate his child. A Sassenach this beautiful would cause havoc everywhere she went.

Lydia could not remember ever feeling so nervous. Coming so far away from the world she knew meant that she simply *had* to make this posting a success. Dimly she recalled the day in Mrs Gray's agency and her almost immediate decision to accept this post. Her own insouciance now astounded her.

How could I have given away all I know, to travel to another world?

Eilidh had pointed out the door to the dining room, explaining that wee Mairead would be brought there directly, but that Lydia was first to meet the Laird in the next room. Lydia had smoothed her skirts nervously, squared her shoulders, and opened the door.

He had been pacing in front of the fireplace, it seemed, but on hearing her enter, he turned. Lydia's first impression was simply how tall and well-formed he was, but then she took in the other details. He was in full Highland dress, with a long red kilt marked with black lines and tied with an impressive leather belt. She had come across similar dress before, worn by the Highland Regiments in London, although their kilts, she remembered, were much shorter.

Swiftly, her eyes swept upwards, past the well-tailored short jacket which showed off his strong figure to perfection, until her gaze reached his face. *Oh, Lord!* He was handsome, with a strong jaw, blue eyes and a strong, straight nose. His dark hair was in some disorder, as if he had been raking his fingers through it. For an instant it felt as though time had stopped as she eyed the man who was her new employer. Something in his form and presence rocked her and she was unsure why. Scrambling to force her mind to function again, she returned to the thought that had been foremost in her mind as she approached the door. This was the Laird himself. The man who was key to whether she stayed or left. What manner of man was he?

She blinked as he stepped forward, a polite greeting on his lips and an outstretched hand of welcome. He asked about her journey and she answered with genuine gratitude, for her journey, challenging as it was, would have been a hundred times worse on a public stage-coach, or without decent accommodation. His reply was rather blunt, clarifying that it had been Mr Crawford who had made the arrangements. She was unsure what to say to this and there was a taut silence.

'Shall we go through to dine, Miss Farnham? I have no doubt you will be more than ready for a home-cooked meal.' He indicated the way and she preceded him out of the small parlour. He fell into step beside her. 'My daughter dines with me every evening. You will accompany her, naturally.'

'She does? Oh, yes, of course, sir.' The habit in the previous households where she had worked was for children to dine with the servants until they neared adult-hood. Most parents, in her experience, did not relish spending extended periods of time with their offspring.

'This surprises you?' There was an edge to his tone, something she could not quite fathom.

Keeping her expression neutral, she replied carefully, 'Each household is different, sir. In many ways.'

Inwardly, she continued to attempt to assess him. Despite an initial hint in his eyes that he found her attractive, his expression now was shuttered and he was making no attempt to leer at her. He had not even tried to touch her arm to guide her to the dining room. So far, so good.

Then they were inside and the people already at the table rose—or at least, most of them did. Lydia's gaze flew to the small girl propped on an enormous chair on the left side of the table. Her first impression was how tiny she looked, and how delicate. Pale skin, long dark hair tied with a blue ribbon, slim arms lacking colour and curves—oh, this child looked sickly indeed!

The Laird was busy making introductions and Lydia smiled and murmured appropriately. The gentleman in the red and green was Iain Crawford, while the young gentleman and young lady were brother and sister, and cousins to the Laird. Eilidh and Angus MacDonald, he named them.

That was four MacDonalds and two Eilidhs already and she had only been in the castle for a matter of hours.

Lord, how am I to recall everyone's name and place?

They sat, Lydia being placed between Angus and Mairead, and the servants immediately moved to bring silver-covered dishes from the sideboards. Lydia's mouth watered at the delectable scents of good, homely food. She helped herself in turn to pie and potatoes, vegetables and some sort of meatloaf that was entirely delicious. There was also freshly-baked bread and yellow butter, which was surprising at a formal dinner. In addition, the food was served by a mix of men and women—in London, only menservants were permitted to serve at table.

So many differences! As the meal went on, Mr Angus MacDonald engaged Lydia in gentle conversation about her journey and she was conscious that the entire party, including the servants, were all likely listening, despite the murmur of other chatter. Mr Crawford and Miss Eilidh MacDonald were engaged in some easy raillery to do with a horse, while the Laird himself was quietly speaking with his child. Mairead was eating very little, Lydia noted.

When he turned to converse with his cousin Eilidh, Lydia saw her chance to speak quietly with the child. 'It is good to meet you, Mairead—or is it Margaret? How is it that people here have two names?'

'Well, you see,' said the child with great animation, 'we have English names, for the writing down, and then we have our *real* names, which is who we really are.'

'So your real name is Mairead? I see. I am happy to meet you, Mairead.' She sighed dramatically. 'Sadly, I have only one name—Lydia.'

Mairead frowned. 'That is sad indeed. I shall ask my father for your real name, for he knows everything. Papaidh!'

He turned, smiling indulgently. 'Yes, dear?'

'What is Miss Lydia's real name?'

His brow furrowed. 'Her name is Miss Lydia Farnham.'

'No, but what is her—her *Ardmore* name? Her *Benbecula* name?'

His expression cleared. 'Ah, she does not have a Gaelic name, child. You may address her as Miss Farnham.'

'Or Lydia,' Lydia interjected, having already some sense of an air of informality here that she had never encountered before. 'The others may call me Miss Farnham, but you can call me Lydia.'

'Lydia,' Mairead echoed, as if trying it on her tongue. 'I like it! *Tapadh leibh!*'

'Does that mean thank you?' Mairead nodded. 'I see we shall be able to teach each other things. You can teach me Ardmore words and I can teach you other things.'

Mairead threw her a suspicious look. 'What things?'

'Whatever your father wishes for me to teach you.' She glanced up at the Laird, to find that he was watching her intently.

'Make no mistake, Miss Farnham—' there was about his words a decided air of implacability that was in sharp contrast to his previous reserved formality '—I expect you to be excellent at your work and to attend to Mairead's needs with great diligence!'

Rather taken aback, she responded instantly. 'Naturally, sir! I would hardly come all the way from London unless I was fully engaged with my responsibilities.'

His blue eyes bored into hers, his expression one of remote annoyance. 'See to it that you remain so, or you will find yourself back in London in a flash.'

This struck Lydia as bordering on unjust and she retorted unthinkingly, 'Hardly a flash, sir, since I left London nearly a fortnight ago!'

Instantly, she cowered inwardly. She must not be impertinent towards her employer. *Lord!*

His eyes narrowed, but he said only, 'Your lessons will begin on the morrow. Come to me after breakfast and I shall outline my expectations.'

'Yes, sir.' Dropping her eyes to her plate, she resolved to speak only when spoken to for the remainder of the meal.

This she did, and she was pleased to find that Mairead seemed interested in her and was clearly desirous of a deeper acquaintance. Remembering the child's sceptical look earlier, Lydia resolved to uncover in the coming days whether her wariness about lessons was of the universal variety, or something more specific.

* * *

After dinner the table was cleared and then a set of glasses was brought in, along with a bottle of amber drink. It was an unusual colour—too pale for brandy, too dark and still for beer. Perhaps it was some sort of Scottish alcohol?

Each glass, she observed, had a flaw in the stem in the shape of a teardrop. The glasses themselves were all shapes and sizes, but the teardrop remained constant. With great ceremony, one of the manservants filled every glass—even the child got a small drop, well diluted with clear water.

The Laird raised his glass. *'Slàinte mhath!'* he declared. *'Agus slàinte mhòr!'*

The party all echoed his words—presumably a Gaelic version of the 'Cheers!' she had heard so often over the years in England. Tentatively, she sipped at the liquid. It was strongly flavoured, yet smooth, and it burned her throat in a way that was both delightful and disconcerting. She took a deeper mouthful. *Oh, yes.* This was wonderful.

Glancing up, she realised she was the subject of the gaze of numerous pairs of eyes. 'Well?' asked the Laird. 'What think you of our whisky?'

'Whisky?' She smiled. 'It is wonderful!'

'We call it *uisge beatha*—the water of life,' Angus explained with a grin.

She raised an eyebrow. 'I should hazard a guess that too much does not make one very lively the following morning!'

They all laughed—or at least, all but the Laird. 'True, true,' said Angus. 'Still, an appreciation of whisky is a necessity for anyone wishing to make their home in the islands.'

Home. *What a strange notion.* Not having had a home for so long, Lydia had all but given up on the very idea. For these people, life was simple. They had their homes and families, their history and traditions. Even their own language. Whereas she was doomed to be ever the outsider. Pushing back against the self-pity that threatened to rise up, Lydia applied herself to her whisky.

Alasdair refused to join in the general fêting of Miss Farnham. While she had shown reasonable skill in engaging Mairead in conversation, he was yet to assess her credentials as a teacher, never mind her behaviour as a woman who could not fail to be aware of her natural advantages. If she thought she could rely on her pretty face to cause havoc, or to avoid her responsibilities, she would soon learn otherwise! He had no regrets in reminding her that she was here on sufferance. He was not so desperate for a governess yet that he would be forced to accept someone unsuitable. Mairead was yet young.

Indeed, one of the risks at the front of his mind was that the governess would behave well for a short time in order to dupe them, then gradually reveal her true nature. He had direct and personal experience of just such a deception and it had cost him—and his child—dearly.

He continued to watch Miss Farnham surreptitiously, frustrated to note that closer inspection revealed no flaws in her physical beauty. Although they were hiding it well, he had little doubt that both Iain Crawford and cousin Angus were conversing with rather more animation than usual. He sighed inwardly, seeing myriad troubles ahead.

Lydia climbed the two little steps at the side of her high bed, slipping between the clean sheets with an audible sigh of relief. Journey's end had finally come—and it had come with unforeseen complications. Blowing out the candle, she lay back on the soft pillows, considering. Mairead was clearly quick-witted, the child's sharp intelligence contrasting strongly with her pale, weak body. Already Lydia's mind was considering approaches and strategies to engage the child, for she knew that a trusting relationship between a governess and her charge was essential in ensuring the child enjoyed her lessons. She had noted that, at the end of the meal, the child had been carried off to bed by one of the servants.

Does she not walk at all?

The family and servants had, so far, been only polite, warm and welcoming. Experience, however, had taught her not to relax her guard. Somewhere among them there would be a lecherous male or a jealous female. Often it took time for people to reveal their true nature, so she had learned over the past five years to be wary of everyone.

Her thoughts drifted to the Laird. *My, you are a handsome one*, she thought, echoing the housekeeper's words to her earlier. In her mind's eye she pictured his strong, regular features, blue eyes, dark hair and tall, strong form, and the curious reaction she'd experienced on seeing him for the first time. *Probably the Highland dress.* Normally, she was even more wary of handsome men, for many seemed to find it inconceivable that she should not admire them.

The Laird, however, she was forced to admit, had made no attempt to flirt with her. If anything, he seemed to hold her in some disdain, which she found decidedly puzzling. Returning to their conversation earlier, her stomach twisted at his threat to dismiss her if she was not 'excellent' at her work. How did he define 'excellent'? She knew herself to be a gifted teacher, with a natural affinity for children, but she also knew that at times parents' expectations of their children could be entirely unrealistic. Recalling the Laird's tone towards her earlier, she bit her lip in the darkness.

Still, disdain left her safer than admiration. She would take it and not worry over it, and be grateful. Turning on her side, she allowed sleepiness to wash over her, taking away the worries about her new place, at least for now.

Chapter Four

'Miss Farnham, thank you for coming to see me. Please, sit.'

As requested, Lydia had presented herself in the small parlour off the dining room, which Eilidh had explained was the Laird's favourite room. Breakfast was finished and the servants were taking Mairead to the room beside Lydia's bedchamber, which she knew already was to be their schoolroom.

Nervously, she took her seat in a sturdy leather armchair and the Laird seated himself in the facing chair. A fire had been lit in the grate, and the room was comfortably warm. Despite some decidedly draughty corridors, Lydia had noted that the main rooms themselves were well maintained, with good fireplaces and chimneys, and plenty of hangings and carpets to ensure comfort.

The Laird came straight to the point. 'I have here a letter from a Mrs Gray, who has provided your reference, including a summary of your previous posts. She describes you as a highly talented teacher and informs me that you previously worked with another sickly child. Is that so?'

Lydia felt herself colour a little. 'She is too good! I enjoy teaching, it is true, and I believe myself to have some skill in teaching children.' Taking a breath, she asked the question that had been burning within her since Mairead's suspicious glance the night before. 'Tell me, sir, is your daughter a keen student?'

He gave a bark of laughter. 'Indeed not! Despite being as sharp as a dirk, she has evaded all attempts to persuade her to book-learning. Numerous people, including my cousin Eilidh, have tried to teach her, but the little rascal distracts them with questions, refusals and diversions, and ends by not practising either her letters or her arithmetic. Mrs MacLeod, who has been the person to most recently attempt to contain my daughter, has met with little success. Indeed…' he eyed her challengingly '…it was she who insisted I hire a proper governess.'

'I see.' Lydia considered this. 'A challenge indeed.'

'And this is why I am paying you so handsomely. It would be insupportable for the Laird's daughter to remain illiterate, or to be unable to contribute to the life of this household, particularly when she is so quick-witted. Since her body is so weak, she will rely even more on her mind as she grows.' He paused. 'You will no doubt be wondering about her weakness. She developed normally as a baby, but fell prey to a bad illness nearly two years ago. We thought the fever would never break—in truth, we thought she would not live. Yet she did.' He shook his head. 'That indomitable spirit of hers!' There was clear affection in his tone, which was reassuring. Little Mairead was loved, obviously. At least Lydia would not have to mend a broken heart this time, as she had so often had to do when working with the ignored children of London's high society.

'She recovered from the fever, but never walked again. Nor did she regain her healthy looks and size. She remains thin and weak and prone to every cough and cold. She tires easily, so you will have to balance her education with her weakness.' His hand, Lydia noted, was gripping the arm of his chair so tightly that the knuckles had turned white. 'Never to run and play, nor climb Rueval, nor milk a cow. Never to know the joys of solitude, for she must always have company, for fear she falls from her chair.' He looked at her directly. 'It is not the life I wanted for my daughter.'

'No,' she agreed softly, not knowing what else to say. She swallowed. 'I assume they—people tried to help her?'

'I brought the best doctors from Edinburgh—even one from London. They could do nothing. Some fever poison got into her, they said, and made her unnaturally frail. Her legs are too thin to hold her up.'

'I see. How does she move about the castle?'

'She is carried everywhere.' He laughed harshly. 'She is so small and slight that even the lightest of maidservants can take her about on their hip.'

'She will not always be so small.'

He eyed her sharply. 'You have a suggestion?'

'The child I worked with in London…they made him a chair with wheels on it, so that—'

'No!' His expression was thunderous. 'My child suffers enough indignity! She will not be carted around in a cart, or a barrow! I shall not hear of it!'

'Of course.' She spread her hands placatingly, though

inwardly, she was not yet ready to concede. John Pickering's wheeled chair had made everyone's existence easier—including his.

I shall keep my powder dry for another day.

He grimaced. 'Do not misunderstand me. We look after everyone here. Old Mrs MacKinnon does not walk and the Mattesons have a daughter who cannot hear. We also have a number of people, young and old, who are prone to illness. They are no less important to us than anyone else. We adapt to their needs, we include them in every way possible and we think no differently of them than of anyone else. Just because Mairead is sickly and becomes easily exhausted, that does not mean we love her any less.'

'Of course!' Despite his gruffness, she took this as evidence of a good heart. 'Our bodies are only the—the *containers* within which we exist. I have often wished for people to see me as a person and not simply as—' she gestured vaguely at herself '—as a face or a form.'

His eyes widened briefly, then he shook his head. 'I have accepted that Mairead cannot return to the good health she enjoyed previously. But her quick mind must be nurtured. Despite all of our efforts, she seems to believe herself incapable of many things. She has even been known to engage in a battle of wills with those who try to teach her. That is why you are here. You will teach her to write and to figure. You will ensure she knows French, the globe, and logic.'

Lydia nodded. All such subjects were well within her abilities, although the 'battle of wills' sounded daunting. 'I would also suggest painting, music, and history.'

Perhaps if I begin with subjects that are more divert-

ing, I might have more success. 'I speak German and Italian as well.'

He raised an eyebrow. 'Such an accomplished lady!' Something in his tone made her grit her teeth. 'You may paint all you like and try her with other languages. However, you are to leave the teaching of history to me. She needs a true understanding of our past—and one free from an English interpretation.'

Slightly taken aback, Lydia could only ask, 'And music?'

'Most people here can sing and play one or more instruments. Our bards are renowned. We have no need of Sassenach music.'

'And what of the classics? Beethoven, Mozart…?'

'We are not uncivilised, Miss Farnham, whatever you may believe. Indeed, Herr Beethoven arranged at least one of the Airs from the Burns collection.' He raised an eyebrow. 'You are unaware of it?' Rising, he walked to the desk near the window, returning with a bound publication.

'The Scots Musical Museum,' she read, then flicked through. 'But this is wonderful!'

He grunted. 'We are proud of our music, Miss Farnham. Perhaps you may learn as well as teach while you are here.'

She smiled and he blinked. 'I have no doubt of it, sir!'

'Yes, very well,' he said gruffly. 'You may go and see if you can make any progress with her.'

Lydia rose. 'I shall do my very best, I assure you. But you must allow me to use my judgement in how I work with her.'

'Your *judgement*?' His lip curled. 'If that is your

proxy for laziness, or avoidance of your duties, then I assure you, you will not get away with it here!'

'It is no such thing!' she replied hotly. 'I simply mean—'

He stood, dwarfing her. 'I care not what you mean. I wish you to be clear about what *I* mean. You are here to work. Your time here will revolve around Mairead and you will ensure she learns. Is that clear?'

'Yes, sir.' Lydia mouthed the words, although she knew her eyes were flashing fire at him. How dared he accuse her of laziness? 'Good day, sir.'

'*Slàn leibh,*' he returned. Had he deliberately used the Gaelic form to intimidate her? Well, he would soon learn that she was not so easily cowed. Whatever it took, she would somehow get Mairead working with her—but she would do it in her own way and at her own pace.

Alasdair watched her go, saw the outrage in the stiff line of her back, the angle of her head. Perhaps he had been a little blunt, but she would have to learn that, in these parts, plain speaking was admired and deception abhorred. Striding to the window, he gazed out, unseeing. Did she truly intend to shirk her duties, for which he was paying a pretty penny? Did she hope to charm them all into doing what she willed, just like…?

He recalled her smile just now—the first genuine smile he had seen from her—and the impact it had had on him, like a punch to the gut. If she went about Ardmore Castle bestowing such smiles on males or females, she would have anything she wished. 'Allow me to use my judgement.' He gave a cynical bark of laughter. Perhaps she was a good governess, perhaps not. But

he would not assume it just because she had a smile fit
to dazzle the hardest of hearts. He had learned to mis-
trust beautiful women through the harshest of experiences and would not be easily deceived.

*I shall stay away and allow her to do what she can.
At least for now.*

He refused, however, to acknowledge that the relief
that went through him at this decision had little to do
with Miss Farnham's skills as a governess and everything to do with her blinding smile.

'And now,' said Lydia, having just checked the
weather through the narrow window, 'it is time for us
to go outside.'

'Ah, Lydia. Must we?'

After only a week, Lydia and Mairead had reached
something of an understanding. They had made a pact,
which Mairead continually tried to renegotiate, but the
essence was that they each took turns to be the 'teacher',
deciding what they would do for the next hour. Mairead
liked to talk and to sketch, and to have stories told to
her, and in return she co-operated to some extent with
the basic lessons that Lydia had introduced. The child's
mind was too quick for patience, but she was, Lydia
thought, quietly pleased at her attempts to form the letters of her own name on the slate. Mairead was beginning to believe in herself.

'Do not tell Papaidh yet,' she had urged Lydia, who
had smilingly agreed. The Laird clearly believed Lydia
to be lazy and useless, and the painstaking work she
was doing with Mairead would take some time to show
fruit, so she was perfectly content to *not* keep him in-

formed in great detail about her work with the child. To be fair, he had not pressed her and each evening at dinner they exchanged only the most cordial of conversation. She remained a little wary of him, but thankfully he had neither attempted to flirt with her, nor had he repeated his autocratic demands.

Mairead, enjoying the role of teacher, had decided to teach Lydia what she called 'Benbecula words', and Lydia, who already spoke three extra languages with a fair degree of fluency, was enjoying the challenge of learning another. Gaelic was tricky, for it seemed they began every sentence with a verb, and used specific words, rather than word order, to ask questions. She encouraged Mairead to speak Gaelic to her as much as possible and was beginning to get a feel for the rhythm and cadence of the language, if not the complicated grammar.

'Can we not stay here, inside?' Mairead's tone was wheedling. For some reason she disliked going outdoors and the castle staff indulged her. Lydia, however, reckoned that children all needed some time outside each day, with sunlight and fresh air. To her, it was simply good sense that it would be healthier.

'We can only stay outside for half an hour today,' she offered placatingly, 'for we shall need to prepare for dinner.' Reaching out her arms, she raised an eyebrow at the child. 'You have worked hard today, Mairead. I am pleased with you.'

The child's face lit up with happiness at this and she reached up for Lydia to lift her. 'Thank you, Miss Lydia,' she muttered into Lydia's neck, making her smile. Definite progress! 'I always worry about not doing things right,' she added.

Lydia leaned back to look at her. 'You do?'

The child nodded shyly. 'I cannot do things like other children. They can write and read, and run, and I cannot.'

Lydia replied carefully, 'Ah, but you can talk and laugh, and sing, which not everyone can do. We all have things we are good at and things we are not so good at. When you work hard and try your best during lessons, even if you do not succeed, you have won. The prize is in the *trying*.'

Mairead stuck her lip out at this. 'No. There is no prize for not doing it. It would be silly to give prizes to those who cannot!'

She would not be persuaded and so Lydia, sighing, changed the subject.

Mairead's skirts had been sewn in an unusual manner, with a seam up the front and back, almost like very wide breeches. This was to facilitate her being carried easily by various people around the castle. When she was seated, her clothing looked like a normal dress, but when she was being carried, balanced on an adult's hip, the split skirt meant there was much less likelihood of stumbling or dropping her. As she walked through the castle, carrying her featherlight burden, it occurred to Lydia to be grateful that Mairead's ailment was different to poor John Pickering's. John's legs, when he was carried, had used to fall like dead things, while Mairead was able to move herself a little and bring her knees into a more comfortable position. She was—

Lydia stopped, halfway down the main staircase.

'What is it, Lydia?' Mairead was looking up at her, puzzled.

Recovering herself, Lydia smoothed out her features, saying only, 'Oh, nothing. I just had the queerest notion, that is all. Now, where shall we sit today when we go out? In the courtyard? Or outside the walls?'

'The courtyard, please. Perhaps we might see the chickens, or there may be a horse and cart. Who knows?'

Now that Mairead had accepted the inevitability of the 'outside' part of today's lessons, she was clearly becoming more enthused by the idea. Lydia suppressed a smile. Not only would Mairead benefit from the fresh air, her mind would be stimulated by all she could hear and see.

Once they were settled—seated on Lydia's cloak in a cleanish corner of the courtyard—Lydia began the lesson. 'How many chickens are out today, Mairead? They are moving around so much I declare I cannot keep track of them!'

Mairead rose to the challenge, eventually declaring there to be eight hens and a rooster.

'And can you imagine if there were *three* roosters, instead of one? How many chickens would there be then, all in all?' The child frowned, working it out, and Lydia challenged her with a few more addition puzzles. Feeling increasingly confident of Mairead's abilities, she decided to stretch her a little. 'Remember the story I told you of the sly fox?' Mairead nodded. 'Here is a riddle for you. If the fox were to take two of these hens, how many would be left?'

'Silly! We do not have foxes here!'

'Ah, but we are *pretending*! It is fun to pretend sometimes, is it not?'

She considered this, tilting her head to one side. 'It is! I pretend sometimes that I can walk and even run! It makes me happy.' She frowned. 'And then it makes me sad.'

Lydia swallowed. 'It is perfectly fine to pretend and to feel happy. *And* to feel sad sometimes. We all do.'

'Even you, Lydia?'

'Even me.'

Lydia was used to following her instincts with children and she sensed that now was too soon to delve further into Mairead's feelings about her limitations. Instead, she diverted the girl into a conversation about the lack of foxes in the islands and how lucky these chickens were, compared to the chickens in the stories. She then gently repeated the arithmetical riddle and, this time, Mairead decided to co-operate.

While the child puzzled it out, Lydia took a breath, feeling as though the auspices might be reasonably good. Today, for the first time, she was starting to feel hopeful here. Not secure. Not comfortable. But, yes, definitely hopeful. Perhaps she could make a difference for this child.

She closed her eyes briefly, raising her face to the weak March sun. The feeling of sunlight on her skin was welcome and she never worried over such things as freckles. Why should anyone care?

Mairead gave her answer, triumph clear in the tone of her voice, and Lydia smiled and congratulated her. 'Now let us imagine,' she said, 'there were seven hens and the fox took three of them. How many would we be left with then?'

Carefully, she continued with the game of basic arithmetic which, since there were no slates or pencils involved, Mairead would not perceive to be a 'lesson'. Clapping her hands each time the child calculated correctly, she ensured Mairead continued to see such learning as simply a pleasant pastime. Being entirely focused on her charge, she failed to notice the Laird standing at a window in the keep and gazing at them both.

Six o'clock, and the party assembled as usual for dinner. Lydia had taken to carrying Mairead downstairs herself, as one of the servants generally took the child off to bed directly after the evening meal. Settling Mairead in her usual chair, Lydia ensured she was safely positioned on a high cushion in the centre of the large seat, then took her own place. The Laird signalled to the servants and the meal began. As ever, Mairead ate very little and Lydia had taken to gently tempting her with morsels of the delicious repast, trying to understand the child's tastes.

Tonight, in contrast to his usual disengaged politeness, there was an air of vexation about the Laird. Lydia could not have said how she knew this. Perhaps his carriage was a little stiff, his expression grim rather than detached. Or perhaps she was imagining it. Regardless, she was conscious that, in his presence, she was intensely aware of him in a way that she had never before experienced with anyone else. It was a mix of curiosity and wariness, she told herself. Why else should her pulse be running a little faster than usual and her mouth feel a little dry? Yet she noticed him in a way that she had never done with anyone else. His facial expressions. His accent. His hands. He had beautiful hands, she knew, although she could not have said what was so beautiful about them.

Mr MacDonald and his sister had gone the day before, with a promise to return the next week. They were regular visitors, it seemed, and behaved as though they were entirely at home in the castle. It must be wonderful, thought Lydia, a little wistfully, to have extended family and more than one home. Since her parents had died she had had neither people nor a place to which she belonged. She herself had been an only child and her mother's sister, her only other relative, had died many years ago. *Alone. I am alone.*

Still, the children in her care were her family, she supposed. Or at least they became so, for whatever time she was given to be with them. Already, she was developing a strong bond with little Mairead.

Tonight, then, there was only the Laird and Mr Crawford, Lydia and Mairead. Partly to distract herself from the Laird's air of brooding displeasure, Lydia responded brightly to Mr Crawford's conversational sallies—despite the fact that he was sitting across the table from her. Never would such manners be permitted in London, although Lydia had to confess to a sneaking appreciation for the informality of the Laird's household.

So far, none of the men in the castle had accosted her either, for which she was profoundly relieved. She continued to keep her interactions with men to a minimum, but was getting to know some of the women already. Mrs MacLeod was just as warm and motherly as she had first seemed, young Eilidh was helpful and hardworking and Miss MacDonald—the other Eilidh—had shown her nothing but kindness. Lydia's appearance seemed not to bother her—but then Eilidh herself was a good-looking young lady, with pale blue eyes and divine red curls.

Mr Crawford who, like the Laird, was probably in his late twenties or early thirties, had been friendly towards her whenever she had encountered him, yet she had not so far felt any alarm in his company. Over recent years she had become quite the expert in discerning which gentlemen were of good character and which were prone to inappropriate behaviour. Confusingly however, even 'good' gentlemen had occasionally tried to hold her hand or make declarations towards her, which had left her mistrustful of all men.

There was a pause in Lydia's discourse with Mr Crawford and the Laird filled it by addressing Mairead. 'Well, *mo nighean*, how are you getting along with your lessons?'

Lydia tensed. The Laird had not as much as glanced in her direction as he spoke, yet this question, she knew, was directed as much to her as to Mairead.

'Very well,' said Mairead. 'We have had stories and songs, and I have been drawing pretty pictures.'

Lydia groaned inwardly. Quite without meaning to, the child was creating trouble for her.

'Stories and songs, eh?' Now his gaze did turn to Lydia and she felt the full force of it. Her heart began to beat a little faster and her stomach was suddenly unsettled.

She set down her fork. 'Stories and songs are important, sir. They are in themselves a form of learning.'

'Reading and writing are also important, would you not agree, Miss Farnham?' His tone was mild, yet his meaning could not have been clearer.

'Indeed! In fact—' She caught the appeal in Mairead's gaze. *Do not tell him!* the child was saying. *Not yet!* 'In fact,' she continued, 'I mean to make progress with Mairead's reading and writing during this coming week.' *There!* That was the truth. The fact that Mairead was co-operating with learning her letters for, apparently, the first time, was not Lydia's secret to reveal. Not yet, at any rate. She did not hold with the view that children's wishes and needs were unimportant. To reveal Mairead's progress so far, in direct contravention of her agreement with the child, would breach the trust they were gradually building between them.

'And what were you doing in the courtyard earlier? You seemed to be quite at your leisure, both of you.'

'We were looking at the hens, Papaidh.' Mairead was all innocence.

'Looking at the hens...' His gaze swung to Lydia, his jaw tight. 'And for this I have spent a near fortune securing a so-called expert from London?'

Lydia bristled. 'You must allow me, sir, to know my own work. Would you direct a carpenter, or a cook, in the detail of their role?'

'I would indeed,' he retorted, 'if I spied the carpenter or the cook sunning themselves in my courtyard when they should be working!'

Mairead was looking from one to the other, frowning. 'Papaidh, do not be *crosta* with Miss Lydia! She is the bestest teacher!'

His gaze softened as it dropped to his daughter. 'The *best* teacher, *mo nighean*, is one who can get you reading and writing and counting. She must be more than an expensive playmate.'

'But we *were* counting! I was counting the hens, then counting when the fox would take some away!'

He looked puzzled. 'What do you mean?'

'Well,' said Mairead, 'first you have to know how many hens and roosters there are. Then you imagine the fox takes two away. Or perhaps four. And then you imagine how many are left.'

His eyes widened, then he gave a startled laugh. 'And this is what you were doing in the courtyard?'

'It was,' said Mairead, nodding firmly.

'But,' offered the Laird, with a decided twinkle in his eye, 'there are no foxes in the islands!' He was grinning at his daughter and Lydia felt her insides tighten at the way it had changed his face. He looked younger, somehow. Smiling suited him. If only he would do it more often!

'That is *exactly* what I told Lydia! Did I not, Lydia?'

Now they were both looking at her. 'You did, Mairead. Chickens here are extremely fortunate, are they not?'

'Everyone is fortunate who makes their home here,' murmured the Laird, 'whether they realise it or not.' His gaze had become unfocused and Lydia was unclear if this was directed at her.

'So you see, there is no need to be *crosta*. Miss Lydia was being perfectly strict and I was counting.'

'And you were very clever at counting, Mairead,' Lydia affirmed. 'Shall we show your *papaidh* how the game works?'

The child agreed and Lydia gave her a series of additions and subtractions, based on the story of the fox and the hens. The Laird and Mr Crawford both pronounced themselves to be impressed by Mairead's cleverness and allowed her to set them some sums in turn. They all ended by laughing, the mood at the table decidedly lighter than it had been.

'Miss Farnham,' declared the Laird then, all graciousness, 'I must apologise. You clearly *do* know your work and I should not have doubted you.' He raised his glass towards her and she could not help but feel pleased. His gaze lingered a little too long and she was conscious of a sudden breathlessness.

She shook it off. 'I should perhaps have explained sooner that my ways of working—particularly with children who are rather, er...*strong-willed*, may be less obvious to others.'

'Including to the child in question,' he murmured.

'Precisely.' They eyed each other, for once in perfect charity, and she was surprised to find her heart racing again, but this time not from fear. Something in the way his gaze touched hers was sending shivers of emotion through her. It was an entirely novel sensation and she knew not what to make of it.

'What is "strong-willed"?' Mairead's tone was one of suspicion. 'And is it a good thing, or a bad thing?'

Sensing the danger, the Laird made haste to reassure his daughter that being strong-willed was a very good thing, most of the time. 'It means you are determined, *mo nighean*. And strong.'

'But...' she frowned '... I am not strong. And my legs and arms are not strong.'

'Well, no. Your heart is strong and your mind is strong, and those are much more important than legs and arms.'

Mairead sighed. 'I just wish my legs were strong-willed, too.'

The Laird's grip on his cutlery had tightened, Lydia noted. The lump in her own throat was pronounced, as Mairead's words rippled into a terse silence. Dropping her eyes to her plate, Lydia realised her appetite was entirely gone.

Thankfully, soon afterwards the Laird signalled for the table to be cleared. Following the formal whisky toast, Eilidh came to carry Mairead off to bed. The child insisted on embracing Lydia as part of her good-nights—the first time she had ever done so. Lydia's heart warmed at this clear evidence of progress in her connection to the girl. She rubbed Mairead's little face. 'I shall look forward to the morrow, Mairead.'

'I, too.'

After she had gone, and with Mr Crawford momentarily distracted by an enquiry from one of the servants, the Laird took the opportunity to say, in a low voice, 'She has really taken to you, Miss Farnham.'

'I know.' She did know. Children always took to her. This was what made it so hard when she, as inevitably happened, was forced to leave. Despite her best efforts, she had never been able to close her heart to the children. She looked directly at the Laird. 'I know.'

* * *

Alasdair was mired in confusion. Miss Farnham, he now knew, was indeed a gifted governess—or at least, so it seemed. He had to acknowledge that the fox-and-hens method of teaching arithmetic was new to him, but perfectly suited to dealing with his strong-willed Mairead. Still, by itself it meant nothing, other than that perhaps Miss Farnham, in all her London posts, had developed some strategies for dealing with a wide range of children. It did not mean she would continue to work hard once the novelty of her arrival had worn off. It did not mean she would stay. He frowned, remembering another lady, another time. *Hester did not stay...*

He shook himself. The past was done. His focus was here and now. A new shadow, unforeseen, had now revealed itself. What if Mairead became too attached to the governess? What would it do to his daughter when Miss Farnham left, as she inevitably would? No soft Sassenach could ever fully adapt to island life. Why, even Hester, who had been raised in Edinburgh—

He cut off the direction of his thoughts, realising he had once again fallen into the past. He tried to think of Mairead's mother as little as possible.

'I know,' she repeated softly. Her voice, gentle and low, somehow managed to pierce right through to his heart.

'Do not hurt her,' he muttered. 'She is not to be hurt.' *Not again.*

'I have no intention of doing so.' Miss Farnham's tone was firm, her expression one of earnest solemnity. Yet he could not take a chance on her apparent sincerity. Although she would need to spend hours each day with Mairead, he would need to ensure that Mairead also maintained strong bonds with others—including himself. Bonds that would be needed when the time came for Miss Farnham to go, as she inevitably would.

'How do you prevent your charges from becoming over-dependent on you?' The question emerged from him before he had fully considered it.

She shrugged. 'I must admit I find it impossible. Children are naturally affectionate, I have found—particularly towards adults who have a genuine interest in them.'

'Aye. And yet you have left behind a number of children over the past few years. How did you prepare them for your departure?'

A furrow appeared on her brow and she opened her mouth, then closed it again. His keen eye also detected a slight flush along those perfect cheekbones. 'I—I cannot say, sir. I have always found it…difficult.'

His next question was an obvious one. 'So why, then, did you leave them?'

'Oh,' she replied airily, 'Various circumstances.'

His attention sharpened further. 'Such as?'

'Alasdair.' It was Iain. 'There is a problem in the kitchens. The second scullery has flooded again.' His attention swinging abruptly away from Miss Farnham, he saw Iain's worried expression, saw, too, that Mrs MacLeod was in the doorway.

'Very well.' He rose, bowing to Miss Farnham. 'Goodnight. We shall speak of this again.'

She nodded, but he could clearly sense the relief emanating from her. Something was off-kilter and he meant to discover what it was. Fox-and-hens games were all very well, but this English governess had a long way to go to earn anything like trust from him.

Chapter Five

Weeks passed. The weather began to become more settled, as March gave way to April and the storms coming in off the western shore became less frequent. Mairead continued to make good progress with her reading, writing and numbers, despite a decided lack of belief in her own abilities, and she and Lydia were becoming ever-firmer friends. Young Eilidh had also taken to Lydia, who was teaching her French in the late evenings after dinner.

Lydia's grasp of Gaelic, while still weak, grew better by the day. She could now recognise a number of common words and phrases, and was able to greet the castle staff with *'madainn mhath'* and thank them with a *'ta-padh leibh'* in quite a relaxed way.

She had continued to puzzle over the mystery of Mairead's affliction and had discussed the matter with Mrs MacLeod. Apparently, following a severe fever two years earlier, Mairead had been left too weak to walk, or play. Her appetite had never returned and she tired easily. Because of this, the staff had begun to carry her around. While their own local doctor had pressed them to insist on Mairead walking, this had been met with resistance from both the child herself and those around her, who had wanted only to care for her. By the time she had fully recovered from the fever, Mairead's leg muscles had become wasted and weak and, despite every effort, no-one had been able to get them working again.

So far, Lydia had not broached the subject again with Mairead. She sensed that the Laird would not want her to speak of it—mainly to save his daughter from distress, but also, Lydia had realised, because he himself was uncomfortable whenever it was mentioned. She could not fail to observe his responses when the topic had come up at dinner, which was generally the only time she saw him.

Indeed, dinner with the Laird had become the highlight of her day, despite the fact that he had been horribly judgemental at first. They now enjoyed a relationship that was perfectly cordial, although... She stopped. *Cordial* did not do justice to the confusing feelings he engendered in her. Yes, she was relieved that he now seemed less hostile and cynical about her dedication to her work, but *cordial* was much too mild a word for the strong emotions she felt each time she saw him. Nervousness was paramount, but beneath it was a swirl of warmth and fear and confusion, along with a thudding heart and racing pulse.

Thankfully, the Laird had not again questioned her about her reasons for leaving her previous posts, although she had sensed his curiosity at the time. However, their dinner-time conversations had moved beyond the polite and they now enjoyed stimulating discourse about books, art and even history.

He—and Iain, when he was able to join them—had given her a little insight into Scotland's history as understood by the Scots, which she was perfectly open to exploring. Emboldened, they had gradually inveigled her into full discourses about Bonnie Prince Charlie, the Royal lines of succession, and the ban on Highland dress, which had only been reversed in their lifetime.

'So your family did not always wear the Highland dress, then?' she had asked the two men.

'Here, we never stopped wearing it. Travelling to Glasgow, or Edinburgh, our fathers were forced into English habits.' The Laird's expression had been grim, Lydia recalled. 'Yet another reason why they were always relieved to return to the islands.'

Iain had agreed with him and Lydia had tucked away this detail as another piece of the puzzle that was this place and these people. Her fascination though, went beyond an intellectual interest in the islands and islanders. Something about the Laird himself fascinated her. The way he spoke. His rare smile. His hands. The way he held himself.

In his company, she had noticed a definite tendency for her heart to beat faster—particularly when he spoke to her directly. When his eyes met hers, her stomach would do strange somersaults, or a knot would develop in the centre of her chest, or she would find herself losing her train of thought...

'I am done, Lydia!' Mairead declared, bringing her back to the present. She had set the child a writing task, to which Mairead had applied herself with great determination.

'Why, this is excellent, Mairead!' Lydia smiled at her. 'I think we shall be ready to show your *papaidh* some of your work soon. Perhaps you might write something for his birthday next month?'

Mairead beamed happily and Lydia's heart swelled to see the child's confidence was slowly improving. Mairead sent her a sideways glance, asking saucily, 'Is it my turn yet?' Their pact had continued, with alternating hours for each of them to choose their tasks. A side benefit was that Mairead was, quite without realising it, learning to tell time.

Lydia glanced at the clock. 'Not quite. Can you see that the long hand is still to the side?'

'It is nearly at the top though,' Mairead offered, with hope.

'It is.' She took a deep breath. 'Now, I wonder if, for these last few minutes of my turn, we could perhaps talk about your arms and legs.'

The child's eyes widened. 'What of them?'

'Tell me what you think about them.'

'Well, they do not work. They are not strong, or strong-willed. And so I cannot walk or run, and I cannot hold heavy things for very long.'

Lydia nodded, all attentiveness, ensuring that no pity was obvious in her expression. 'Did you know that I was governess to another child who could not walk? His name was Master John.'

'Was he the same as me?'

'Not exactly. His legs were completely dead and

would not move at all, whereas I think yours can move a little.'

'Oh, yes,' said Mairead calmly, 'Look!' She moved her right foot up and down, then her left. Concentrating hard, she lifted both legs outwards, straightening them from the knees. She also lifted her arms in the air, holding them up briefly before dropping them again. 'I have always been able to move them a little. But that is not the same as walking.'

Lydia sank to the floor beside her. 'But that is wonderful! Can you do it again?'

Mairead complied and Lydia clapped her hands. 'Mairead, I must be honest with you. I do not know if it is possible for your arms and legs to get stronger, but if you wish it, I can help you.'

Mairead looked at her blankly. 'But everyone knows my arms and legs do not work. I am like old Mrs Mackinnon—although her arms are strong. It is her legs that do not work.'

Lydia shook her head. 'I am very glad that Mrs Mackinnon is so well thought of by everyone. Why, it is clear to me that she does not need to walk to be important and valuable to everyone here. Her knitting and sewing skills are legendary in the castle, I believe. But your case may be different, Mairead. You have just shown me that your arms and legs do work. They just get tired, that is all.' Lydia tried a different tack. 'Have you ever seen a baby who could not walk?'

'Well, of course! There are always babies and they never walk!'

'How do they go from not walking to walking?'

'I—I do not know. They just do.'

'I have cared for many babies and I have seen them change. First they roll over, then they sit and after that they work out how to hold themselves on their hands and knees.'

'Yes! And then they learn to crawl!'

'They do all of those things *before* they try to stand or walk. And they change from just having their mama's milk to eating proper food and they eat more of it as they get bigger. Maybe we could try some of the things that babies do? It would mean lots of practising, just like your handwriting—but maybe your legs might become a little bit stronger.'

Mairead considered this. 'I do not like to eat. They make me have breakfast and dinner every day, but I only eat it because I must.'

Lydia shrugged. 'No-one can force you to eat more. But I think that the food may help the muscles in your arms and legs to get stronger. Only you can decide, Mairead.'

'And I shall walk again?'

Lydia shook her head. 'I cannot say. I make no promises, Mairead. Do you understand? I do not know, and you do not know, how strong your legs and arms may become. But we can make a game of it, do you not think?'

'Can we do it now?' The child's eyes were shining. She glanced at the clock. 'It is my turn anyway! I choose babylegs as my lesson!'

Babylegs?

'Very well.' She smiled. 'Let us begin by sitting on the floor then, as babies do.' Thinking quickly, she rose and took an apple from the bowl on the side table. 'I am going to place this apple beside you and you must reach for it and pick it up.'

This Mairead did with no difficulty, so Lydia placed the apple in various places around her, gradually increasing the distance so that Mairead had to lean more and more to reach it. This she did, her stomach muscles and balance proving themselves up to the task. She even ate the apple—something that Lydia had not seen her do before. Carefully, Lydia did not comment on this.

Next they worked on rolling over and Lydia was pleased to see that Mairead's legs moved to assist her as she clumsily and slowly manoeuvred herself from back to front and back again. Clearly pleased with her own efforts, the child pushed herself into a seated position.

'Master John was not able to roll,' Lydia told Mairead quietly. 'His legs would not help him.'

'Then I am sorry for him. But I am happy that I can roll!' She rolled again, slowly making her way to the edge of the carpet and back again, giggling at her own efforts. 'This is very amusing, Lydia!'

Lydia grinned. 'I am glad to hear it!' Mairead's face was flushed with a healthy colour, she noted. *Children should be active.* 'Perhaps for our outside time, if it is dry later, I could take you to that small hill where we sit sometimes. You could sit there and practise reaching for things without toppling over.'

'No!' Mairead's tone was sharp. 'For we could be seen from the windows if we go there.'

'You do not wish to be seen?'

Mairead took both Lydia's hands in hers, looking up at her with a pleading expression. 'We are going to tell

Papaidh about my reading and writing soon and then I shall have no surprise for him. This—my babylegs— will be the next surprise.' She shrugged. 'And if it does not work, then at least he will not be sad.'

Lydia, tears stinging her eyes, enveloped the child in a warm hug. 'You are very wise, Mairead. And very kind.'

'Tapadh leat,' Mairead whispered and Lydia's heart sang at the child's use of the more familiar form of address.

'Now,' she said, all practicality, 'how are your poor legs and arms feeling after all that hard work?'

'My legs are burning, Lydia. They feel very warm.'

'That is a good thing, I think. May I stretch them? That might help.'

Mairead nodded and Lydia gently lifted Mairead's right leg. There was little muscle in the calf, but Lydia could indeed feel warmth through the fabric of the child's split dress. Gently, she stretched Lydia's foot and ankle, bending and rotating it, then stretching the calf by bending the foot upwards. After doing the same with the child's knee and lifting the leg to gently stretch the upper leg muscles, Lydia repeated the same with the other side. 'And that is enough for now, I think. Time for lunch!'

Inwardly, she was suddenly quaking, questioning whether she was doing the right thing. What would the Laird say if he knew? Mairead was his child, after all. Still, strengthening Mairead's ability to roll over easily was no bad thing, surely? If ever she took a spill from a chair, she could at least attempt to sit herself up— altogether more dignified than flailing around on her back or stomach, awaiting assistance. Like Mairead, Lydia was possessed of a strong independent streak and sensed that the child would value the sense of control this would bestow—even if it were limited control.

She sighed. The danger was not there. The true danger was that—despite deliberately trying not to—she might have given the child false expectations. *I hope I do not break her little heart.* That was the part that the Laird had every right to object to. And the fact that Mairead wanted it kept from him did not help. Indeed, it compounded Lydia's sense of guilt, for he would not even know of his child's hopes.

This was not the first time that Lydia had experienced a dilemma to do with her care of a child. Frequently, she had used unorthodox teaching methods—methods that she knew would be unacceptable to the children's parents. Teaching outside was one of her favourites. She was not so old herself as to have forgotten the tedium of a dreary classroom. The same tasks in fresh air seemed easier, somehow. Thankfully, Mairead no longer protested about outside time and had even been known to groan in disappointment on a rainy day.

Today, her memory just as strong as her determination, Mairead insisted Lydia carry her well out of sight of the castle, to a part of the island where there were few houses. Gentle hills covered in crisp brown and bright green vegetation abounded and Lydia was flushed and perspiring before they reached a spot at the top of a hill that satisfied her charge.

'Here!' she declared imperiously, reminding Lydia of the Laird. He occasionally got just such a look on his face and used that tone, when he was at his most laird-ish.

There was a small bush nearby and Mairead amused herself by counting the green caterpillars that were swarming all over it. 'Seventeen!' she declared in triumph. 'That means there will be seventeen butterflies in a few weeks.'

'Unless the birds eat some of the caterpillars.' Lydia sent her a wicked smile.

'No, no, Miss Lydia.' Mairead wagged a finger at her. 'You shall not trick me into playing fox and hens with the caterpillars!'

Lydia laughed. 'Very well. Let us rest here a while then, for I do declare I am exhausted from carrying you all this way, child!'

'Then you must rest, Lydia, for I mean to practise my rolling!' Before Lydia could stop her, she had lain down on her side, pushing herself into motion, then shrieking loudly as she rolled swiftly down the hill. Horrified, Lydia rose as quickly as she could, racing after the delicate child as she moved towards the bottom with alarming speed. She came to a halt just as Lydia reached her.

'Oh, my dear, are you well? Mairead!' She turned the child towards her, astonished to see Mairead's eyes alight with devilish glee.

'That was wonderful! I must do it again!'

'Oh!' Lydia sank down amid her own skirts, overwhelmed with relief. 'You gave me such a fright!'

'Please carry me to the top again, Lydia.'

'Oh, no!' Lydia's tone was firm. 'My job is to keep

you safe, and rolling down hills is not in the least safe. Why, you might have struck your head upon a rock!'

'But there are no rocks in this part, look! It is all bog moss!' Mairead pointed out. Blinking, Lydia was forced to admit the child was correct. The green moss adorning the hillock was soft and springy—perfect for Mairead's rolling.

'And this will be good for my legs and my arms. Please may I do it again? Even once more?'

Seeing the unusual flush of healthy colour in the child's cheeks, and the bright sparkle in her eye, Lydia found herself powerless to resist. 'Oh, very well. But just once more, mind.'

This time, Lydia walked down to the halfway point before signalling to Mairead to go. The child's shrieks resounded around the hills, but now Lydia recognised them as signalling delight, not fear. Afterwards, she spent a good ten minutes taking pieces of heather and moss from Mairead's hair and clothing while the child munched on another apple, before picking her up and making for the safety of the castle. Really, the little rascal was becoming quite a handful!

That evening, at dinner, Lydia stole a glance at her charge. Gone was the hoydenish child with a head full of vegetation. In her place was the usual Mairead— neat, tidy and self-contained. Naturally, she was asking questions, but in a reasonably calm manner. When her *papaidh* asked what she had been doing all day, she made mention of their trip, but only to ask him the name of the hills. He told her, then moved on, and Lydia let her breath go a little. 'Miss Lydia and I have been working hard, Papaidh, and we shall have something to show you soon.'

'Indeed?' He raised an eyebrow. 'May I know what it is?'

Shyly, Mairead glanced towards Lydia, who smiled. 'You may tell him.'

'I can write some things now, Papaidh. And I can read many words. I have been working very hard on my letters, have I not, Lydia?'

'Indeed you have, my dear.' Her voice thickened with sudden emotion, Lydia swallowed, looking at the Laird. 'She is clever and she has been working very diligently, so her letters are coming along nicely.'

He was beaming with delight and, as he spoke to his daughter of his pride in her, Lydia's heart turned over. *These two!* Underneath the table, she bunched her hands into fists. While she had usually come to love the children in her care, she had never before been so taken with one of the parents. Indeed, she had never before been so taken with any gentleman!

Yes, he had a tendency to glower and he had been terribly rude towards her when she had first arrived, but Lydia understood that his primary concern, naturally, was Mairead. Father and daughter had a firm friendship, and it delighted her to observe their interactions. Sometimes, when they were speaking Gaelic to each other, she would allow the rhythm of the beautiful language to wash over her, dreamily watching them both.

Naturally, she knew that developing a tendre for her employer was forbidden, but years of hiding her feelings in company gave her a reasonable level of confidence that he could have no notion. Never before had she encountered a gentleman who combined honourable behaviour with a fine face and form, and the combination was too much for her lonely heart. It would pass, she knew, for she had heard of such things before. In the meantime, she must be careful to not allow anyone to see her growing regard for the Laird—particularly the Laird himself.

Mairead had turned her attention to her food and Lydia was delighted to see that, tonight, the child was showing signs of an increased appetite. Perhaps rolling down hills and moving one's arms and legs was of benefit in that way, too. Or perhaps this was simply a reflection of Mairead's determination to help rebuild her strength. Gaining confidence in reading and writing seemed to be changing how Mairead saw herself.

They were seated side by side and Lydia suddenly became aware that, under the cover of the table, Mairead was continuing to exercise her legs. Lydia could sense the child moving her feet, gently straightening one leg, then the other, and seemingly lifting her legs to balance her feet on the cross bar of the tall chair. Six years old and such determination! She glanced at the Laird. Oblivious to his daughter's surreptitious activity, he was currently conversing with Iain about arrangements for an upcoming wedding in the castle. Noting his firm jaw and the decided way in which he was directing his steward, Lydia had to hide a grin. It was clear where Mairead got her strong will from!

'Something amuses you, Miss Farnham?' His tone was mild, but the look he threw her was piercing.

'Oh, I am just—just pleased to hear there is to be a wedding. It is always such a happy occasion, is it not?'

He raised a sceptical eyebrow. 'Indeed? I am delighted to hear of your pleasure at the prospect. I must disagree with you, however. Not all weddings are happy occasions, even if they seem so at the time.'

'Who is getting married, Papaidh?'

'Màiri is going to marry Calum MacLean in two weeks. You know—the Màiri who works in the kitchens.'

'Oh.' She looked crestfallen. 'I thought it might be Eilidh.'

'Which Eilidh? Eilidh Òg or Eilidh Ruadh?'

Aha! *Òg* was young, Lydia knew, and *ruadh* meant red-haired. *So this is how they differentiate.* Eilidh Òg would be the maid and Eilidh Ruadh the Laird's red-haired cousin.

'Eilidh Òg. She helps me and Lydia. She likes Dòmhnall Mòr. I think they should marry each other.'

The Laird glanced at Lydia, a clear question in his gaze. She replied with a shrug and a crooked smile.

I have no idea what Mairead is referring to.

'Does she now?' the Laird murmured. He glanced towards Iain and the two exchanged a knowing look. 'She could do worse.'

'Dòmhnall Mòr is a good lad,' agreed Iain. 'No fortune, though. All he's done so far is work the kelp. They'll need a cottage and he a trade.'

'He's good with livestock. Perhaps put him with the cattlemen.'

'Aye. Leave it with me.'

Lydia watched this exchange with great interest.

Young people, then, were able to choose their partners here? She shook herself. Naturally, servants and
farm workers could always choose their mates, even
in England. It was the aristocracy who tried to arrange
marriages with 'suitable' partners for their offspring.
Lydia had seen the outcome when such marriages did
not go well—couples who could barely stand the sight
of one another, children damaged by being caught up
in a battle that was none of their own making. Happy
marriages like that of Lord and Lady Barnstable, and
her own dear parents, were rare. Was that what the Laird
had been referring to, with his oblique comment just
now? Or had it been something more specific?

For the first time it occurred to her to wonder about
Mairead's mother. According to the limited information
she had gleaned in passing from the castle staff, Lady
Hester had been young and beautiful and the Laird had
been besotted with her. She had died when Mairead was
still a young baby. Sadly, the child had no memory of
her mother, Lydia knew. Had Lady Hester died in child-
bed, or of milk fever? Or had illness or accident carried
her off? Either way, it was a tragedy, Lydia knew, for
any child to lose her mother. Lydia's own mama had
died only a few short years ago, but Lydia missed her
yet. Loneliness was her lot now and she had given up
on the notion of marriage for herself. Her experiences
with men had made her withdraw from any notion of
being closer to any of them. Oh, she knew in her mind
that some marriages could work. She just did not feel
it in her heart.

Turning her thoughts back to the death of Mairead's
mother, she felt an ache of compassion for the child.

But it was not only Mairead who had lost a loved one. It was a tragedy, too, for the grieving husband left behind. Lydia stole another glance at the Laird. He had his 'business' face on as he discussed with Iain the numbers likely to attend the upcoming wedding and the food that should be provided. The two men had lapsed into Gaelic, but Lydia was still able to understand the gist of their conversation. *My understanding of Gaelic is improving.* As people became more used to her presence, Lydia had observed, they were less likely to remember to speak English in front of her, although they always did so when addressing her directly.

Her mind drifted back to the two men's plan to ensure the other soon-to-be groom had a trade. The way the community here looked after each other was heartwarming. While similar things sometimes happened with servants in the households where she had previously worked, here the nets of support reached out to cover everyone in the islands, it seemed.

Mairead was taken off to bed soon afterwards and Iain was called away, leaving Lydia alone with the Laird. These were the best evenings, when they would talk quietly together, sometimes for hours. Tonight, he was in a jovial, relaxed mood. They shared some whisky, discussed the trivial matters of the day and rested at ease with one another.

Recalling the conversation earlier, Lydia grinned as an unexpected thought occurred to her. The Laird, noting this, immediately asked her to share her thoughts— as he had before. He often seemed to wish to know what she was thinking. 'Oh, it is nothing,' she replied airily.

'I am just wondering if poor Dòmhnall Mòr has any notion of marrying Eilidh!'

He laughed at this and her gaze travelled to his firm jaw and strong throat. *So handsome!* How, she wondered, had she gone from suspicion of all men to actually developing something of a tendre for one?

It is this place. No-one had accosted her, no-one had attacked her, no-one had declared themselves to her. She had been in the islands for less than two months, but she had begun to believe that perhaps here was a place where she could feel safe. Oh, she had seen admiration in some eyes, but the men involved had behaved properly at all time. *Mrs Gray was right. There are different expectations of men here.*

'Yes, perhaps we should consult the young man himself, before we have him married! While my Mairead is very discerning and often notices things that others miss, perhaps we should leave the matter between Eilidh and Dòmhnall for the present.'

'Absolutely! It must be difficult enough courting in a place where everyone knows everyone's business, we should not make assumptions that may be ahead of the couple themselves.'

'That is true,' he replied slowly, clearly pondering her reply. 'Such affections may develop suddenly, like a flash of lightning, or more slowly, like the rising of the sun.' He seemed almost to be speaking to himself. 'And lightning, while it may feel dramatic, can do great harm.'

'I would not know, sir.'

His gaze swung back to her, laughter dancing in his eyes. 'Of lightning, or courtship?'

She declined to engage, saying merely. 'Is that the time? I must retire, for no doubt Mairead will be awake bright and early on the morrow!'

Mairead was not only awake early, she had clearly been pondering over the dinner table conversation herself. The very next morning, while Eilidh was seeing to the fire in the little study room, she asked the maid directly, 'Eilidh, do you like Dòmhnall Mòr?'

The girl blushed a fiery red and stammered something about having plenty of friends, and that she supposed Dòmhnall Mòr was not unlikeable.

Ah. So there is no understanding between them.

'Miss Lydia,' Eilidh said, avoiding looking at Mairead, and clearly trying to leave the topic of Dòmhnall Mòr behind, 'I have mended the hem on your yellow dress.'

'Why, thank you so much, Eilidh. I have been used to doing all my own mending, so you really do not have to do this.'

'I was wondering though, what will you be wearing to Màiri's wedding?

Lydia shrugged. 'I confess I had not given the matter much consideration. What should I wear?'

'The blue,' Eilidh declared, without hesitation. 'Though I would wish to alter it a little.'

Lydia laughed nervously. 'I do not wish for my bosom to be on display to the world, Eilidh!'

'Of course not, miss. But your dresses in general are too large for you. Would you allow me to take this one in and see how you like it?'

To wear a dress that fitted her, that looked pretty and

not dowdy? Caution warred with vanity within her and, for the first time, she allowed vanity to win. 'Oh, very well, then. Why not?'

Chapter Six

Why not? *This was why not!*

Lydia stood before the mirror in her chamber, biting her lip. It was the day of the wedding and Eilidh had finished the dress. It was stunning. Eilidh, clearly a gifted needlewoman, had not only taken it in, she had made it hug Lydia's figure to perfection. The dress had been a gift from Mrs Pickering before the rift between them—an old dress, she had said at the time, from before an excess of plumpness had come on her.

Lydia, always glad to receive her employers' cast-offs, had thanked Mrs Pickering, who had been both taller and generally larger than Lydia. She had had to take the dress up a little at the time, but ensured that it remained wide enough to hide the lines of her shape. Eilidh had uncovered those lines and revealed every curve of Lydia's body. Yes, the lace *fichu* was firmly in place—very little skin was on display—yet the cerulean silk with its gauze overdress hugged every part of her form. There were her hips, her stomach, her breasts and her waist. All visible. All on display.

She took a breath, tried to look at the image in the mirror as if she were seeing some other person, at a party, perhaps. Seen in that way, with a degree of objectivity, Lydia realised that the dress was not particularly unusual. It was pretty, in fact. Eilidh had added lace at the sleeves and a little on the bodice, and the effect was wondrous. *It is the prettiest dress I have ever worn.*

To make matters worse, Eilidh had insisted in styling her hair and Lydia's tresses had been swept up into an elaborate chignon, with pretty golden side curls framing her face. To Lydia, who had spent all of her adult life trying to disguise her looks, the effect was terrifying. Eilidh, of course, was only delighted.

'Ah, Miss Lydia, you will outshine even the bride today!'

'But I have no wish to outshine her! This is Màiri's day. I would not do anything in the world to take that away from any bride!' She shook her head. 'You will have to tell them I am indisposed. I cannot possibly go down looking like this.'

Mairead, who had been listening to this exchange with great interest, chose this moment to interject. 'Do you not like your dress, Lydia? I think it is very pretty!'

'It is not that. It is just—' She bit back her words. Never could she admit aloud that she did not welcome her own good looks.

Mairead tilted her head on one side. 'Eilidh worked very hard to fix your dress and your hair. And—' she added, twisting the knife 'I know very well that you are *not* indisposed, and you always tell me how important it is to be truthful.'

Lydia closed her eyes briefly.

I declare this child will be the death of me.

'Very well. But I intend to retire as soon as I may.'
She reached for the child, who slipped into her arms
and nestled comfortably against her hip as if she were
meant to be there.

Mairead's own dress was of white muslin, trimmed
with blue ribbons, and with a split skirt as usual. The
long fabric was a perfect disguise for little legs that were
gradually getting stronger, and already, to Lydia's delight, had some actual visible muscle. In the past fortnight, as well as perfecting her rolling and sitting up,
Mairead had been practising kneeling and she was now
able to kneel up for quite ten seconds at a time, before
her strength gave out.

What could not be disguised however, was the
healthy colour in Mairead's cheeks. Some of the staff
had made comment about her rosy complexion, which
had gladdened Lydia.

I am not imagining it, then.

The Laird, if he had noticed, had made no comment so far. He and Lydia had taken to moving to his
parlour after dinner each evening, to play cards, drink
wine and converse on matters big and small. Iain frequently joined them, but most evenings, it was just the
Laird and Lydia.

Lydia was feeling increasingly easy in the company
of both men—which was entirely surprising to her,
given her previous experiences. While Iain had occasionally had a warm look in his eye towards Lydia, he
had done nothing to make her feel uncomfortable and
she was hoping that, for once, she might be able to call
a man 'friend'. He was a good person and she had come

to like what she knew of him, but he left her heart and body unmoved.

The Laird, on the other hand, showed no signs of attraction towards her. He was unfailingly polite—warm, even—but Lydia, who had been hounded by men all her adult life, was rather put out that this man, of all men, should show her nothing but cordiality. Despite her assumption that her fluttering innards would eventually settle themselves, they were showing no signs of doing so. Just being in his presence was enough to make her heart skip and her stomach complete strange tumblings. *Wonderful!* she thought wryly as she descended the main staircase, Eilidh by her side and Mairead in her arms. *Finally, I am attracted to someone and he does not feel the same.* Indeed, there were occasions when she still believed he disapproved of her.

It was as yet unclear exactly why. She knew he had been sceptical about her teaching abilities. Was he yet? He frequently quizzed her about Mairead's lessons and Lydia provided the information with a calmness she generally did not feel. There was always a certain nervousness that accompanied discussing children's progress with their parents, but it was even more pronounced with him. No matter how much she assured him of Mairead's progress, she never felt that he quite trusted her.

'Ooh!' Mairead breathed, as they reached the top of the stair leading to the Great Hall, Eilidh beside them. Below them, the space had been hung with greenery and flowers, in celebration of Màiri and Calum's special day.

'How pretty!' Lydia breathed, echoing Mairead's response. The greenery had been intertwined with flowers from the machair and the marshes—pretty primroses and buttercups gleaming bright yellow and contrasting with the deeper hues of marsh marigolds and the golden frothiness of lady's bedstraw.

So intent was she on identifying the flowers—some of which she had never seen before coming to the islands—that Lydia entirely failed to notice the Laird, standing to one side with Mrs MacLeod and looking up at them descending.

Alasdair always felt a certain ambivalence about weddings. They were a frequent occurrence in the island community, but he never knew whether to be hopeful and delighted for the marital couple, or cynical and pessimistic of their chances. Reason told him there were many married couples within the castle and the wider Ardmore community who were perfectly content with each other, even after many years.

Yet when his thoughts turned to his own marriage, and to Hester's death less than two years after they had exchanged their wedding vows, he felt only a cold emptiness. Despite what the islanders believed, his fixation with his beautiful young wife had not long survived the reality of living with her.

He had courted Hester in the glowing candlelight of Edinburgh ballrooms and married her within two months of meeting her. Memories shuddered through him. The thrill of bringing her here to the castle for the first time. The hurt that had pierced him when she had seen only its imperfections.

Standing with Mrs MacLeod in the Great Hall, with the excitement of the upcoming nuptials in the air, his thoughts drifted to Calum and Màiri. *They are both from Ardmore. Both from the same world*, he reminded himself. Islanders understood one another. *Outsiders will always be outsiders.* In his mind, he used the Gaelic word 'Sassenach', which, naturally, drew his thoughts to the governess. Her status as an outsider, combined with her striking beauty, meant that she was dangerous. An outsider could never be truly content here in the islands, he knew. He knew it and yet could never understand it. It mystified him, for he knew Ardmore to be as close to Paradise as was possible in this world. Still, experience had been his teacher. Harsh experience.

Yes, Miss Farnham would inevitably leave and his main concern as a father was to ensure Mairead did not become over-reliant on the woman. He was rather pleased that, up until now, he himself had managed not to succumb entirely to the governess's charms, although it had taken every ounce of self-restraint to do so. So far, he had succeeded in maintaining a balance between developing something like a friendship with her—a novel situation in itself—without yielding to the temptation to let his eyes or his touch linger on her.

To be fair, she had no airs to attract, being possessed of a down-to-earth practicality which contrasted greatly with her angelic beauty. In that sense she was very different to Hester, who had used her looks to wheedle, cajole and persuade people to comply with her wishes.

If Miss Farnham had been even a little flirtatious, she would have caused havoc in the castle. Indeed, it had surprised him to notice how she kept to herself and chose the company of other women—going as far as to avoid even conversing with men, apart from himself and Iain—and *that* was of necessity. She was, he knew, generally liked in the castle—*liked*, rather than simply admired for her looks.

If he were completely honest, he might confess to enjoying her company every evening—hers and Iain's, naturally. She had a good mind and he enjoyed informing her of Scottish history and hearing some details of her life before coming to the islands. And if, in the dead of night, his thoughts of her were of a more intimate nature, he could set this aside in the cold light of day. He was a man, after all, and no man could fail to be inspired by her beauty.

His musings returned to her tales of London life. Although she had provided plenty of information about the various children she had cared for—their character and habits, their ages and dispositions—she had never explained why she had left each family. To listen to her, one would assume that she had been devoted to every one of her charges. Yet she had left every one of them.

Having noted this, he still could not fault her current diligence towards Mairead. She spent most of every day with his daughter, even on Sundays, and frequently carried her off for jaunts out across the low hills and moors. They went to the beaches, too, he knew, for Mairead was assembling an impressive collection of seashells. Despite his worries that she might succumb to a chill, the child actually looked healthier now than she had before. She was eating more, too, which might have been a coincidence. Or it might not.

Grudgingly, he admitted that Miss Farnham was doing a reasonable job so far. Catching his thoughts, he frowned. That was unfair. She was being conscientious and was getting results, both with Mairead's lessons and with the child's general appearance and demeanour. If a woman from the islands were achieving as much with Mairead, he would have been delighted. But Miss Farnham's status as an outsider, combined with her impossible beauty, served only to increase his wariness of her.

A sudden lull in the Great Hall chatter brought him back to the present. People were nudging one another and eyes were turning to the grand staircase. Naturally, he, too, looked up—and caught his breath.

Miss Farnham was descending, Mairead on her hip. Someone else was with them, but for the moment his attention was fully captured by the governess. Never had he seen her look so beautiful—and he was well used to the knowledge that she was divinely pretty. *It is the dress.* It hugged every delectable curve and confirmed his previous suspicions that her body was every bit as perfect as her face. Greedily, his gaze roved over her form—those breasts! And the hips!

Abruptly, he caught himself. *I am no callow youth, to be so taken by an attractive woman.* Yet his body, frustratingly, disagreed. He slammed his jaw shut, belatedly realising it had sagged in hungry reaction. She had reached the bottom of the stairs and was hesitating, looking decidedly uncertain. *I should go to her.* Yet he did not. The hunger in him was too strong. He needed to get himself under some sort of control before he attempted to converse with her. The last thing he needed was to give her any sort of indication that he found her attractive. Therein lay the path to ruin.

Hester had played him like a master musician played

the harp. He, blinded by emotion, had entirely failed to understand his young wife and tragedy had ensued. It was his fault and his failing that he had not realised Hester was unsuited to island life. And that he himself was not someone a beautiful woman could truly love. He had been too wedded to his duty, unable to give Hester the attention she had craved...

He forced himself to focus on Mairead. As if conscious of all the staring eyes, she had nestled deeper into Miss Farnham's embrace and was currently hiding her face in the governess's neck. *The governess who will inevitably leave us all.*

This was exactly the inducement he needed to shake himself out of sentimentality, fear, regret and desire. Quite before he knew what he was doing, he had marched towards the bottom of the stairs. 'Give her to me!'

Even he heard the commanding tone. It was not a tone he often used, so it was little wonder that Miss Farnham's eyes widened in startlement and—was that fear?

'Of course.' Her voice shook a little. 'Look, Mairead, here is your *papaidh*!'

Mairead was already lifting her head. He held out his arms and, for the briefest of moments he wondered if she might refuse him. His blood ran cold. Then she reached for him and his heart began beating once again.

Danger!

'Miss Farnham, I have been considering and I have decided I should like to observe some of my daughter's lessons.' He had not, in fact, been considering it at all, but now that the words had been spoken he saw the sense in it. 'Each day after nuncheon I shall spend an hour with you both.'

'Yes, of course, sir.'

He could tell that his words were causing her some nervousness, but the feeling that Mairead was becoming much, much too attached to her governess terrified him. 'Good. We begin tomorrow.' He looked down at Mairead, who was balanced on his hip. 'Now, *mo nighean*, we must take our places, for the wedding is about to begin.'

Striding away from the governess, he did not look back. And yet, indelibly etched in his mind's eye was an image of her almost frightened expression just now—eyes huge in her pale face, a face perfectly framed with the addition of fashionable guinea-gold side curls. As if she was not beautiful enough!

A few moments later the ceremony began. While it might have seemed to others as though he were attending to it, his thoughts were elsewhere. Actually, there were very few coherent thoughts. Instead there was a whirlwind of swirling emotion—fear of losing Mairead, regret at his own curtness, concern at having distressed Miss Farnham, a sense of righteousness at having reminded her that Mairead was his daughter… underneath it all, and threading through everything else, was a damnable attraction towards her that he could no longer deny.

Lydia watched him stride away, shock holding her immobile. Eilidh, who had stood quietly nearby during their entire exchange, slipped an arm into Lydia's. 'Let us find a place to sit, for they will begin shortly.'

In something of a daze, Lydia allowed Eilidh to lead

her to two seats near the back of the hall. *I knew this was a mistake!*

They had almost reached the bottom of the stairs before Lydia had realised that numerous people were staring at them. A governess, she knew, should never be *forward*, never seek attention. She should remain in the background, quietly and unobtrusively dealing with the children. She should certainly not be wearing silk and lace and sporting saucy side curls. As she recalled the Laird's thunderous expression, her innards tightened with nervousness and regret.

I should never have worn this dress!

Her heart was pounding. She felt distressed, upset— tearful, even. Where had her friend disappeared to? The person who had talked with her so easily each evening? In his place was a laird, a distant figure giving commands in an imperious manner. It was a side of him she had seen less and less as time went on and it was a shock to be reminded of it.

Thankfully, the wedding ceremony began soon afterwards and so there was no longer any requirement for conversation. Years of hiding her feelings allowed her, she hoped, to appear outwardly serene, yet inwardly turmoil raged. The Laird was displeased with her—so displeased that he had behaved with more impoliteness than she had ever seen from him. Part of her secret admiration had grown, she, knew, from watching him respond with understanding to difficult issues and controversies among the castle—urgent challenges to do with disagreements which he mediated with unfailing good judgement and equanimity.

Such equanimity had been absent just now, when

he had made his displeasure towards her crystal clear. There had been nothing of composure in his harsh tone and dark scowl. Never had she seen such incivility from him. She felt chastised, uncertain, lost—as though she herself was a recalcitrant schoolgirl and he her angry tutor. She had come to expect harshness from employers when they found out about men importuning her, but this felt so much worse—partly, she owned, because she had been beginning to trust him.

This time, no man had attacked her, despite her foolish decision to dress in a way that could only draw attention to her looks and form. A sudden thought struck her. Perhaps the Laird was angry at her new dress, her fancy hairstyle and the attention it had generated—attention she had never wished for.

The failing was hers. Yes, her gown and hairstyle had been fashioned by Eilidh, but Lydia herself, in a fit of vanity, had succumbed to the temptation. And now she was to pay dearly for it. Whatever the Laird's reasons were for mistrusting her, she had added to them. It was all her own doing. No man had importuned her, it was true, but the Laird had made his disapproval of her transformation clear.

As the ceremony continued and her thoughts flitted about like butterflies in a garden, there was one clear thread running through all of the agitation within her.

Please, please do not send me away!

Chapter Seven

Three hours later and Lydia's agitation had calmed somewhat. She had not actually been dismissed, and so she still had hope that the Laird would allow her to remain at least a while longer. So he wanted to observe her lessons with Mairead? However much he might have judged her for her vanity, at least she could be confident in her own abilities as a teacher. Reminding himself of the innate fairness and sense of justice she had seen in him, she dared to hope that perhaps he would allow her to know her trade, just as he had during the fox-and-hens incident.

Throughout the wedding banquet, she listened with half an ear to the Gaelic conversations going on all around her, while inwardly she was planning tomorrow's lessons. She needed to demonstrate that not only was she a good teacher, but that Mairead was already making real progress with her learning. The child was preparing a birthday missive to her *papaidh*—on parchment, no less. She had written some lines in Gaelic and in English in her best handwriting and was now adding small drawings as decorative flourishes around the edges—mainly flowers, butterflies and sea shells. It lacked a fortnight until the Laird's birthday and part of the child's gift to him was, Lydia knew, the progress she had made in writing. The child relished the notion of how surprised and pleased her *papaidh* would be when he saw the missive.

The other secret work—that of helping the child regain her strength—was also unknown to the Laird. Mairead's comment earlier about truthfulness had pricked Lydia's conscience. Would the Laird not wish to share in Mairead's delight as she developed a new skill, or sustained her own weight on her knees for a little longer each time? Or would he, as Lydia had initially feared, be furious at her allowing the child to have hopes that might well be dashed?

Surely, she thought, he had noticed the improvement in Mairead's appetite? The colour in her cheeks when she returned from an outing? Her general animation?

'*Gabh mo leisgeul*, miss. Excuse me.' It was one of the castle menservants. 'I need to move this table.'

'Oh! I am sorry!' she replied automatically, then repeated it in Gaelic. '*Tha mi duilich.*' She stood, as others all around her were doing, and moved towards the edge of the hall. They were clearing all of the tables away to the sides, leaving an open space in the centre. Seeing a chair free in a particularly dark part of the room, she made for it rapidly. Safe in the shadows, she exhaled with relief, then glanced nervously around, seeking the Laird. There he was, still at the top of the room, now conversing with the bridegroom and his parents. Allowing herself the indulgence of a perusal of his fine form, she could not help but reflect on how well all the gentlemen looked in their Highland garb. *Particularly*—she forced herself to look elsewhere.

On the small dais where the priest had stood, two fiddlers now began tuning up, triggering a thrill of reaction around the room. Before long, the musicians were ready and the space filled with men, women, and older children all ready to dance. Younger children also abounded and many were now running around the hall, chasing each other or play-fighting. The customs here were tolerant of children—no, not simply tolerant. They positively *liked* children in the islands. It was another way in which this place was bewilderingly different to the life she had known.

Good different.

The Laird, she noted, was one of the first on the dance floor, leading his cousin Eilidh Ruadh by the hand. *Where is Mairead?* Ah, she was seated on Mrs MacLeod's knee and looking contented. Such a pity she could not run and play with the others. Perhaps Mairead would enjoy some time with other children… Lydia stored the notion away, to be considered later. She knew that just now she should cross the room and offer to look after the child, but frankly she wished to draw no attention to herself. This dark corner suited her.

The music began and Lydia's eye returned immediately to the Laird. The music was wild, lyrical, and lively and seemed to her to have a different resonance here. She had heard many reels and jigs in London ballrooms, yet here, she knew, the music *belonged*. It was of the islands and the spirit of the islands soared through every note. *I am being fanciful!* she told herself, shaking off the thought. The Laird was, she noted, a good dancer—but then, so was every person here, it seemed. Astonishingly, people of all ranks and roles were dancing together—servants and farmers mingling as equals with the Laird and his family.

Rank is also seen differently here.

The dance steps were new to her, but she could feel joyfulness all around the hall. Some in London considered dancing to be unseemly—particularly the livelier dances—yet Lydia saw nothing but delight on the faces of the dancers before her. Calum and Màiri had led the dance and were now working their way towards the bottom of their group. Her eyes roved on. There was the other Eilidh—Eilidh Òg—dancing with an extremely large young man who must be the famed Dòmhnall Mòr. She grinned, now understanding the significance of his nickname. Mòr meant big or large, yet in English they frequently referred to him as 'Wee Dòmhnall'. The humour here was delightful. Dòmhnall was smiling at Eilidh, who was herself beaming with happiness.

Mairead is clever!

She had somehow noticed the two young people were interested in each other. Not that either of them were trying to hide it today. Lydia glanced towards the child again. Mairead was now clapping in time with the music and looking wistfully at the dancers. A pang went through Lydia. She understood the wistfulness, for it was hard to simply *watch* such a joyous exhibition.

As Lydia watched, someone bent to speak to Mrs MacLeod and the housekeeper stood, placing Mairead on the chair before leaving to sort out whatever it was that required her attention. Knowing her duty, Lydia rose, hoping that she could cross unnoticed to where

Mairead sat, looking lost and alone in a chair that was much too big for her slight frame.

Thankfully the music continued, and she reached her charge without incident, having moved carefully around the edges of the room. Mairead greeted her with gratifying enthusiasm and Lydia took Mrs MacLeod's place on the large chair, placing Mairead on her knee and asking her to say who the various people were.

Having lost herself in a surfeit of MacDonalds, Mac-Mhuirichs, MacRurys, Buchanans, and MacLeans, Lydia allowed the child's chatter to wash over her, allowing herself for a moment to imagine herself in Eilidh Ruadh's dance slippers. The Laird's cousin was in fine fettle, skipping and hopping her way through the set with impressive skill. She looked beautiful, too, in a dress of green velvet trimmed with cream lace. As if sensing her gaze, Eilidh looked across and their eyes met. The Laird's cousin smiled at Lydia and gave a little wave and Lydia smiled back. Both Eilidhs were sweet girls and she had frequently wished Eilidh Ruadh would visit more frequently, as she would dearly love to make a friend of her. Naturally, as Eilidh was of the Laird's family, and Lydia herself a servant—albeit a higher servant—such a notion was impossible.

Eilidh seemed to frown briefly, then made a point of saying something to the Laird. Immediately, he glanced her way and Lydia felt the force of his gaze. Instantly, the world seemed to waver a little, as if she were once more on the deck of the *Mercury*. What had his cousin said to him? She was sure it would have been nothing unkind, yet even if it had been something good, it had had the unfortunate effect of bringing his attention to her.

A few moments later the dance came to an end, the dancers all laughing, or hugging, or seeking cool refreshment after their exertions. The fiddlers, too, were taking a break and being served with their choice of beverage. Through the crowd, Lydia briefly noticed the bridegroom's mother, who seemed to be crying. Before she could be certain, the crowd shifted again, blocking Mrs MacLean from Lydia's view.

'Here you are, Mairead and Lydia!' It was Eilidh Ruadh, the Laird's cousin. Pulling a chair closer, she sat herself down next to them. 'What a pretty dress, Mairead!'

The girl smoothed the fabric over her thin knees. 'Thank you, Eilidh. Yours is pretty, too!'

'Indeed it is!' Lydia agreed. 'I love the velvet, Eilidh.'

She grinned. 'When I get too warm from dancing I shall no doubt wish I had worn something lighter.' She eyed Lydia's own dress. 'What a beautiful gown! Was it made in London?'

'Yes and no.' Lydia laughed. 'It certainly came from London, but our own Eilidh Òg took it in and added the trim.' She grimaced. 'You do not think it…too much?'

Eilidh looked at her blankly. 'How? No! Of course not!'

'But I am just the governess—'

'You are *just* nothing! Look around you!' She indicated the wedding guests with a gesture. 'Everyone is equal here. We simply have been given different roles to play. Farmers, castle workers, governesses—we are all equally important. No one is idle here. Despite being

Angus's sister and Alasdair's cousin, I busy myself with everything from weaving to caring for the sick. I could not imagine a life of idleness.'

Lydia gaped at her. 'But surely ladies and gentlemen do not *work*?'

'To *not* work would be wrong. We all depend on one another here. Yes, Alasdair has time to read and study, but his book-learning helps him understand more of the world. He has a responsibility to mete out justice, to think deeply about his responsibilities and to learn from leaders in all places and times, if he can. Surely you, as an educated woman, understand this?'

Lydia nodded thoughtfully. 'Work of different flavours. Yes, I begin to see. I had sensed something of the way in which all the people here seem…connected, somehow. That was not my experience in London society.'

Eilidh nodded. 'Even in Scotland, outside the islands, our way of life is less common now. The Highlands used to be full of clansmen, all loyal to their clan. Since Culloden their way of life is gone and lowland culture becomes more prevalent.' She pursed her lips reflectively. 'I was sent to a school for young ladies in Edinburgh, you know!' Her eyes lit up mischievously. 'They taught me how to behave if I were to ever find myself in the midst of London society. It all seemed like foolishness to me.' On the dais, the musicians were preparing to play another tune. 'I must go, for I promised this dance to Peadar Donn.'

'Enjoy the next dance!'

'You, too!' With this cryptic comment, she sped off. A moment later, the fiddlers began, playing a short introduction to the next dance, and people swarmed into the dancing area. Amid all of the bustling movement, Lydia could not find the Laird at all. Despite his rudeness earlier, she remained foolishly fascinated by him. Where was her sense of containment? Where had her inner calmness gone? She sighed inwardly. *I have become nonsensical.*

'Miss Farnham.'

She jumped in shock, turning her head to see he was standing next to her. His nearness instantly made her heart race and her mind freeze. 'Oh!'

His eyes narrowed at her reaction. 'Come and dance!' He held out a hand, the gesture just as lordly as his tone.

Why is he asking me to dance, when he seemed so cross with me earlier?

'Oh, no!' Finally, she had found her voice. 'I cannot. That is to say, I *should* not... My place is here, with Mairead.'

'Your *place*, Miss Farnham, is wherever I say it is! Come!'

'Yes, dance with Papaidh, Lydia,' Mairead added.

'But I do not even *know* these dances!'

'Papaidh will teach you, will you not, Papaidh?'

'I shall certainly endeavour to do so!'

Was that a glint of humour in his eye? It was hard to work out, particularly when her insides had melted so completely. And she knew exactly why they had done so. It was because of *all of it*. The Highland dress. His height and breadth, and good looks. The way he pronounced words ending in the letter 'r'. The way he was looking at her...

Or perhaps not. When she straightened after set-

tling Mairead in the chair, all she could see in his expression was cool reserve. He offered his hand and she
took it, allowing him to lead her to the dance floor. All
around her, couples were doing the same and she wondered how many were experiencing the thrill she was
sensing in the place where his hand was gently holding
hers. His fingers were enveloping hers, his skin smooth
and warm, and little tingles of excitement—or was it
nervousness?—were shooting through her.

Couples were lining up with four gentlemen facing
four ladies in each group. Looking around for a set that
still needed a pair, the Laird directed Lydia to her right,
then placed her at the bottom of the set, taking his place
in the line of gentlemen opposite. To Lydia's right, the
three other ladies looked relaxed—none seemed to be
worried about not knowing the steps.

'I must confess,' Lydia offered tentatively to the
woman beside her, 'I have not danced this before.'

'Not to worry, lass, you'll soon pick it up. You're last,
so you can watch all of us dance it first. This one is the
Weaving Dance, which is a favourite in these parts.'

Before Lydia could reply, the music began in earnest.
With a fixed attention tinged with more than a hint of
desperation, she watched as the first couple danced together, then worked their way down the set, the lady
spinning with each of the men in turn, while returning
to her partner in between each encounter. When they
reached the bottom, the lady spun with the Laird, while
the gentleman indicated with a gesture that he would
spin with Lydia next.

Showing willingness, she reached out her hand
to him at more or less the correct time and skipped

briefly around in a circle with him before returning to her place. The man then worked his way back up the set, spinning each lady in turn. Finally, he and his partner went down the set again, this time both simultaneously turning the men and women opposite and meeting in the middle in between. When they reached the bottom, they stood beside Lydia and the Laird and the new top couple began their turn.

Frowning with concentration, Lydia continued to watch carefully. She must not make herself look foolish! Half-afraid, she glanced at the Laird. He was eyeing her steadfastly and something in his gaze made her blush a little.

'Perfect!' he mouthed, his demeanour one of support and encouragement, and she felt herself bloom under the warmth of his approval. By the time the next two couples had completed their turn, Lydia was feeling hopeful that perhaps, she would not go wrong. Stepping forward, she reached for his hand and he gave it, and their first turn together was faultless.

Remembering her role, Lydia turned to the first man in the set and off she went. Coming back to the Laird each time felt like coming home. For these few moments he was hers and she was his, and the notion made her feel as though she were flying.

When they reached the bottom, he began spinning the ladies, returning to Lydia each time, and she moved her way up the set, maintaining her constant awareness of him. Finally, they spun their way back down and Lydia, realising she had made no major errors, began to relax a little. To her surprise, once they had finished

their turn as the last couple, the music did not stop.
Leaning forward, he bent close to her ear.

'Now we do it all again.' He straightened, smiling.
'You did well, Miss Farnham. However—'

However? Had she gone wrong somehow?

'—it is permitted to *enjoy* oneself while dancing. Indeed, some might say that is the best part!'

She could not help it: she laughed, recognising that
she had just completed a full figure of dancing wearing a frown of concentration. Instantly his eyes widened briefly, then he seemed to shake his head a little.

'I apologise, sir. I was afraid of going wrong and so
I had to concentrate.'

'I could tell.' He was grinning again. 'And call me
Alasdair.'

'Alasdair.' She smiled. Now that he had offered her
this privilege she realised how much she had longed to
be able to speak his name. She had learned that the informality of the castle extended to some of the staff—
those more senior in age or occupation—calling him
Alasdair as frequently as calling him sir, but never
would she have dared to do it without permission. It
gave her a warm feeling inside that she could now do so.

Before long, it was their turn to lead the dance again
and this time she took her place with confidence. Now
she could not help smiling, for surely this was the most
entertaining dance she had ever taken part in! She said
as much to her neighbour, who seemed delighted that
she was enjoying herself. Finally, the dance did end
and, while others spontaneously hugged their partner,
or bowed and curtsied in quite a formal manner, the
Laird simply lifted Lydia's hand and kissed it, thank-

ing her for the dance. His eyes met hers as he did so, as if seeing her reaction mattered to him.

Gasping at the sensation of his lips on her skin, she managed a reciprocal word of thanks, before blurting out, unthinkingly, 'Then you do not disapprove of my dress?'

Instantly, his gaze travelled lazily over the gown, before he raised his eyes to hers again. 'Not at all. In fact, I strongly approve of it. Why do you ask?'

So it was not the dress. Then what?

Her body was still tingling from the effect of that lingering gaze, but he was awaiting an answer. 'I—As a governess, I have always before been expected to keep to the shadows. I have never been invited to dance at an event such as this. My place is normally—' she gestured to the area where Mairead sat '—with the children.' Mairead, she noted absently, was currently being well entertained. She was seated on Eilidh Òg's lap, Dòmhnall Mòr crouching down beside them, and the three of them were laughing about something.

This seemed to give him pause. As if recollecting something, he stiffened his frame and his expression became remote. 'Naturally, you are an employee here and I expect you to see to Mairead. But...' he shrugged '...everyone at this wedding should be able to enjoy themselves, too. The dancing is part of that.'

'I wholeheartedly agree with you, Alasdair!' They both turned. There was Angus, the Laird's cousin, grinning from ear to ear. 'Miss Farnham, will you dance the next one with me?'

Now the Laird was positively glowering. *Oh, dear!* What had happened to change him from the warm and friendly dance partner of a few moments ago, to this? Aloof, cold and decidedly cross.

'If the Laird permits?' she offered firmly.

I have had enough of trying to guess what he is thinking.

The Laird paused, looking from one to the other. 'Oh, very well! But then you should spend some time with Mairead.'

'Of course!' She bit back an angry retort.

I would have been perfectly content to stay with Mairead all evening!

It was he, after all, who had taken her away from Mairead. Really, the man was as contrary as the weather in the islands, changing from one half-hour to the next!

Alasdair watched her dance, his disapproval giving way to helpless amusement on seeing that frown of worry furrow her brow again. Would she gain confidence during the course of the dance, as she had with him? Angus, he noted, was being particularly attentive as a dance partner and seemed to be taking every opportunity to converse with Miss Farnham as they went through the steps. When she sent his cousin a grateful smile, Alasdair ground his teeth together in—what? Anger? Frustration? He could not be sure. His feelings towards the governess were so contradictory he could barely make them out. The attraction was unarguable. He had conceded her beauty from the first moment he had laid eyes on her. His body craved her, his eyes followed her...he knew himself to be a heartsick fool.

Yet his mind would have its say. His distrust was well founded, given his experiences with Hester. So he allowed the burning jealousy its place within him, but resisted asking her to dance again himself.

It being an Ardmore castle wedding, by this stage in the evening plenty of drink had been taken and the party was beginning to show signs of raucousness. Perhaps Mairead should be taken to retire for the evening? He glanced across at his daughter. She was smiling happily and watching the dancers intently. *No, I cannot end her enjoyment too soon. She has little pleasure in her life.* Besides, once Mairead was in bed, Miss Farnham would be officially free to enjoy her evening in whatever way she wished. Which, judging by the speculative looks of some of the unmarried men, might include dancing all evening, if she so chose.

He took another sup of whisky, wondering if his own behaviour just now had been influenced by the haze of languid contentment provided by alcohol. He did not normally imbibe so freely, but at a wedding, it was almost expected. Reflecting on his brief encounter with the governess, he was able to reassure himself that his behaviour had been unexceptional. For the most part.

Giving her permission to use his name was not inappropriate, he reassured himself, since most of her senior colleagues already did so. He frowned. Hearing his name on her lips had sent an unexpected thrill through him. *Danger!* Again, his instincts were on alert. Not only might she threaten his closeness to his daughter, she might also be perilous to his peace of mind.

Once before, he had allowed himself to be dazzled by an unsuitable woman—a woman who was an outsider and whose beauty had distracted him from understanding her true character until it was too late. Raising his glass, he drained it in a single swallow.

Much too late.

Despite numerous offers, Lydia steadfastly refused to dance any more sets. The Laird's clear disapproval made it imperative that she behave as she ought. It was not unreasonable, she supposed, for her employer to permit her to enjoy just one or two dances. Anything more might look as though she were neglecting her duties.

Besides, her role here was no less precarious than any of her previous situations. She had lost too many positions because of the unwanted attentions of men. The last thing she should be doing would be to encourage any man to believe they could woo her. *I am a governess here*, she reminded herself for the hundredth time. *I am not available for wooing.* So she politely rebuffed the pleading looks and cajoling entreaties of a series of perfectly reasonable men, laughingly telling them all that she had no wish to dance any more tonight.

Having returned to Mairead, she was now cuddling the child on her knee and absent-mindedly responding to her questions and comments. Young Eilidh brought Dòmhnall Mòr to meet her and Lydia liked what she saw. He was tall, broad and handsome, with a crooked smile and a decided light shining in his eyes when he looked at Eilidh. *Quite right, too.* After a brief conversation with Lydia and Mairead they returned to the dance floor. *They mean to dance together all evening,* she thought, somewhat wistfully.

As she watched the dancing, her eye fell on Angus, currently traversing a set with a pretty young woman with long dark hair. A pang went through her as, briefly, she indulged herself with thoughts of her two dance partners tonight.

Angus was a good man. She knew it in her bones. He would not dream of pressing unwanted attentions on a lady. He would, she guessed, make an excellent husband and father for someone. Such a man, if she had met him in London and he showed signs of admiration, she might have permitted to woo her. As a practical soul, she knew well that a sensible marriage would end many of her worries about her future security. A husband who was a man of character, and with reasonable prospects, could ensure that never again would she feel the crippling terror of being set adrift, anchorless and incomeless, in a world that, it seemed, wished only to cause her suffering.

The fact that Angus was also handsome, young and strong would have been an added bonus. There was but one barrier to Lydia even theoretically considering Angus as a possible suitor. And that barrier was currently glowering by the staircase, while throwing back whisky.

Her gaze became unfocused. This unexpected *tendre* for the Laird was decidedly inconvenient, for it was affecting her ability to think clearly and practically about her options. It would not last, she was sure, for such feelings were generally held to be no more than a passing fancy. While it held her in its grip though, it made her vulnerable to errors of judgement. Like wearing this dress. Like dancing. Like dreaming of a kiss from him…

Stop!

Such thoughts were unhelpful. Her position here was already perilous, without her adding to it with improper notions of the Laird. Perilous because, sooner or later, a man might importune her. Perilous because the Laird disapproved of her at times. Perilous because she had never managed to keep a position for longer than a year or two.

Mairead snuggled closer, clearly tiring, and Lydia clasped the child closer. Here was her true purpose in Ardmore. 'Would you like to go to bed, little one?' Affection thickened her voice.

Mairead is a darling.

'No,' the child murmured. Then, more loudly, 'No! I am wide awake, Lydia, see?'

Lydia smiled sympathetically.

Neither of us wishes to retire.

'Yes, I do see. Very well, we shall stay a little longer. But soon it will be bedtime for both of us.'

The music had been paused and now the fiddlers seemed ready to resume. Something different was in the air, for this time the musicians began calling all of the guests to make a circle around the newly married couple. Lydia watched them assemble, fascinated, until Mrs MacLeod bustled across to them. 'Come on, Mairead and Lydia! You must be part of this, too!'

Lydia stood, Mairead on her hip, and noticed with a heart-skip the Laird making his way towards them. He took his place in the circle beside Lydia and held out his arms to his daughter, who went immediately to her *papaidh*. All around the room, guests of all ages were making a single, enormous circle around Calum and Màiri. Some were joining hands. Lydia stood awkwardly, not daring to offer her hand to the Laird. Her pulse, though, was racing at the very possibility that she might feel his touch again.

Next, the bride and groom's parents stepped forward, the four of them making a small circle around the newly-married pair. Then the music began. The people in the large circle began moving clockwise and more hands were linked. The Laird, without looking directly at her, shifted Mairead on to his right hip, then took Lydia's right hand with his left one. A moment later the lady on Lydia's other side took her left hand. All around Lydia could see hands being joined as the circle formed around the edge of the space. On the Laird's right, a young girl rested her hand on Mairead's arm, completing the circle.

Alasdair's hand was warm in hers and Lydia's heart was now pounding so hard she was sure it must be obvious to everyone in the Great Hall.

Calum and Màiri, in the centre, joined both hands and also moved clockwise, while their parents moved around them in an anti-clockwise direction. The fiddlers, outdoing themselves, repeated the three tunes, each one faster than before. In the frenzy of movement, and emotion, and wild, wild music, Lydia was conscious of only two things: her feeling of belonging to this community and her feeling of connection to the man and child beside her.

The music built to its inevitable crescendo and when the final, soaring bars rang around the Great Hall, people broke into applause and tears, and more spontaneous hugs. Beside her, Lydia sensed the Laird turn towards her, dropping her hand and instead embracing her with

his free left hand. She turned naturally into his embrace
and he brought her and Mairead together in the circle
of his arms. She raised her eyes to meet his and what
she saw there made her heart burn with desire and connection, and…something else. Sliding her arms around
both of them, she kissed the child on the cheek. At the
same time, she felt his lips brush her cheekbone and
thought she might actually die from happiness, if such
a thing were possible.

The whole thing lasted no more than a few seconds,
then they separated again. A melee of embracing was
taking place throughout the Great Hall and Lydia herself was hugged with great force by Mrs MacLeod, who
told her she was a 'good lass', by Eilidh Ruadh and by
Angus, whose embrace was gentle and somehow respectful. Then the music began again, and this time the
party joined in a rousing chorus of 'Auld Lang Syne',
a song which Lydia had frequently heard sung in the
drawing rooms of London. Never before, though, had
it made the hairs at the back of her neck stand to attention. The entire community was singing in unison, and
she was a part of it, as though she belonged there. She
had never experienced anything like it.

Calum and Màiri's parents had closed in on their
offspring with a fierce four-person embrace and Lydia
was moved and astonished to see they were all six crying as if their hearts would break.

As the song ended, but the tears continued, Lydia
appealed to Eilidh Ruadh in bewilderment, 'But why
are they so distressed?'

Eilidh wiped away a tear with a lace-trimmed handkerchief. 'Calum and Màiri are leaving tomorrow for Canada. It is likely we shall never see them again.'

'Why should they leave, when it seems they do not wish to?' The grief on faces all around was clear to see, now Lydia had an explanation for it. 'Can they not stay here?'

Eilidh looked grim. 'The islands have little in the way of prospects. There is a meagre living to be earned by burning kelp for potash, or making twill, but those who have even a little savings know their opportunities will be greater in the New World.' She laughed harshly. 'If that part of our land had not been taken by an absentee landlord who charges increasing rents, but does not invest in the land or the people, perhaps we would have a chance. For Calum and Màiri, their best option is to leave, although it breaks the hearts of everyone here.'

'But—who is this landlord? Can Alasdair and Angus not do something? That cannot be right!'

'It is not right!' The Laird had been approaching, Mairead still nestled in his arms, and he had clearly caught the end of their conversation. 'It is not fair, nor just, but our hands are tied. Even now, Angus and I are trying to negotiate to buy back a few hundred acres of land from an English lord who had no right to it in the first place! His name is Burtenshaw. We have written to his agent in London, but the negotiations are monstrous slow!'

'I—I am sorry!' Lydia felt terrible, as though she and every other English person had personally betrayed the Islanders.

This led to near-identical grins on both MacDonalds' faces, as they made haste to reassure her.

'Oh, no, Lydia! We did not mean to suggest—'

'We do not blame the English people, nor the lowland Scots, nor even the lost Highlanders,' the Laird said soberly. 'This is down to a handful of entitled aristocrats who believe themselves to be in the right.' He shrugged. 'The Bonnie Prince should have prevailed.'

'And this is why your history is important, even now,' Lydia mused thoughtfully.

'Yes, for the injustices created are an open wound. We cannot change history. All we can do is mitigate the impact on our people. Sometimes, like today, we fail.'

Abruptly, he turned away and Lydia knew instinctively he feared showing distress in public. She watched him unblinkingly as he strode across to Calum and Màiri and their parents. He stood calmly, awaiting his turn as they were surrounded by well-wishers, then embraced them all, handing a small roll of notes to Calum, who enveloped the Laird in a heartfelt hug.

It was too much. Fearing that she would break down in tears, Lydia distracted herself by announcing that it was time for Mairead to retire and that, tonight, she would see to her herself.

Mairead did not even protest and as the little girl nestled in to her on the way up the grand staircase, Lydia allowed herself for just a moment to imagine what it must be like to say goodbye to your child, knowing you would never see them again. She had some experience of hurt, having lost her parents, and having been forced to say farewell to numerous children over the past few years. But something about the grief of Calum and Màiri's parents tonight had pierced her deeply.

She hugged Mairead fiercely as she settled the child

into bed, then made her way to her own chamber, undressing by rote and desperately holding back tears. It would not do! She was becoming much, much too involved with this place and its people. A growing love for Mairead, a tendre for the Laird, and now this—an unlooked-for sense of connection to the island community. The more she allowed herself to feel things now, the more it would hurt when she was eventually, inevitably forced to leave.

Inevitably? Yes.

Why should this post be any different to any other? Wishing to stay had never helped her before. As she knew well, wishes did not come true.

Chapter Eight

Alasdair, wincing at the bright morning light, made his way back inside the castle. The staff were still clearing up after last night's festivities and their cheerful, noisy activity was somehow grating. Most had, like him, made free with the whisky, but most seemed to have escaped the half-headache that was draining him this morning. *Morning?* He corrected himself. It was just past noon and he was expected in the schoolroom.

What had seemed a clever notion last night now seemed the height of foolishness. He knew he needed to spend more time with Mairead, for since Miss Farnham's arrival their daily time together had diminished. To be fair, this was not the governess's doing. It was more the case that, prior to the governess's arrival, Mairead had spent time every day with him, with Mrs MacLeod and with whomever else could be spared to mind her. Miss Farnham, who seemed very conscientious, had developed the habit of spending most of the day with his child—from after breakfast until dinnertime—and, quite simply, he missed his daughter.

However, the solution was clearly *not*, as he had assumed, for him to join in their lessons. It was for him to simply organise his day so that he had time with the child. If he had been more clear-thinking, he would have dealt with the whole situation more appropriately.

Sighing, he made his way to the part of the castle where Mrs MacLeod had housed the governess. *A fairly comfortable bedchamber*, he recalled, then flushed at the improper thoughts that had instantly sprung to mind. He had barely slept last night, his mind and body distracted by memories of Lydia in that blue gown and out of it. To allow his attention to remain on such thoughts in daylight would be the undoing of him.

Forcing his attention elsewhere, he spared a thought for Calum and Màiri, who would be crossing to South Uist about now. *Never to return to Benbecula. To Scotland.* The notion was appalling.

Calum's family were from near Rueval, the hill that dominated the island. Unfortunately the land was now owned by that absentee lord whom he and Angus were trying to negotiate with. If a lord could not—or would not—care for his people, then, in Alasdair's view, he should no longer be the owner. *We might have to go to London, if we must.* The notion unsettled him, for he was fairly sure he would dislike it immensely.

Yet I like Miss Farnham.

The thought was startling, the truth blinding in its novelty.

I like her.

He had known he desired her, but now he had to acknowledge that he enjoyed her company, their discussions, the time he spent with her. It was unlooked for and, he acknowledged grimly, unwelcome in many ways—mainly because she was so desirable. He did not *wish* to like Miss Farnham and he could certainly make no generalities about London society based on one governess. Previously, he had considered that what was developing between them was some sort of friendship. Now he knew it for certain.

He had reached the door. Inside was Miss Farnham's bedchamber, which led directly to the schoolroom. Bracing himself, he knocked.

There was no response. Naturally there would not be, for his scratching would be impossible to hear in the schoolroom. Tentatively, he opened the door a little, then spoke a few words, just in case she was there. *Nothing.*

Feeling as though he were trespassing, he opened the door wider. The chamber was empty. In some relief, he strode across to the schoolroom door. Despite himself, he had taken in too much with his one, fleeting glance. Two miniature portraits on the side table. *Her parents?* A hairbrush. A book. *What is she reading?*

The bed.

Her bed.

He swallowed, his inner eye suddenly flooded with notions best kept to lonely nights. Here she slept, here she undressed, here she bathed. Oh, but he could imagine assisting her with her bath, rolling with her in the bed, sleeping with her locked tightly in his arms...

'Come in!' His mind distracted by a flurry of thoughts and emotions, he had knocked without even thinking about it.

In he went, as though he were somehow going to his doom.

'Papaidh!'

All dour thoughts dissipated instantly at the sight of his daughter's smile. 'Well, child, I told you I would come, did I not?' He turned to the governess. The side curls from last night were still in evidence, although today she had returned to one of her ugly shapeless gowns. His disappointment was acute, although he knew, logically, that the shapeless gowns were much, much better for his peace of mind. 'Good day, Miss Farnham.' Unbidden, his mind threw at him memories of their brief embrace last night, the feeling of her soft skin as he had kissed her cheek. He felt himself flush and had to force himself to not fidget in an unbecoming manner.

She had stood to greet him and now made a graceful curtsy. 'Sir.'

'I told you to call me Alasdair,' he growled. Even if he had instantly regretted it, he would not go back on his word. Besides, he was all at sea, with no idea at present how he felt or what he wanted.

She inclined her head. 'Good day, Alasdair.'

Her pronunciation was in the Gaelic style and it sent an unwelcome shiver through him. She did not, he noted, offer him the courtesy of calling her Lydia. A pang of what felt remarkably like disappointment went through him. Yet, given his recent behaviour towards her—one minute disapproving, the next warm—how could he blame her for seeking a formal distance? It was, after all the most sensible solution for both of them. And so it was with formality that he addressed her.

'Very well. I am here to observe your methods, Miss Farnham.' He glanced about the room, then pulled up a hard chair from near the window. 'You may begin.'

Part of him knew he was being harsh, that behaving in ways that would seem cold and judgemental would not lend itself to any employee performing well, but he could not help it. Just being in Lydia's—in *Miss Farnham's* company was enough to unsettle him and he did not like to feel unsettled. He had to resist this damnable, un-looked-for attraction and remember that she was here as a governess, not anything else.

Without any hint of nervousness, she turned to Mairead, suggesting they begin by showing Mairead's *papaidh* how well she was learning the Globe.

How serene she is! How accomplished and calm her manner!

He watched, as much fascinated by Miss Farnham as by his daughter's progress. A few minutes later, he had to admit to being impressed.

'Mairead is a quick-witted child and a good learner,' Miss Farnham declared, making his chest swell with pride.

'Of course she is,' he retorted gruffly. 'Now then, Mairead, where is Benbecula?'

'That was the first place Lydia showed me.' She spun the globe, placing her finger unerringly on the small dots representing the archipelago that was the Outer Hebrides. Her mouth turned down. 'We are so small, compared to all these big places.'

'Ah, that is because the islands are precious!' He made haste to reassure her and to defend his beloved homeland. 'I believe the islands have been well hidden, so that only the lucky ones can even find them, much less live here.'

'That is what Lydia said!'

'She did?' Dumbfounded, he glanced at the governess, who looked a little put out.

'Mairead, let us try some French for your father.'

Half listening as Miss Farnham put his daughter through some simple French words and phrases, his mind was puzzling over her defence of the islands. As a non-islander she could not have meant it, of course, but at least she had had the wit to say it to the child. Hester had seen only the remoteness of the Hebrides. *Perhaps*, a small voice whispered inside, *perhaps she is not like Hester.*

The French lesson was drawing to a close, so he praised his child, adding a 'well done' in French.

'So you can speak French, too, Papaidh?' Mairead seemed astonished.

'I can. The French have always been our friends, so it is important to learn their language.'

Miss Farnham was eyeing him quizzically and he laughed, somehow knowing exactly what her look signified. 'I shall admit,' he offered, 'if you force me to, that Napoleon has perhaps become a little too ambitious. He ought to have stayed in France, looking after his own people. The urge for conquest can never be admirable.'

'I am glad you think so,' was all she would say. 'Now then, Mairead, it is time for some reading and writing.'

He leaned forward, keen to see the progress the governess had been made with this. Prior to Miss Farnham's arrival, Mairead had fought, distracted and denied everyone who wished to teach her to read or write—including himself. Holding his breath, he watched as Miss Farnham wrote some simple sentences on the slate and asked Mairead to read them. This she did, running her finger underneath and sounding out any words that she seemed less familiar with. She then painstakingly copied each one, forming letters that were reasonably clear. Despite Miss Farnham's frequent reassurances, actually witnessing Mairead reading and writing was strongly affecting him and he had to make a tight fist out of sight of the others, in order to prevent tears starting in his eyes.

My Mairead!

By the time she had finished, he had his emotions somewhat under control, but when Mairead showed him her work, with a clear sense of pride, he did not hold back. 'I declare I am astounded! Mairead, you are doing wonderfully well and working so hard at your lessons. And as for you, Miss Farnham, you are exceptional!'

His child beamed with happiness, while Miss Farnham looked decidedly flushed. Her beautiful face glowed with pleasure and he was unaccountably pleased at being able to praise her so fulsomely. 'Thank you,' she managed to say, before Mairead interrupted.

'I have been doing some more writing, Papaidh, but I cannot show it to you yet!' She giggled and she and Miss Farnham made a great show of exchanging 'secret' signals. Mairead must have written a message for his upcoming birthday.

Making a great show of checking his pocket watch, he then looked at them both, asking with exaggerated confusion, 'Excuse me? I missed that. Did you say something?'

'No, no, nothing at all,' declared Miss Farnham with a studied air of innocence. Mairead mimicked this, clearly enjoying the game.

His eyes met those of the governess and hers were brimful of humour.

She is a treasure!

Somehow, he found he could not look away and the gaze deepened, becoming something else—something deliciously dangerous.

After a long moment Miss Farnham blinked, as if recollecting where she was, then looked away, busying herself with wiping the slate clean. Alasdair cursed himself for a fool. Had he learned nothing from Hester? Although his instincts were currently screaming at him that Lydia was not Hester, he knew he should not be letting down his guard. To do so risked not only his own happiness, but Mairead's as well. If he risked trusting the governess, letting her get ever closer to both of them, what would then happen when she went away? She would break Mairead's heart, and he could not allow that to happen.

'Miss Farnham,' he said mildly, 'you may take some time off this afternoon, for I intend to spend the rest of the day with my daughter.'

Mairead must not become over-reliant on her governess.

Instead of welcoming this, she looked almost panicked for an instant, before her features smoothed into polite neutrality. 'Yes, sir—er, Alasdair. Enjoy your afternoon.'

'I shall.' Resisting the urge to ask the governess about her reaction, instead he turned to Mairead. 'Well, *mo nighean*, what should we do today?'

Miss Farnham half raised a hand. 'Er...before you

go, there is something I should like to ask you.' Miss Farnham sounded unsure, which was not like her.

'Yes? What is it?'

She glanced at the child, then rose. 'If you please, sir?'

He followed her out of the room. Clearly, she did not wish to speak in front of Mairead. Turning to face him, she seemed to almost brace herself, and he wondered, in some bemusement, what she was about to say.

'Sir—' Checking herself, she began again, her face tight with what looked remarkably like anxiety. 'Alasdair, I hope you are satisfied with my work and with Mairead's progress.'

'I am more than satisfied, Miss Farnham. She is making tremendous progress. I know not what witch-craft you have used, but it is very effective!'

Her shoulders relaxed a little. 'Then—you are contented to keep me on for a little longer?'

A little longer? 'What are your intentions, Miss Farnham?'

'My intentions?'

'Yes,' he replied tersely, suddenly conscious they were in her bedchamber. There in front of him, just over her left shoulder, was her bed.

'I intend to work hard with Mairead, if that is what you are asking?'

'I am asking whether you have plans to leave,' he retorted bluntly.

'To leave? No, no—' she shook her head '—I plan to stay for as long as my being here is satisfactory to everyone.'

This was not particularly clear. 'To *everyone*? Including yourself?'

She nodded, although still wore a confused look. 'Yes, naturally. Actually, on that topic—' She lifted her chin. 'If I *were* to leave for whatever reason, would you be willing to pay for my trip back to London?'

'Well, of course! To do anything less would be dishonourable, since it is I who have brought you so far from home.'

Her trip back to London!

His stomach sank, but he maintained an uninterested air. His voice, though, dropped a little, almost as if he were afraid to ask the next question. 'Do you miss it?'

'Miss what?'

'London. Your home.'

She shrugged. 'Not especially.' Her eyes danced. 'Although I do miss being able to frequent Hookham's Lending Library.' She thought for a moment. 'And Gunter's.'

'Gunter's? What is that?'

'It is a teashop in Berkeley Square. They serve ices there. And sorbets.'

He raised an eyebrow. 'We have no icehouse in Ardmore, it is true, but do remember your book allowance. Iain can arrange to order any book you wish.'

'I would prefer to order more teaching materials. Slates, pencils, readers and the like.'

'Why?'

'With your permission, I should like to teach some of the other castle children. I believe it would be beneficial for Mairead to spend more time with other children.' Her tone was animated; she was clearly passionate about the matter.

'I would not wish for you to become distracted. Mairead has only just begun to accept being taught...'

In her enthusiasm she briefly laid a hand on his arm. 'Oh, I know, please do not fret. I genuinely believe she would do better if some of her lessons were alone, but some with others.'

'Let me think about it.' He needed time to consider the matter. For now, his mind was still in tumult from the notion that she would leave. From the way she had touched his arm. From the knowledge they were standing in her bedchamber.

'Thank you, Alasdair.'

'You are most welcome, Miss Farnham.' He paused, then when she said nothing further he bowed, before leaving her to collect Mairead from the schoolroom. When they passed through, she was in the window alcove, moving her chair into the shaft of bright sunlight. Why would she not offer him the privilege of saying her name?

Lydia.

He tried it in his head, feeling his tongue taste her name.

'Goodbye, Lydia!' Mairead called cheerfully.

'Goodbye,' she returned.

His last image of her before he turned away was of her outline—over-large gown, elegant arms, bare neck, blonde hair—haloed by the sun streaming through the casement behind her. Momentarily, he had a sense of being blinded—not, this time, by her beauty, but simply by her own self.

Lydia.

Chapter Nine

Over the following weeks a daily routine emerged. Around noon each day, the Laird would come. He generally stayed for an hour and Lydia became progressively more relaxed with his presence in the schoolroom. Mairead made clear progress every week and Lydia now knew she had little to fear on that score. Alasdair even joined in the lessons, seeming to particularly enjoy simple conversations with Lydia in French, for Mairead's benefit. He would jest with her, asking silly questions about Lydia's and Mairead's favourite colours or favourite foods, and Lydia loved seeing this more carefree aspect to him. She also loved their evenings together, which had continued unbroken and where the friendship side of their relationship had strengthened again following the tension of the wedding.

After the noon-time lesson, the Laird would then take Mairead for an hour or two and Lydia would use the time to teach the children who were too old to share Mairead's lessons. Finally, for the last hour before dinner, Mairead would return, and with her three other castle children of a similar age.

As Lydia had anticipated, this had multiple benefits. Mairead, with a head start on her lessons, felt more than equal to the others, despite her affliction. Her belief in herself was growing stronger week by week. The parents of the other children were delighted and the children themselves, despite some initial trepidation, had settled well.

The Laird's birthday came and Mairead presented him with his handwritten gift. It had to be admitted that he looked decidedly emotional as he read the child's message and Lydia was moved to make it clear that, while she had helped Mairead with spelling, the words were the child's own. One again, she was struck by the clear love between father and child—something that was commonplace here, but rare in her previous experience of aristocratic families.

Lydia's own birthday followed unnoticed three weeks later, on June the seventeenth, and as she prepared for bed that night, she was tempted to wallow in a little self-pity. Since her parents had died, forcing her to leave school at eighteen and begin her work as a governess, no-one had known about or celebrated her birthday. Still, it would serve as a useful reminder that, however much she might admire and like the people of the islands, she could not ever truly be one of them. They were family, bound by the ties of blood, history and clan. She was to them a visitor and she should not forget it.

Her mind drifted back to that conversation with the Laird in this very bedchamber, exactly a month ago. While it had been reassuring to know he would pay for her passage back to London, he had not directly answered her question about keeping her on a little longer. Still, he was evidently pleased with Mairead's progress, which gave her some reassurance. Stepping up to the window, she was astonished to note that there was still a great deal of brightness in the sky, although the clock informed her that it would soon be midnight. Midsummer meant very little darkness this far north. The moon was full and serenely beautiful in the pale evening sky.

Lighting a candle, she closed the shutters and the heavy curtains, enjoying the sensation of warmth and safety. Glancing around, she realised that she loved her chamber and her schoolroom, and, yes, the children she taught. She loved the castle community and the beauty of the island, and she loved—she *loved*—she shook her head. She had a great deal of *fondness* for the people she spent most time with—Mairead and her father. It would, she told herself, be unnatural not to have developed an affection for them. However, she would be wise to protect her heart as best she could, in preparation for the day when she might have to leave them all behind.

Eilidh Òg, too. The maid was making great progress with her French and was now, she had shyly confessed, 'walking out' with Dòmhnall Mòr. Lydia had made a point of cultivating an acquaintance with Eilidh's young man and approved of him more and more. She and Dòmhnall Mòr had developed a teasing repartee, where she would gently bait him about his sweetheart and he would correct her Gaelic grammar.

Eilidh, Dòmhnall and some other young people were

planning to row across to a nearby island for a picnic next Sunday afternoon and Eilidh was working until late in the evening remaking an old dress for the occasion. Lydia smiled as she undressed, delighted by thoughts of the girl's evident happiness.

Inevitably, once she was in bed, her mind returned to the Laird. *Alasdair.* He was never far from her thoughts, the tendre she had developed in the early weeks here having, surprisingly, not weakened at all. If anything, Lydia reflected, her admiration of him was becoming ever deeper. It could not be reciprocated, of course. Alasdair's opinion of her, she suspected, was entirely coloured by her being an outsider. No matter how much he might appreciate her company at times, or her skills as a governess, she was something 'other' to him. To all of them. She could not say how exactly she knew this: she simply did.

Not for the first time, she wondered about the death of Lady Hester, the Laird's wife. From casual comments made by various Ardmore residents, she had come to understand that Lady Hester had died in a carriage accident while on her way to Edinburgh. The Edinburgh detail had been stated as though it were of some significance, but its meaning was entirely lost on Lydia. Lady Hester, while not born on the islands, had been Scottish. Not an outsider. Not a Sassenach.

Mairead—although she had never known her— would sometimes speak of her mother in passing, as did the castle staff. The Laird, though, had never mentioned her in Lydia's presence. Not once. Was that significant? *Perhaps*, she ruminated, *he still grieves for the loss of her.* The notion made her sad. She, too, had known loss and the idea that he was grieving and mourning the loss of his wife in the way she had mourned her parents disturbed her. She did not want him to be unhappy. He did so much for others—carrying the responsibilities for the entire community. Yet his own burdens could not be shared, nor even spoken of. A dead wife, a sickly child…

Her heart skipped. Mairead continued to increase in health and the child's progress with her 'babylegs' was gaining momentum. She could now pull herself up to lean against furniture in a position that could arguably be called 'standing', although she had not yet been brave enough to let go. Lydia's chest burned with pride at Mairead's fierce determination. She longed to reveal the secret to Alasdair, but Mairead was insistent.

'No!' she would declare. 'I fear I would not try so hard if this were not a secret. When my legs are sore and I want to stop, I remember Papaidh and it makes me keep trying.'

This had a certain logic to it—besides, Lydia would have found it impossible to betray the child's trust. So they continued with their secret exertions, both in the schoolroom and during their jaunts out. Now that the weather was milder, they often went to one of the many beautiful beaches or sandbanks, where they would both daringly remove their shoes and stockings and allow the tiny waves to tickle across their feet and ankles. *I shall take her to the sandbanks at Rarinish again tomorrow.* Drowsiness was beginning to overcome her, accompanied by a delightful feeling of purpose and contentment—for however long she would be here. Turning on to her side, she blew out the candle.

* * *

The trip to Rarinish, one of the islets north of the castle, was going well. Mairead enjoyed splashing in the sea with Lydia holding her and her dress was damp up to the knees. When Lydia tied it up for her, she was surprised to see that the child's legs now looked almost normal—pale, yes, but one could no longer have described them as being 'weak' or 'wasted'.

They spent a little time sitting on the sand and watching the greedy oystercatchers feeding on cockles exposed by the low tide, then Lydia decided to be daring with Mairead's exercise. Her heart pounding, she asked Mairead if she would like to try standing by herself, since the soft sand would cushion any fall. Mairead looked uncertain and so Lydia persuaded her to pretend to 'fall'—in other words, sit down with a bump—numerous times. This done, she held both the girl's hands for a moment, then gently let go of one.

'No! Do not let me go!'

'I shall not,' Lydia replied soothingly. 'Remember, you may sit down any time you choose. Now, just enjoy the sensation of standing up, with only one of my hands for balance.'

Frowning with concentration, Mairead steadied herself, a slow smile growing on her face. 'I am standing, Lydia, like a proper girl!' She was clutching Lydia's hand tightly and her balance was shaky, but she was indeed standing.

'You are! Oh, you clever, clever girl!' She stood for almost a full minute, before balance and tiring muscles betrayed her and she sat down hard on the sand. Lydia dropped to her knees and hugged her then and Mairead clung to her fiercely.

'Again!' she mumbled into Lydia's neck, drawing a smile.

By the end of the trip she had fallen down a dozen times, but her reliance on Lydia's hand was diminishing. She still held it, but at times Lydia could feel the child was barely using her hand at all. Still, they had run out of time for the day.

'Time to go,' Lydia declared, eyeing the progress of the sun across the sky. 'It will soon be midday and you do not wish to be late for your lesson with your *papaidh*.'

'Wait! I want to try by myself, Lydia. Just once.'

'Very well.' She allowed Mairead to pull herself up into a standing position, then let go of one hand. 'You may let go of the other hand whenever you are ready.' She held her breath as Mairead gathered herself, then let go. Her arms were extended for balance, but she lasted a full five seconds before losing her balance and sinking down into the soft sand.

'I did it! Lydia, I did it! I stood by myself!'

'You did! Oh, Mairead, I am so proud of you!'

'I am proud of me, too,' the child said simply, before adding, 'Thank you for teaching me.'

Lydia kissed her cheek. 'It is a delight, my dear.' She picked her up. 'My, you are definitely getting sturdier. I declare you shall be *forced* to walk before long, for you will be too much for me to carry, with those strong girl-legs of yours.'

'Not baby legs?'

'Not baby legs,' Lydia agreed, as she started off across the sand.

* * *

'Where did you go this morning, Miss Farnham?'
The question came unexpectedly as Lydia, Alasdair and
Iain settled themselves in the Laird's salon after dinner.

'Oh! To—to Rarinish.' Lydia gathered herself, hoping her face was not flushed. 'To the sandbanks on the
south-west side, to be exact. It is exceedingly pleasant there.'

'And what do you do there, you and Mairead?' Alasdair's tone was mild, but he was clearly curious.

'Why do you ask?'

He shrugged. 'Mairead seemed in fine fettle when
you returned.'

'I am sorry we were a little late back. We had been
splashing at the water's edge and watching the birds.
I find the sea air and the water to be most efficacious
for health.'

'Efficacious, eh?' His eyes were twinkling. 'I am not
sure that would have been my primary concern when
I was six.'

She smiled tightly, hearing criticism. 'Very well. It
was diverting. You know my approach to teaching is
based on the notion that enjoyment is the best governess. Splashing at the water's edge is something that
Mairead finds amusing and I believe there is nothing
wrong with that.'

'Indeed, and I must admit she is looking the better
for it. She looks healthier than she has done at any time
since her illness.'

'I agree,' said Iain and they both looked at him.
I had quite forgotten he was there.

'Rarinish is a beautiful place,' Lydia declared, in an

attempt to take the conversation away from what else she and Mairead might do there. 'I have not yet visited Flodday or Rossinish, but I expect they are equally picturesque.' She named two of the other local islands and inlets. 'I understand that the young people plan to picnic on Rossinish on Sunday.'

'A good choice.' Alasdair and Iain exchanged a glance, prompting Lydia to reply with a question of her own.

'Why? Is there something special about Rossinish?'

'There is, but it is a thing that only locals know.' Alasdair glanced at Iain again. 'Should we tell her?'

'Absolutely!' Iain did not hesitate. 'I think she has already done enough to earn it.'

Lydia looked from one to the other, all bewilderment.

Alasdair leaned forward in his chair, an air of great significance about his bearing. 'After Culloden, we were in disarray. Cumberland's soldiers were everywhere and they treated the clans with much harshness. The Bonnie Prince himself was being hunted throughout the Highlands, with a thirty-thousand-pound price on his head.'

He paused and Lydia pieced it together. 'The Prince was *here*?'

The Laird nodded grimly. 'Somehow, they found out and two thousand soldiers were sent to the islands, to scour every castle, cottage and farmhouse. We had need to get him off the islands as soon as we could. Iain's grandfather, Captain Crawford, came up with the plan.'

Iain took up the story. 'Our kinswoman, Flora Mac-Donald, had a stepfather with connections to the army. She managed to get a pass for herself and two servants to get to Skye. Despite the soldiers everywhere, we still managed to get him on the boat and over the sea to Skye.'

'But surely they would have checked the servants?'

'They certainly took a good look at Flora's serving-man, a South Uist man by the name of Neil MacEachan. However, the maid, an Irishwoman called Betty Bourk, was allowed to pass without comment.'

Lydia gaped. 'He passed himself off as a *woman*?'

They were both laughing. 'He did, and fools he made of them all!'

Lydia frowned. 'I vaguely remember this being spoken of in London. Mr Johnson and Mr Boswell met Flora MacDonald, I think?' She shook her head. 'The audacity of it is quite astonishing!'

The Laird seemed to be enjoying her reaction. 'They left from Rossinish and I shall make it my business to take you there, and show you the exact bay from whence he left.'

'I should be very interested to see it. But tell me—' her brow creased as she understood the enormity of the tale she had just heard '—you said "we" as though you were present. I know that history is important to you, but these events happened more than sixty years ago, well before either of you was born.'

Alasdair shrugged. 'These events shaped our present. Culloden and the atrocities afterwards seem like yesterday to us.'

She nodded slowly. 'I understand you, I think.' Remembering their conversation at the wedding, she added, 'Tell me, the lands where Calum's family live—'

'Were confiscated by the crown after Culloden and

given to some lord who has never set foot in the islands. He does not care for the people or the land, only for the rent he might receive.'

'Have you spoken to Angus again?' Iain's expression was serious.

'I have. We may yet have to travel to London to apply some persuasion, for Lord Burtenshaw's agent has not responded to our written overtures.'

As the two men talked on, Lydia indulged herself with her favourite pastime—watching the Laird without his knowledge. Oh, it might have seemed as though she were focused on both of them, but in truth she had eyes only for Alasdair. As ever, she felt a strange mix of joy, fascination, and physical desire in his presence. In these moments, she felt more awake, more vital, more *alive* just for being in the same room as him.

'Excuse me?' They were both looking at her and Iain had just said something.

'I wondered how the castle children are doing with their lessons,' he repeated.

'We are making steady progress,' she reported. 'I am delighted to be teaching them.'

'You need not have done it, you know,' said Iain, rather pointedly. 'They already get some schooling from others, when we have the time to teach them.'

Lydia was unsure of his meaning. She shrugged. 'I like to be busy. If I can be of assistance to others, then naturally I should.' She raised an eyebrow. 'After all, everyone here has a similar attitude, so I am not sure why "need not" must come into it.'

'Aye, you are like the islanders in many ways, I think.' Iain smiled.

Lydia flushed with pleasure. 'Praise indeed!' she managed to reply.

Quite why the Laird's expression was now inscrutable, she was unsure.

She is like the islanders.

Iain's statement, despite its innocent intent, was causing havoc in Alasdair's mind. The past few weeks he had been in Lydia's company more than ever before and she was inveigling herself into his thoughts with increasing frequency.

The lessons with Mairead were an absolute delight. Dimly, he recalled how Mairead had used to resist learning with every stubborn fibre of her being. He himself had alternated between trying to cajole and force the child into attempting reading and writing, to no avail. To see her now, positively enjoying her lessons, was both a relief and a joy.

When he recalled how sceptical he had been about Lydia's skills as a governess, he felt rather ashamed and made a point of regularly praising the teacher as well as the student. When he did so, Miss Farnham would rarely blush or dissemble, more frequently responding to his praise with a simple 'thank you'. She was as much a master of her craft as any bard or painter.

The evenings, too, were delightful. Although he enjoyed nights like tonight, when Iain would join them, he had to admit to a stab of disappointment when the steward did so. *I like being alone with her.* Indeed, being with her was fast becoming the best part of his life.

He shook himself. He was no love-addled boy, with little else to worry about. He was a father, a laird, a widower. He had responsibilities. Dòmhnall Mòr could court Eilidh without consideration for anything but his feelings for the girl and whether they were reciprocated. Alasdair had not that luxury. Still, as he climbed the stairs for bed, Alasdair already knew that tonight, as most nights, his last thoughts would be of Lydia.

Sundays always felt special in Ardmore Castle. Lydia was free from her schoolroom duties, the staff all dressed in their best clothing and, after Mass or church, the Laird would join them in the Great Hall for their afternoon meal. Sometimes there would be singing and storytelling, and Lydia's grasp of Gaelic had now improved to the point where she was able to understand most of what was being said around her. Her ability to form sentences herself was improving slowly and they all praised her on her pronunciation. She would always suppress a smile at this, for her pronunciation was based almost entirely on Alasdair's speech patterns, of which she had been a diligent student.

Just as the food was being served, the group of six young friends which included Eilidh Òg and Dòmh-nall Mòr departed abruptly, abandoning their places at the table.

'What is happening?' Lydia asked Mrs MacLeod, who was sitting next to her. The housekeeper checked with a serving maid nearby, then leaned back to pass on the news to Lydia.

'There is a ship anchored in the Minch.' She named the strait to the east of the island. 'It cannot come into the bay as there is a bit o' bad weather on the way, so someone will have to row out to pick up whatever cargo

it has for us. There'll be no picnic today for the young
ones with a squall on the way, but they were eager to
volunteer for this.'

'I see.' Lydia puzzled over this for a moment. The
castle overlooked the sea and had its own slipway
nearby, which had often made her wonder why she had
had to travel so far overland on her arrival. 'So ships
come up this way, too? I was brought to Lochboisdale.'
Life was so strange here. When one was used to wan-
dering through shops and markets, the fact that goods
had to be ordered and awaited for weeks or months took
some getting used to.

'They do. People get accustomed to taking whatever ship is next. Some go up the Minch, along our east
coast, while others, like the one that brought you here,
go on to Canada after South Uist.'

'Aye,' agreed Lydia, hardly noticing that she was now
speaking like an islander. 'The *Mercury* was headed to
Rupertsland in Hudson Bay.' She thought about this for a
moment, hoping the cabin boy and all his colleagues had
made it safely across the Atlantic Ocean. 'There are so
many worlds out there and we cannot live in all of them.'

'I am perfectly content with this one,' declared the
housekeeper. 'And I hope you are, too.'

'Oh, I am. I am very happy here.' It was true. A sense
of belonging was slowly seeping into her bones. Fear
remained, of course, for however much she might like
this place and its people, there was nothing to say that
they would want her to stay forever. Shaking off the
brief melancholy, she returned to the topic of the young
people. 'Eilidh Òg and Dòmhnall Mòr have gone to the
ship, I note,' she said pointedly.

'Aye. Don't often see one without the other, these days. We shall have another wedding before long, wait and see.' Sighing dramatically, the housekeeper added, 'Course, it is never the wedding we all want.'

'What do you mean?'

Mrs MacLeod glanced briefly at the top table, where Alasdair was deep in conversation with Iain. 'The Laird has been alone now for six years. Tomorrow is the anniversary of Lady Hester's death—although we only found out about it a week later.'

Lydia followed her gaze, allowing herself to drink in the sight of the Laird in his Sunday best. *He always looks wonderful in his Sunday kilt.* She turned her attention back to the housekeeper, realising this was her opportunity to find out a little more about Lady Hester. 'What happened to her? Someone mentioned a carriage accident, but it seemed as though there was more to the tale.'

Mrs MacLeod nodded grimly. 'She left him a note saying that she could not bear to stay in the islands a moment longer. Apparently she had persuaded a foolish, infatuated boy to organise their passage to Glasgow, then on to Edinburgh. He died with her in the carriage that day.'

Lydia's mouth fell open in shock. 'Then—she was unhappy here? And she *left* the Laird?'

'Aye—though he was sorely smitten with her. But she made no effort to make herself settle here, if you understand me?'

Lydia shook her head. 'But—Mairead!'

How could she have been so foolish as to leave Alasdair? And her baby?

'She paid little heed to the child. There is many a mother needs help from a wet nurse and nothing wrong with that, but Her Ladyship cared only about regaining her figure and getting her precious sleep!'

'Caring for a baby can be difficult,' Lydia offered dubiously. 'Especially in the early months.'

'Aye, well, we all know that. She had plenty of help, but the baby was *hers*. Not that you'd have known it.' She sniffed. 'At least Mairead never knew what her mother was. If you ask me, the child has had a happier life for it.'

Lydia's mind was still reeling. 'And the Laird…?'

'He shut himself away for weeks and months afterwards and has never been the same since. He used to be full of joy and life. Now, it is a miracle to get a laugh from him. Calum and Màiri's wedding was the first time in years we have seen him so open and natural.' She cast a sideways glance at Lydia. 'Now, what might account for the change in him that day?'

Lydia shook her head, mystified. 'Perhaps his grief is finally beginning to ease. I was unhappy for an age after my parents died, but gradually I began to live again. Six years is a long time to mourn, I think. He must have loved her dearly.'

The housekeeper snorted. 'He was a fool—and I say that with all of my fondness for him. Lady Hester would never have been suited to island life and so he should have realised before he married her!' Her gaze softened. 'But men are often fools for a pretty face.' Her gaze sharpened and she eyed Lydia keenly. 'I do not mean *you*. You, my girl, are much more than your face and so you have proved.'

Uncomfortable with any comparison between herself and Lady Hester, Lydia nevertheless heard the compliment in the housekeeper's words. 'Thank you. It can be difficult for me to be properly seen sometimes.' She pointed to her own visage. *'This* gets in the way.'

Mrs MacLeod patted her hand. 'You are certainly *seen* here and not just by me. I am glad you came to Ardmore.' She eyed her closely. 'You do seem to have settled well. The isolation does not bother you, then? The lack of shops and balls, and being so far away from high society?'

Lydia laughed. 'Not at all! I never valued those things. Indeed, I was never invited to balls or parties in my own right. If I was there, it was only to chaperon my charges and sit in the corner with the other duennas. And before that, when my parents were alive, we lived quietly.'

'But here, you may dance at a wedding like everyone else.'

'Precisely! It was so diverting! I shall look forward to the next wedding, in the hope I can dance again.'

'Well, judging by the antics of Wee Dòmhnall and young Eilidh, we shall not have long to wait.' She winked. 'My guess is that he will find a way to propose to her soon.'

'Oh, how wonderful!' Just for a moment, Lydia considered what it must be like to receive a proposal of marriage from a man that you truly loved. *It would be—* abruptly, she caught herself. Never should she allow her mind to complete that thought. Marriage was not something that might ever come her way and she certainly could not imagine agreeing to a risky marriage—one without respect. One without love.

Concentrating on the life she was building for herself here, as a respected governess, was of paramount importance. She had finally found a place and a community where she felt truly happy. Her focus needed to be on ensuring she did nothing to make them—to make *him* send her away.

Chapter Ten

Wﬁen Eilidh and the others had not returned three hours later, the bell was rung in the castle, the Laird calling for a gathering in the Great Hall. Lydia, having given Mairead into the care of one of the castle maids, hurried down the great staircase. *What on earth has happened to them?* Sensing the tension all around, as she got closer she could see it in the tight shoulders and worried faces.

Ringing in her ears were the maid's words just now. 'Oh, Miss Lydia, what if their boat sank? What if they are drowned?' She had reassured the girl, admonished her to be calm and counselled her to help prevent Mairead becoming distressed. Hopefully the young people were simply sheltering somewhere from the heavy rain. Yet she, like everyone else, it seemed, had to consider this terrible possibility.

Helplessly, she stood among the crowd while the Laird organised the search party. He was planning to lead it himself and there were nine or ten others, it seemed, going with him. They talked of where various boats were located that could be used and were putting together packs that included lanterns, ropes and whisky, all tied in large cloths that, Lydia realised, were actually kilts.

She bent to help with one of the packs and by the time she had stood again, the party was ready to leave. 'Bring them home safe, *a Thighearna*!' they exhorted. That was the Gaelic word for laird, and Alasdair was all laird just now. Grim-faced, clearly deeply concerned that some of his people were in trouble, leading the party that would find…whatever they found.

The next few hours ticked by slowly. So, so slowly. The day, already gloomy from the storm clouds overhead, gradually darkened into evening and still they did not return. Lydia spent some time with Mairead, reciting happy children's tales to her and ensuring she was calm, before kissing her goodnight and returning downstairs. There was a hush about the conversations that contrasted terribly with the usual cheerful activity in the Great Hall, and the islanders' worry was palpable. The rain was still beating down outside—one of the summer storms that came upon them unexpectedly at times—and Lydia could not stop thinking of everyone out in such inclement weather. No-one was speaking English tonight—over the months they had all gradually been using more Gaelic with Lydia anyway—but she was relieved to find that she could hold her own in the conversations. Prayers were said and occasionally someone would cry, but they kept repeating that the young ones would be safe, that the Laird would find them and bring them back. Their faith in him was impressive, yet Lydia, thinking about it from Alasdair's perspective, began to understand the sense of responsibility that he must eternally carry.

It was almost two in the morning when shouts from the courtyard alerted them to arrivals outside. Lifting her head from the table, where exhaustion had finally overcome her, Lydia stood with the others, moving forward to greet the bedraggled party. The Laird was there and he was glancing all about—his eyes met hers and the relief of it made her sag momentarily against the table. Then two people stepped forward to relieve him of his burden and she realised he had been carrying a young woman. *Eilidh!*

As she moved closer, she realised it was not Eilidh, but one of the others who had gone on the ill-fated trip. Looking about, she recognised all of the search party had returned, but with only four of the young people. Four, not six.

A wail went up from the far side of the room. 'No! Where is my Dòmhnall?' It was Dòmhnall's mother, Lydia recognised.

Maggie. Her name is Maggie.

'And Eilidh? Where is Eilidh?' Eilidh's sister Mòrag, who was about fourteen, was rapidly becoming hysterical. Lydia saw Mrs MacLeod cross to her and wrap her arms around her, speaking quietly in the girl's ear.

The Laird was kneeling on the floor beside the girl he had carried home, while a flock of women spoke to her and checked her. He looked exhausted. The girl was conscious and shivering, and a little blue about the lips. A couple of the women were now giving orders for her to be brought to her chamber, where a fire had already been lit. They would be able to strip her there of her wet clothing and begin the process of warming her up. All four of the young people were receiving similar treatment, with the exception that the young men were already being partially stripped as they were moved upstairs. Much as she was tempted to follow the staff upstairs to begin warming up the unfortunate young men and women, Lydia knew she had a more important task to complete. She stood motionless, waiting. Everyone had gone upstairs, leaving just her and the Laird. He had not risen from the floor.

Collapsing down beside him, she took his hand—his cold, wet hand—and looked directly into his eyes. What she saw there almost killed her.

'We could not find them,' he managed. 'The boat crashed on the rocks. These four made it to shore. Dòmhnall and Eilidh—' His face crumpled. 'Lydia, I could not find them!'

'Hush, now.' She wrapped both arms around him and he clung to her in the semi-darkness of the Great Hall. She felt his pain—the helplessness and frustration, grief and loss. Oh, she could hardly bear it. All those days in his company, evenings building a friendship, nights thinking of him...would he trust her enough to take any comfort from her embrace?

'I have failed them all.' The words emerged as if pulled from his soul. Brokenness was in every syllable. The Laird of Ardmore, guarantor of his people's safety. Oh, she knew him so well! And now he was giving her the gift of honesty. Of showing her his true face.

'No! You have not! No-one could have done more,

Alasdair!' She pressed both hands to his face, desperate for him to hear her.

'Lydia!' he managed to say, his eyes locking with hers. Suddenly, something new was in the air, desperate desire crackling between them. *Kiss me!* she thought, then his mouth was on hers and the world spun wildly, as they each sought the connection they craved. Frantically they kissed and kissed again, bodies pressed close together, arms holding each other tightly.

Lydia was lost in a maelstrom of emotion. The need to care for him was uppermost in her mind, while her body revelled in the sensations he was causing within her, and her heart wondered at the miracle of being kissed by him. In the midst of anxiety and death, they sought solace in one another.

Finally they paused, both breathing harshly, forehead resting against forehead. His hands were still busy on her back, gently stroking, and she thought she might go mad from the simple beauty of it.

They kissed again, this time gently, tenderly, then separated a little to look into each other's eyes. Was that wonder in his expression, or was it simply her own reflection? 'Lydia,' he breathed. 'Lydia.'

Her name on his lips sent shivers through her. Was she dreaming?

Footsteps echoing on the great stair above brought them to their senses. By the time Mrs MacLeod appeared they were both standing, suitably distanced, and engaged in a quiet conversation about the search. 'It will be light in three hours,' he said. 'I shall go out again.'

'But you are drenched, Alasdair! And freezing!'

Lydia appealed to Mrs MacLeod. 'How can he go out again so soon?'

'Because he must,' the housekeeper replied grimly. 'He knows his duty.'

This felt like a reprimand. 'Of course. But should he not first—?'

'I have built up the fire in your room, sir, and laid out some towels and dry clothing. I shall meet you here in three hours to see you off again.'

He bowed. 'I thank you, Mrs MacLeod.' There was something strangely formal about their interaction. Whatever it was, it increased the lump in Lydia's throat.

They all separated then, to go to their own rooms for whatever was left of the night. Lydia paced the floor, knowing she would never be able to sleep. Between the boating tragedy and kisses with the Laird, her mind and heart were reeling and she could barely think straight. She opened the shutters and watched the half-moon sailing slowly across the sky. By the time the first hints of dawn were paling the sky, she had made up her mind.

Alasdair could not think, could not rest, could not even pray. Eilidh and Dòmhnall had their whole lives ahead of them. They had to be alive! On the way to his chamber he had paused in Mairead's room, bending to kiss the child's cheek before tiptoeing out again. He could not imagine what Eilidh and Dòmhnall's families were feeling right now. As laird, he was responsible for all of the people, just as though each one of them were his own child, or his brother, or his mother. He had to do what they could not. Lead. Co-ordinate. Think. Plan. Do.

Briefly, he allowed himself to remember kissing Lydia, his heart soaring and his body responding instantly. He had wanted to kiss her for the longest time. Yes, kisses, and more. Thinking of her by night and resisting her by day had been his life now for what seemed like an eternity. In the midst of worry and strain and…maybe death, he had reached for her as naturally as flowers turned to the sun. She was light and heart, and goodness, and with darkness all around, he had needed her warmth.

Just now, he could not regret allowing her to comfort him, nor could he regret the glory of their embraces. It would give him strength for the hours to come.

And what if it was Lydia who was missing? A knife-like pain stabbed through him, causing him to gasp and double over. *She is safe,* he told himself. *And Mairead is safe. My attention must be focused on the task at hand.* Slowly, deliberately, he locked away his feelings, hardened his heart, prepared himself for the tasks ahead. He strode across to the window and opened the shutters. The rain had stopped, but the necessary control within his heart was iron-cold. It was time.

Donning her stoutest boots and tying her overdress up tightly, Lydia put on her warmest cloak and whispered her way downstairs in the pre-dawn paling. They were already there and the Laird frowned as soon as he saw her. 'What on earth do you think you are doing?'

She shrugged. 'Is it not evident? I am coming with you.'

'You are not!' His dark brows beetled together. 'I need you here, where you will be safe.'

She lifted her chin. 'The storm has passed and Eilidh is my friend. I am going to look for her. And for
Dòmhnall Mòr.'

He began to reply to this, but was interrupted by the
housekeeper. 'An excellent notion, Lydia.' She turned to
the Laird. 'You, sir, are too stubborn for your own good.
And too blind to see what is plain to everyone else.'

'What do you mean by that?'

'I mean that Lydia should go with you.' She handed
him the bundle she had prepared. 'Now go, before I decide to accompany you as well!'

Grumbling, he stomped off, Lydia skipping to keep
up with him as he marched through the courtyard in
the pre-dawn light. Turning away from the castle slipway, he led Lydia across the moor, northwards then
east, towards Rossinish. By the time they had walked
for twenty minutes the sun was beginning to appear
on the horizon before them and the Laird had thawed
out a little, even to the extent of conversing with her
briefly about the accident—although neither of them
made reference to their embrace the night before. It
had happened only a few hours ago, yet it might have
been a hundred years, so closed off did he seem. It was
as though last night there had been two different people, Lydia and Alasdair. Today they were back to being
the Laird and the governess. The *sullen* laird and the
governess.

His withdrawn, curt demeanour was, she supposed,
perfectly understandable, given their task today. Lydia,
too, was devastated by Eilidh and Dòmhnall's absence
and anxious about what lay ahead. It had taken all of
her reserves of inner strength to prepare herself for

what they might find today. Even so, she had felt compelled to accompany him. Quite simply, it was better for Alasdair that she was with him. Still, she prayed for a miracle—that somehow, the young people could be discovered alive.

They had passed the Oban Uaine—the Little Green Bay, Lydia translated in her head—and reached the southernmost edge of Rossinish. There, the Laird led her to a sturdy, flat-bedded rowing boat, tethered carefully at the head of one of the many inlets of the Little Minch. It was, he told her, near this inlet that the accident had occurred. Clambering aboard, Lydia remembered her trepidation that very first day, when she had feared sinking. And now the worst had happened and a similar craft had been lost yesterday, falling victim apparently to a shift in the wind which had pushed the small boat on to the rocks. The wind, the islanders had noted sagely, must have suddenly veered to the northwest in advance of the storm. It happened, sometimes. Lydia shivered at the apparent stoicism, then remembered their real distress. Knowing what might have happened did not make it any less troubling.

The boys, knowing their sweethearts would be hampered by their long skirts, had rushed to their aid, and two couples had made it safely ashore. No-one had seen Dòmhnall or Eilidh since the boat had capsized. So, apparently, Alasdair and the others had been told when they had found the four young people on the far side of the islet.

He had repeated this to Lydia in a flat tone and all she could do at the time was nod.

I hope I am some comfort to him. At least he is not alone.

He had given her no indication that he welcomed her presence, but he had at least accepted it. Now he was rowing along the inlet towards the sea, his head turning left and right, desperately searching. Averting her eyes from the bunching of the muscles in his arms as he rowed, Lydia knew that, finally, she had to face up to their task. It was highly likely that they were looking for bodies and entirely possible that the bodies might have been taken out to sea, never to be found. Taking a breath, she, too, began scanning the shore on each side, hoping to find something and also hoping she would not.

At first, she did not even recognise what she was seeing. She stiffened, peering to make sure. Wordlessly, she pointed and Alasdair's head swung round to the right side. There, among the vegetation, was a large dark shape. As Alasdair rowed closer, his face pale and set, Lydia kept her eyes on it. Dark hair. Broad shoulders. Face down in the water, unmoving.

Dòmhnall!

Grimly, Alasdair brought the boat to shore, then helped Lydia out before pulling it safely up the bank a little. 'Wait here,' he said gruffly, taking a rope from his pack and stalking off in the direction where they had seen the body. Lydia, too much in shock to even cry, slumped to the ground, hugging her knees tightly for a few moments. Dòmhnall was dead. There could be no mistaking the matter.

How can this be? And what of Eilidh?

Rising, she returned to the shore, then set off further

to the right, away from where they had found Dòmhnall's body. Trying not to see in her mind's eye the image of Dòmhnall as she had last seen him, she concentrated on each moment. Breathing in and out. Placing one foot in front of the other. Searching for Eilidh.

Even though she was looking, it came as a great surprise to suddenly see, on the bank before her, the shape of a young woman, laying on her back with most of her legs in the water. Breaking into a run, Lydia sped across the damp grass, then dropped to her knees beside Eilidh. Her eyes were closed, her face white, deathly white, yet—was that movement in her chest? Was she breathing yet? Tentatively, Lydia placed a hand on the girl's ribs, at the same time bending down to feel if any breath was emerging from her nose.

Yes!

Eilidh is alive!

'Alasdair!' she rose, calling at the top of her lungs. 'Alasdair!' Moving to stand above the girl, she tried to get her hands under Eilidh's shoulders to pull her up, but had not the strength. Taking a deep breath, she tried again. Eilidh remained unmoving. 'Alasdair!'

Alasdair pulled Dòmhnall's body another couple of feet up the bank, away from the lad's watery grave. His heart was breaking. Such a grand, fine young lad, gone. He turned Dòmhnall on to his back, then closed the lad's eyes, saying a quick prayer for his soul. Not that a boy such as Dòmhnall would be in need of any prayers. A civil, quiet fellow, he had harmed no-one in all his eighteen years.

Just eighteen, and gone.

Alasdair's heart felt as though it might break at the very notion. Abruptly, he stilled, tilting his head.

'Alasdair!'

There was no mistaking Lydia's call. With one final tap on Dòmhnall's shoulder and a promise that he would be brought home to Ardmore, he hurried off in the direction Lydia's voice had come from. As he ran, he saw her then, kneeling down beside—

Lord, no! Not both of them!

'She is alive!' Lydia seemed to be trying ineffectually to pull Eilidh up the bank, her eyes bright with unshed tears. Rather randomly, it occurred to him that Hester would have been having strong hysterics by this point. Not that Hester would ever have dreamed of accompanying him on such a grim mission. 'I cannot get her out of the water.'

Finally he reached them. Lydia gave way and he was able to pull Eilidh from the water with little effort. He picked her up and Lydia helped by gathering the girl's full skirts and tucking them around her where they would not impede his ability to walk. Most of Eilidh's weight, he suspected, was in her heavy, water-filled clothing. She was alive, yes, but could die yet, from the effects of being cold and wet for so many hours. Striding across the rain-damp seagrass, heedless to the lapping of the waves and the calling of the birds, nevertheless he was conscious of Lydia's quiet company. It gave him comfort and strength, somehow, to have her near.

Once at the boat, Lydia managed to pull it down the bank and into the water's edge. She clambered in first, and he gently placed Eilidh into her arms. The girl had not yet woken, but had stirred a little, and Alasdair's heart clung to any sign of life. Jumping in, he reached for the oars, rowing smoothly down the inlet and back towards the land. 'Better to go back directly to Ardmore by boat,' he grunted, 'with Eilidh to carry. The others will return for Dòmhnall.'

They were facing each other, he and Lydia. She was not looking at him, her attention being entirely focused on Eilidh. She had taken off her cloak and was now wrapping it around the girl, tucking it in as best she could and using a corner to dry Eilidh's face. The compassion and concern in her expression and her actions was plain to see. *She does not simply look like an angel*, was the thought that flashed through his mind, *she has all the goodness of an angel also.*

After some time, she spoke. 'How much longer?' Those blue eyes were now locked with his and he found himself momentarily lost for words.

He glanced behind. 'I turn at that headland, then the next inlet is the one that leads to Ardmore. How is she?'

She shook her head. 'Very ill. We need to get her warm and dry as soon as we may.'

Though his muscles ached, arms and legs protesting, he gritted his teeth and rowed faster, harder, putting more effort into it than he had had to do for many a year. As he rowed towards the Ardmore slipway he heard shouts of welcome, and when he finally reached land there were strong hands there to pull the boat in and tether it. Two of the men jumped in, wordlessly taking Eilidh from Lydia's arms and carrying her up towards the castle. The other two lingered as he and Lydia came ashore, one asking, 'Dòmhnall?'

Alasdair shook his head. 'We found his body.'

Briefly, he gave them Dòmhnall's location. 'I shall speak to Donaidh and Maggie now.'

They nodded grimly, one man crossing himself. As they walked up the slipway in silence, Alasdair glanced back. The men had already cast off and were moving along the water with purpose and speed.

He turned his attention back to Lydia. Her lovely face was rather pale and she was shivering, her gown damp from where she had been cradling Eilidh. He tutted and paused to remove his coat. 'Here.' He placed it on her shoulders, his hands lingering briefly, feeling how delicate she was. How delicate, and yet how fierce.

'Thank you.' She looked up at him and he saw in her eyes all the sorrow he was feeling. Wordlessly, she slipped her hand into his and he welcomed it. Just now, he needed an anchor and Lydia was it.

As they finally reached the top of the bank and the last, brief walk to the castle, they dropped their handclasp. It was necessary, yet he felt bereft. Some part of him was screaming a warning at allowing himself to feel close to her, but he could not listen. Not now. Not today.

Then they were in the courtyard and silence fell all around them as they passed through. Conversations stopped. People ceased in their work. The heaviness of the terrible news he was carrying to Dòmhnall's parents walked with him and no-one would look him in the eye.

Mrs MacLeod and Iain Crawford were waiting in the Great Hall, as they should be.

'Where are Donaidh and Maggie?' His tone was clipped.

'In the chapel.' Iain looked grim.

Alasdair nodded, spun on his heel and walked towards the chapel. Duty called him and duty bound him. He had never knowingly shirked it, but if he could, he would have given anything to have different news to impart to Dòmhnall's parents today.

Lydia watched him go, saw the nobility in the way he held himself, the way he contained his own sorrow. Coatless, he looked vulnerable somehow, as though his linen shirt were a soft skin that arrows could easily pierce.

'You found him, then?' Mrs MacLeod's face was creased with grief and sympathy. Lydia nodded sadly, removing Alasdair's coat and handing it to the housekeeper. She felt cold without it. Mrs MacLeod exhaled slowly. 'At least that. We shall have a proper funeral— aye, and a wake, too. It will be of great help to all of us who will mourn the lad.' She squared her shoulders. 'I have work to do. We shall have a steady stream of visitors for the next few days.'

'I, too,' added Iain. 'I shall begin to make the arrangements for the funeral.' His eyes softened. 'Thank you for going with the Laird.'

'Oh, I—' She could not find the right words. 'I had to,' she offered simply.

He bowed and Mrs MacLeod curtsied, and Lydia frowned at the strangeness of it. Why should they salute her? Slowly, she turned towards the staircase. She would change her clothes, check on Mairead, then find wherever they had taken Eilidh.

Chapter Eleven

Within the hour, the castle had been transformed. The clocks were stopped, curtains were drawn and the mirrors covered up or turned to the wall. Some of the youngsters were sent up to the top of the tower, to watch for the return of the rowing boat. Then the bell began ringing once more, calling everyone to the courtyard to welcome Dòmhnall's last return to Ardmore Castle. Four of the men had gone to the slipway carrying a pall and Dòmhnall was carried home draped in a tartan cloth. Lydia shrank to the back of the crowd, feeling somewhat of an intruder, but she could not stop her gaze continually drifting to where Alasdair stood by the castle door with Dòmhnall's family. He was rigid with suppressed grief, while Dòmhnall's mother could not contain herself and cried bitterly the whole time, her grim-faced husband's arm about her. Beside them were two younger boys—Dòmhnall's brothers.

Lydia could not bear to look upon their grief and so briefly turned her eyes to the heavens. Blue skies, sunshine and seabirds gliding. It looked so peaceful, so serene. Why did the heavens not care that Dòmhnall was gone? The skies here always seemed so vast. Today, instead of beauty, their vastness felt like indifference.

At least Eilidh does not have to see this.

The girl had woken up and her own mother had told her of Dòmhnall's fate. When Lydia had gone into her chamber Eilidh had been distraught and they had called for Mrs MacLeod to provide a draught of laudanum. She would by now be unconscious again—a kindness in the circumstances.

The priest led them all in some prayers. Lydia did not know the words in Gaelic, but muttered the Lord's Prayer in English under her breath. Then they trooped slowly inside, where Dòmhnall's body was given into the hands of a group of older women whose job it was to prepare him for burial. Maggie, the lad's mother, went with them, while others lined up to speak to Donaidh, Dòmhnall's father, to express their sorrow at the loss of his eldest son. Dòmhnall's two younger brothers, already dressed in their Sunday kilts, stood unblinking by their father's side, seemingly bewildered, and Lydia saw Alasdair bend down to speak to them.

Lydia suddenly found herself flooded with anger.

It is so unfair!

Dòmhnall was just about to begin his life as an adult. He should have married Eilidh, become a herdsman, sired children of his own. Momentarily, Lydia found herself back in that dark place where she had existed when her papa had died, just a year after Mama.

Grief could burn a person and leave them as ashes. Or freeze them, if they did not allow it to run its course.

In the immediacy of Dòmhnall's loss, Lydia could see how easy it would be to sink into despair.

This, then, is the price I must pay for loving these people.

For love and loss, as she well knew, were but two sides of the one coin.

The three days of Dòmhnall Mòr's wake turned out to be one of the strangest times Lydia could ever remember. The coffin had been placed in a small room off the Great Hall, and a vigil was kept day and night. Maggie, Dòmhnall's mother, would only leave her son's side with the strongest persuasion, and even then she was soon back. Everyone generally congregated in the Great Hall, drifting in to see Dòmhnall and Maggie from time to time. On the second day, Eilidh came downstairs and she and Maggie hugged one another and cried together for the longest time. Eilidh did not look well at all and kept coughing into a linen handkerchief. Later, Lydia saw them laugh together as they told some remembered story of 'Wee Dòmhnall'. It was astounding to see how much the wake itself brought everyone together, helping Dòmhnall's family and sweetheart get through the shock and distress of these first days without him. She herself had hugged Eilidh tightly and cried with her.

'Who will correct my grammar now?' Lydia had asked, making Eilidh laugh-cry. This had turned into a fit of coughing, and Lydia had been concerned to see that Eilidh remained pale and shivering, even in the warmth of the Great Hall. Yet Eilidh steadfastly refused to return to her bed, *needing*, she said, to be part of the wake.

The staff, while engaging fully in the fluid gathering of the wake, were busy cleaning, cooking and preparing for the funeral. Alasdair, Iain and Mrs MacLeod between them were managing the whole thing, while simultaneously dealing with their own grief. Alasdair was everywhere, spending much time speaking to Dòmhnall's family, while also engaging with his senior staff and holding impromptu meetings with cattlemen and fishermen, weavers and Dòmhnall's fellow kelp-burners. He and Lydia had caught each other's eye at times, which even now, in such awful circumstances, sent a thrill through her, but she only had the chance to spend a little time with him when he would approach from time to time to see his daughter.

Mairead seemed bemused by everything and had a hundred questions. These ranged from how *exactly* Dòmhnall had died, to whether he was now with Mairead's mama. Lydia answered all of the child's queries as best she could, while trying to be as reassuring as possible. Lessons, naturally, were cancelled, although they had continued to exercise what they now called Mairead's 'girl legs'. Once, earlier today, Mairead had been sitting on the floor with two of the castle children and had curled her legs to tuck them under her, quite without thinking. No one had commented, but Lydia had held her breath, knowing that, a few short months ago, Mairead had rarely even moved her then weak legs and might have lost her balance while sitting.

Angus and Eilidh Ruadh had come to stay and Lydia was enjoying the opportunity to deepen her friendship with Alasdair's cousins. She had been surprised to discover that Angus was himself a laird in his own right. Eilidh, who had mentioned this fact in passing, shrugged. '*Laird* to us is in a sense only a word. It is a responsibility as much as an honour.' She thought for a moment. 'Actually, the honour comes when a laird is a good leader, when he takes his responsibilities seriously, when he genuinely cares for the people under his protection. It is earned, not bestowed.' She glanced across to where Angus and Alasdair were deep in conversation. 'They are both good men, and good lairds. This—' she gestured around vaguely at the wakehouse '—this is how it should be.'

'I understand.' Eilidh raised an eyebrow. 'I do,' Lydia insisted. 'I know I have lived here only a few months, but the sense of connection between you all is wondrous. Particularly in times of heartbreak.'

'I cannot imagine how people manage without it,' Eilidh replied.

Lydia, remembering the agonies of being entirely alone in the world once orphaned, could only nod, her throat being suddenly too tight for speech.

Alasdair was consciously and deliberately keeping as far away from Lydia as possible. His increasing reliance on her was terrifying, because part of him wished nothing more than to hold her hand again, or tell her of his grief, or…kiss her. Yet he must not. He could not trust his own judgement with women, for he had failed spectacularly on the one previous occasion when he had listened to his heart. And his failure had led directly to Hester's unhappiness… Hester's death. And now with the loss of Dòmhnall, and his current responsibilities to the family and to all his people, he had no room or

time for any consideration other than the most immediate of tasks.

Every moment of every day was a nightmare for
him just now, and it mattered not if he was awake or
asleep. Dòmhnall's death had come at the worst possible time of year for Alasdair. He had naturally not forgotten that Hester had died on this day, six years ago.
July was always difficult, with one painful anniversary
after another lining up to pierce him, to bring him low
and to remind him of just how foolish he had been in
choosing a wife who had been entirely unsuitable and
entirely unhappy.

It was close to midnight. Slipping into his parlour for
the first time in two days, he poured himself a whisky
and allowed the memories to wash over him.

Hester.

Oh, things had gone well at first with their marriage.
Caught up in a honeymoon haze, they had laughed and
loved together in Edinburgh and on a scenic tour of
the Highlands in late spring. It was only when he had
brought Hester home to Ardmore that difficulties had
begun to become apparent. He gradually became aware
that her notions of castle life were based on some sort
of romantic ideal, and chickens in the courtyard and
chimneys that occasionally bellowed black smoke into
chambers did not suit her expectations. He had been
patient and encouraging, and supportive—as best he
could, anyway—yet she could not adapt. She missed the
Edinburgh shops. She missed her friends. She missed
her mama.

Well, of course she had! He shook his head now at
his own blindness. *She was little more than a child her-*

self when I brought her here! He stopped. She had been
three-and-twenty, just two years younger than he, and
had turned down numerous offers before accepting his
suit. He, caught up in a sense of achievement at being
the one to win the Beauty, had not known to look beneath the pretty face and flirtatious smiles. What he
discovered, when it was entirely too late, was that she
had been selfish, indolent, and prone to vindictiveness.
Rather than embrace her responsibilities as Lady of
Ardmore, she had, it seemed, anticipated a life of ease,
surrounded by servants and comfort. She knew how to
order servants about, but not how to see them as Ardmore people, to be cared for.

The day he had come upon her beating a kitchen
maid—the young girl cowering, crying and trying to
escape—had been the day he finally realised what a terrible mistake he had made. Hester had already by that
point denied him access to her bed, but from that day he
found he had lost all desire for her. It had been too late,
though, for they had already conceived their child—a
honeymoon baby. Once her situation was confirmed,
she used it to gain every possible advantage for herself
in terms of attention, comforts and excuses for bad behaviour. When Mairead was born she had shown little
interest in the child, bidding the maids 'take it away and
find someone to feed it'. He had wondered if perhaps
she was experiencing a lowness of spirits which some
women were said to go through after giving birth but,
in truth, he acknowledged grimly, she was in essence
no different to how she had always truly been.

Mairead had been born in the depths of winter, and
Alasdair now understood that Hester had decided to

leave him soon afterwards. Her constant remarks about having satisfied the requirements of a wife by giving him a child, her references to the way islanders thought girl babies just as valuable as boy babies, even her refusal to be a mother to Mairead…looking back, it was as plain as day. At the time, though, Alasdair had simply carried on as best he could, trying to please her, trying to help her adapt. *And at least I have Mairead!* he thought fiercely. He and Hester had made each other deeply unhappy, but she had made him a father and for that he was grateful.

'Sir?' It was Mrs MacLeod. 'They are looking for you in the Hall.'

He rose, shaking off memories inwardly as though they were raindrops on a cloak. 'Very well. And, Mrs MacLeod?'

'Yes?'

'Please go and rest.'

Lydia saw him as soon as he entered the Great Hall. This was mostly because she had been watching, hoping to see him again before she retired for the night. He spoke to a few people including Iain before going to see Dòmhnall's parents in the side room. Afterwards, he came to Lydia.

'How do you, Miss Farnham?' His formal words belied the warmth in his eyes as he looked at her.

She shrugged, hoping her feelings were not too obvious. 'As well as anyone, I suppose.' She gave a half-smile. 'And please, call me Lydia.'

'Lydia.'

They both paused, as though something of great significance were happening.

'Lydia,' he repeated, then he coughed slightly. 'I—er—thank you for seeing to Mairead. I have had much to do these past days, since...'

'Of course.' She eyed him closely. 'Are you getting any rest?'

Now it was his turn to shrug. 'Some.' He gestured vaguely. 'There is much to do. After tomorrow...'

'Yes.'

He looked at her again and she maintained her gaze, and her heart swelled with emotion.

'Lydia, I—' He swallowed, then bowed, before turning on his heel and walking away.

Wary of curious eyes, Lydia immediately dropped her eyes to the book in her hand, as though nothing momentous had just occurred. In reality, though, she knew now, knew for certain, that something was new and that she was changed for ever.

Alasdair walked towards the stair leading down to the kitchens, shaking his head ruefully at his lack of resolve. Despite all his worries and regrets, despite all the freshly reawakened memories of Hester's departure, he had found himself unable to resist speaking to Lydia just now. He felt bare, exposed, thin—as though a breath of wind or a chance word might break him. *It is the lack of sleep,* he told himself. *And Dòmhnall's death.*

Yet the cause mattered not. The effect was that he felt vulnerable, barely able to function, peeled and raw for all to see. It had been impossible to hide from Lydia just now. He had no idea what was in his heart. He only knew that he had allowed her to see it and that she had not run away, or rejected him. He meandered around the castle, along quiet stairwells and empty corridors, with what he hoped was a purposeful air. Inwardly, though, he was all turmoil. Reaching his chamber, he paused only to pull off his boots before lying on the bed and sinking into welcome oblivion.

The day of Dòmhnall's funeral dawned. When Lydia opened her shutters, the skies were grey, low and suitably dour. 'Good!' she muttered to the clouds. 'The weather should not be pretty on such a terrible day.'

She had offered her services to Mrs MacLeod, as the funeral meal—unlike those in England—was to be held *before* the service itself. Mrs MacLeod found her in the kitchens, helping the scullery maids to wash dishes, and tutted in shock. 'Miss Farnham, you should not be here!'

Lydia froze briefly.

Have I erred?'

'Oh! I am sorry, Mrs MacLeod. I was trying to find a way to be helpful, that is all.'

Mrs MacLeod was full of dignity. 'That work, we give to our youngest maids—those beginning to learn their trade. You are a senior member of this household and should never have to complete such menial tasks.'

Lydia, drying her hands on a soft towel, frowned in puzzlement. 'But I understood that you were not focused on hierarchies and regimented expectations. It is one of the aspects of life here that has most impressed me.'

Mrs MacLeod bade her accompany her with a ges-

ture and Lydia fell into step beside her. 'You are confusing *value* and *order*, Lydia. Everyone is valued, but
we each have our roles, based on our age, experience
and aptitude. Each to his or her own strengths.'

'I am glad to hear you call me Lydia again! I had
thought I had done something unforgivable when I
heard myself addressed as Miss Farnham.'

This earned a chuckle. 'I was momentarily taken
aback, that is all. Now then.' She ushered Lydia inside
her own housekeeper's room. There was a fireplace, a
neat bed in one corner, a dresser with china and books,
and a polished wooden table. She spread some papers
across it. 'Here is my plan for the Great Hall. We have
brought all of the extra tables and chairs down from
various places in the castle, but with the crowds we
shall be feeding today, I have had to think carefully
about the placing of the tables. The staff have already
begun to lay the place out, but it would assist me enor-
mously if you could ensure that they follow this plan. It
will allow the kitchen staff to serve everyone with the
least difficulty.' She sighed. 'I was there ten minutes
ago, and there is much to be done. I could not stay to
organise them for I am needed in the kitchens. We are
to serve the full seven courses, as tradition demands.'

'Seven! My goodness!'

'Exactly. I need to spend the next half-hour down
here. It would reassure me to know you were directing
the laying out of the Great Hall.'

'Of course! I shall go there at once!'

It was all very well, Lydia thought, to *agree* to do a
thing. The actual *doing* of it, though, was much more
complicated. Surveying the chaos of the Great Hall,

with numerous men and women moving about, shifting furniture seemingly at random, and then undoing each other's work, Lydia had some sympathy for Mrs MacLeod's frustration. She stood for a few moments, simply watching, only moving to the dais when she had figured out what was needed. Her heart skipped a little as she stepped up on to the raised platform.

Will they even listen to me? Who am I to try to direct them, after all?

She tried to call out, but no-one was attending to her. She bit her lip, then lifted her chin. Picking up a wooden spoon that was resting on a bench, she banged it repeatedly on the sturdy wooden table. Now she had everyone's attention. Looking at all of the eyes turned her way, she almost baulked.

Senior member of this household. Senior member of this household.

She took a breath. 'Mrs MacLeod has asked me to assist you in the preparations for the feast. This is her plan.' She held up the paper. She had spoken in English, as she was not sure her Gaelic would be up to the task, but now she switched to half-English, half-Gaelic. 'Sandy, could you and Peadar bring that big table up here, on to the dais? This one can go back down. And can you three then move the heaviest tables to the middle—' she pointed '—along here?'

They agreed and jumped to carry out her requests with alacrity, sending relief coursing through her.

Whew!

Stepping down from the dais, she then approached the remaining staff with specific instructions as to where the smaller tables should go. Thankfully, they,

too, seemed happy to comply. Setting down Mrs Mac-
Leod's plan, Lydia joined in with the work, pulling tables into position, then beginning to place chairs and
benches around them. As a governess, she had always
had a necessity to direct children at times, although
she much preferred when she did not have to give orders. This was the first time in her life that she had in-
structed a group of adults and she felt simply relieved
that it seemed to have gone well.

Alasdair stood at the top of the stairs, watching and
listening with great interest. He sensed Lydia's anxiety as she prepared to speak and grinned with delight
when the staff, naturally, obeyed her. Descending, he
joined in the work himself, moving chairs and benches
into position, and in doing so, gradually working his
way towards her.

'Miss Farnham,' he offered, his tone deliberately severe, 'I hear that one of my tables has sustained some
damage?'

She eyed him in puzzlement. 'One of the tables? Oh,
dear, which one?' She glanced anxiously about and he
waited until her gaze returned to his face before re-
plying.

'The damage, I am informed, was caused by the ro-
bust application of a wooden spoon.'

'A wooden—oh!' The entire wake had been like
this—sadness permeated by moments of humour. She
loved how the islanders were able to do this.

Light and shade, even on a day like today.

'You are roasting me, sir.'

'Alasdair,' he reminded her.

'Alasdair.' Her eyes danced. 'And I have asked you to call me Lydia.'

His tone darkened. 'I believe I already have.'

The humour faded from her eyes, being replaced by a flash of something that looked remarkably like hunger. 'I remember.' She withdrew a little, then twinkled at him. 'That first time, you ought not have called me "Lydia" until you had my permission, you know.'

He leaned closer, until he was sure his breath would fan her cheek. 'Sometimes, it is best not to wait for permission.'

She licked her lips a little nervously and his breath caught at his own reaction to her.

Lord, what am I doing?

Berating himself for both foolishness and a shockingly poor sense of timing, he withdrew.

I have not flirted with anyone since I courted Hester.

Setting aside the thrill of exhilaration that was coursing through him, he sternly reminded himself that they were preparing for a funeral. Making a general remark to Miss—to *Lydia*, he allowed himself to be taken away by one of the men. When he looked back, she had calmly returned to setting out chairs.

What a woman!

As his desire settled—for now—and his mind reasserted itself, he allowed himself to remember Hester. This day six years ago his wife was already dead, but he had not yet had the grim news. This, then, was still the period when he had been reeling with the shock of Hester's departure. That she should leave him, leave Mairead and leave Ardmore! Her note had said nothing of the farm worker who had accompanied her, but his absence was quickly remarked upon and within hours the news had come that they had been seen on the road to Lochboisdale, her trunks in the back of his cart. He had been a handsome boy, Alasdair recalled. Handsome, and clearly under Hester's spell. He sighed. He could not complain, for had she not bewitched him, too?

The shame of it lingered. No man could wish to be cuckolded so publicly, and it had been mortification more than loss that had caused him to withdraw from everyone for weeks and months. Any warm feelings he had held towards Hester had been long gone by the time she had left. He had not wished her harm, though, and had shed genuine tears when word came through of the carriage accident that had killed her and her young beau.

Closing his heart to women, he had devoted himself to his daughter and his duties. When Mairead had almost died of fever as a previously healthy four-year-old, he had thought it some sort of judgement from the heavens for his foolishness in marrying Hester and making her so unhappy. He shrugged, acknowledging the truth. He still believed it, if he were honest.

He moved another chair into place, now only half-aware of the Great Hall and the people around him. Why else had Mairead been left so weak and sickly, if not punishment for his foolish decisions? No matter how hard he worked, how seriously he took his responsibilities, he could not ignore the facts, or shake off the sense of guilt buried deep within him.

And now young Dòmhnall was gone, lost to the sea. Oh, he knew what people said here—that the sea took a price now and again. People were permitted to travel across from islet to island, peninsula to mainland. They could fish for salmon and dig for shellfish. They could harvest kelp for burning and seaweed for fertiliser. The sea would allow it, on the understanding that, occasionally, she would claim a life. Rationally, he knew that Dòmhnall was not Hester, and that he did not have to feel guilty for the young lad's death. But the time of year, his duties as laird…it was all a muddle in his heart and, today, his burdens felt weighty indeed.

There! The Great Hall was ready. Ready to mourn and celebrate a life cut short. While Hester had been young, silly and selfish, she had not deserved to die. And Dòmhnall, big, strong, handsome Dòmhnall, certainly had not.

Bracing himself, he disappeared into his parlour to prepare the lament.

The feast was done, the Great Hall replete with mourners. Lydia, from her carefully chosen seat halfway down, kept her eyes on the dais where the Laird sat with Dòmhnall's family. The events of the past few days had not given her much time for reflection, but during the unusually sombre meal, she had begun to consider what she now knew about the Laird and his wife. How terrible it must have been, for Lady Hester to leave him and for everyone to know of it!

Some marriages were desperately unhappy, she knew. Having lived at close quarters with a number of families, it was not difficult to tell when a couple genuinely cared for and respected each other, and when they did not. Marriages among the *ton*—London's aristocracy—were often contracted through family connections, with parents and guardians of young ladies frequently deciding whom their daughters would marry. Sometimes it worked out to everyone's satisfaction, while on other occasions it most definitely did not. Mrs MacLeod's words had suggested Alasdair had chosen his own bride. Had he, then, loved her?

The story of Hester's departure made it clear that she had been unhappy, had *chosen* to leave Alasdair and Mairead. Lydia did a quick calculation in her head. Mairead could not have been more than a few months old when her mother had gone. Lydia shook her head, unable to understand any of it. How could Hester have left such a man as Alasdair? How could she have left her baby behind?

Selfishly, Lydia was fiercely glad that she had, for otherwise Mairead, too, might have perished in the carriage accident. Pain knifed through her at the thought of anything happening to her beloved Mairead. And then they would have had no need of a governess.

Even now I might have been back in Mrs Gray's agency, seeking a new position following the London Season.

Recalling the sense of bewilderment she had felt during her long, long journey to the island, Lydia now nodded to herself. Despite her doubts, she had found more happiness here than she could have believed possible.

Even on a day such as today, when grief was everywhere, inside and out. The pain she felt for Dòmhnall's loss was just a shadow of what his family must be feeling, what Eilidh must be feeling, what the islanders must be feeling.

I am not a proper islander, yet today I feel part of

this. And it is a privilege to share in their grieving, to support them as best I can.

Alasdair was talking quietly with Donaidh, Dòmhnall's father. Studying his face, Lydia revelled in how well she knew each feature, each angle. She knew his moods, too. Just now he was, naturally, under some strain. His shoulders were bowed, lips tight with unspoken grief. He was listening to Donaidh, his head tilted towards the shorter man, and Lydia read respect and dignity in the undivided attention he was granting to Donaidh. Abruptly, her eyes stung and she looked down at her empty plate, worried she might give way to unseemly emotion.

'Thank you!' She managed a half-smile for the maid who was collecting the dishes from their table, then swallowed hard.

Do not think too much!

She did not dare remember the kiss, or the teasing way in which he had spoken to her earlier. It would be perilous, she knew, to refine too much upon such things. Had she not, after all, fended off a hundred kisses over the years? Men set little store by such casual embraces.

And yet, she reflected, there had been such intensity in their kiss. It had been fuelled as much by shock and grief as by desire—the need to do something life-giving in the midst of death. Either way, she could not hope for it to be repeated. He was the Laird, she the governess—and a Sassenach, at that. Whatever comfort he had taken from her, she was glad of it. She refused to regret kissing him, even if the moment had held more meaning and depth for her than it had for him. Men, she reminded herself, might kiss and embrace and then forget.

Ignoring the dissenting inner voice trying to tell her that Alasdair was different to other men, she directed her attention back to the dais, where he had stood and was making ready to speak.

Ten minutes later she, along with almost everyone else in the Hall, was in tears. There was no shame in it, for men and women alike were wiping tears and blowing into handkerchiefs. Alasdair spoke eloquently of Dòmhnall Mòr, eldest son of Donaidh and Maggie. He recited the young man's strengths and gifts, along with anecdotes showing both the young man's kindness and his ability when younger to get into scrapes. Laughter punctuated the tears and somehow made the sorrow both sweeter and more painful.

Offering his own sorrow to Dòmhnall's parents, brothers, wider family and his sweetheart, Eilidh, the Laird then led them in a brief prayer. He finished with a toast and they all rose, calling Dòmhnall's name as they supped their whisky.

Uisge beatha, Lydia recalled. The water of life. *If only...*

This led the way for a series of speeches and toasts, men and women rising at random, it seemed, to share their thoughts and add their condolences. Caught up in the moment, it took some effort for Lydia to step outside the occasion briefly to notice how the rituals of these past days had served not only to support the grieving, but to further deepen the bonds between all the Ardmore people. Each individual, each family would give support, knowing that when they inevitably suffered a bereavement themselves, they would receive the same succour.

Following the formalities, people stood, stretched their legs and began conversations with acquaintances from other tables. Lydia went to check on Mairead, who was in a large chamber in the newer side of the castle, with a dozen other children. The funeral feast had been restricted to adults, babes in arms tied to their mothers with shawls and near-adults, while the little ones—those aged about two to fourteen—had been entertained by some of the younger servants. Mairead was quite content, laughing and jesting with the other children, and it warmed Lydia's heart to see it.

Hurrying back to the Great Hall, Lydia saw that Mrs MacLeod was directing people to clear a space in the centre. Two lines of chairs were arranged and a platform with long struts on either side placed there. Silence fell as Dòmhnall's coffin was brought in and placed on the chairs. The priest stepped forward, beginning the prayers, and eight women lined up, four on each side of the coffin. Maggie was at the front and to the right, her chin quivering, but her tears bravely contained. When the priest paused in his litany six of the women, working together, hefted the coffin to waist height, working in pairs, using the struts to lift the coffin. Maggie, her head held high, picked up a cord attached to the front of the coffin and led the party forward, while the eighth woman took up a similar cord at the back. Slowly, they stepped forward and others moved swiftly to clear the chairs. As they walked towards the door, Lydia wondered how the women were managing so stoically, for Dòmhnall was neither small nor light.

Feet-first, they brought him to the castle door, where eight men, led by Donaidh and Alasdair, moved ahead to receive him. Passing their precious burden on to the menfolk, the women did not cross the threshold, but instead stood back to allow all of the men to exit. The moment when Maggie passed the leading cord to Donaidh was particularly poignant.

Here is our son.

The only sounds Lydia could hear were the shuffling of shoes on the stone floor, the cry of gulls outside and an occasional sob from someone in the Hall.

The men moved off, carrying Dòmhnall to his grave, and the women gathered together inside the doorway, craning for a view as the sad procession moved through the courtyard, beneath the arched gate, and away. To her left, Lydia spied Eilidh Òg, who was being held up by her mother and sister.

'The poor girl,' said Mrs MacLeod, who had moved towards Lydia as the women moved away from the door. 'To lose her sweetheart at such a young age.'

'It is truly dreadful,' agreed Lydia, knowing her words were inadequate.

'Still, she may love again,' the housekeeper added. 'There's many a one thinks their life is ended when their loved one goes. But there are choices, always choices.'

Lydia frowned. Was she still speaking of Eilidh?

'An rud nach gabh leasachadh, 'S fheudar cur suas leis,' Mrs MacLeod added. 'What cannot be helped must be put up with. When my own husband died I was too old to seek another. Besides, my children were grown, so I had plenty to see to me. It is a different matter for young Eilidh.' She eyed Lydia keenly. 'And for the Laird.'

'The Laird? You think he will marry again?' The thought sent an arrow of pain through her.

'I know not if he *will*. I only know he *should*. The child needs a mother and he needs a wife. A good wife.' She moved off and began directing the clearing of the tables and chairs.

Helping the other women, Lydia could not help but ponder this. *A good wife*. What would that mean, in terms of Alasdair? The answer came to her immediately. Someone who loved him. Someone who would share his burdens. Someone who understood his responsibilities.

Then the other thoughts. Someone from the islands. Not an Edinburgh wife, this time. And certainly not a Sassenach. Someone of his own status. Despite the more relaxed approach to rank and position here, she found it telling that Lady Hester had been the daughter of an Edinburgh noble. Yes, they could talk all they wished about the lack of focus on status and station, yet when it came down to it, like married like. Perhaps, in some ways, the islands were no different to the *ton*.

Since her arrival on Benbecula, Lydia had not been further than a few miles from Ardmore Castle. Yet the islands, she now knew, were many, all close together in a chain over a hundred miles long. An t-Eilean Fada, they sometimes called the archipelago—the Long Island. She rehearsed the names in her mind. Lewis and Harris in the north, then North Uist, Benbecula, South Uist, and Barra, with myriad smaller islands and skerries all around. There were lairds, captains and heads of houses dotted through the islands and Alasdair could no doubt have his choice among the local maidens of rank if and when he decided to remarry.

A mother for Mairead. Her chest clenched with sudden anguish at the notion. While she had spent longer than a few months with some of the other children she had cared for, there was something unique about her relationship with Mairead. Only Master John Pickering had hitherto come this close to her heart, and she was interested to note that both children were much more dependent on her than children who could run about and play freely.

Of course Mairead deserved a mother and Lydia would not begrudge her the opportunity if it occurred. But could she stay here in Ardmore, once Alasdair married? The thought made her senses whirl. She loved it here, she truly did. But she loved him more.

I love him.

Sinking down on a nearby chair along the back wall, she brought her hands to her face.

I love him.

Chapter Twelve

I love him.

Well, of course she did. Never having experienced this sort of love before, it was no wonder she had failed to recognise it before now. Love to her previously had been the affection she had felt for her parents, for the children she looked after. It was warm, steady and good and she knew it to be real. It made her want only the best for them, even if the people she loved were occasionally difficult or irritating. It had commitment in it, and self-sacrifice, and a knowledge of the other person gained through time and proximity.

This love was more. It had all of those qualities in abundance. Yet it was also a burning conflagration— a passion so sharp it felt like fever. It had begun with a small flame—a tendre which she had tried to tell herself was a passing infatuation. Yet the flame had grown and spread until it was deep within her, burning internally with heat and with force. Everything he did fascinated her. Everything he was inspired her. Even when he was cross, or burdened, or curt, she never doubted his character, his nobility, for an instant.

One thing though, one crucial aspect of love, was missing. Closing her eyes, she tried again to sense the love she had shared with her mother and father, with the children. It had thrived in an atmosphere of reciprocation and mutuality. Mairead loved her back. As had John. As had her parents.

In that sense her love for Alasdair was not the same. While she believed he had come to respect her, and might even call her 'friend', there was nothing to suggest any deeper feeling, not to mention anything like the passion she felt for him. Oh, he had kissed her. He had even teased her in an enticing way earlier. The memories did wonderful things to her insides and made her curl her fingers and toes. Even the way he had looked at her sent delicious thrills curling through her body. Yet she knew better than most maidens how men could be slaves to passing desires. She had little doubt that the numerous men who had claimed to 'adore' her in an attempt to bed her had now quite forgotten her. Not one had sought her out after she had been dismissed from whatever post she had held. Not one.

Men behave differently here.

The thought came unbidden, with echoes of Mrs Gray's words, yet she could not trust in it. Yes, islanders were more respectful generally and Eilidh Ruadh, in one of their more intimate conversations, had revealed that it was expected that both men and women would go to the marriage bed as virgins. Yet men were, after all, men. Were they not?

A cry went up from the other side of the Hall. Opening her eyes, Lydia saw a group of women clustered around someone and made haste to join them, anxious to discover what was amiss.

'Get her to her chamber,' one of the women said. 'We shall need the doctor, I fear.'

Reaching the group, Lydia discovered that young Eilidh had collapsed, her face paper white and a blueness about her lips that looked ominous. Working briskly, the women loosened her stays, then together they carried her upstairs. Lydia went along in the hope she could be of service, but the Ardmore ladies were briskly, kindly efficient. Eilidh was put to bed, a hot brick at her feet and the fire lit. By this time she had come round and was crying bitterly, while enduring fits of coughing. She seemed to find it difficult to get her breath and Lydia could see the concern in the eyes of the women, Maggie among them.

Lord! Here am I, in a haze of self-pity, while Eilidh has nearly drowned, lost her sweetheart and now looks to be seriously unwell.

The doctor, she was informed, lived near Nunton on the other side of Benbecula, and it would take a couple of hours for some of the younger women to fetch him, particularly if he was from home. The men were still at the funeral and no time could be wasted awaiting their return. In the meantime Mrs MacLeod gave Eilidh a pungent tisane, which the girl took without demur.

She knows herself that she is very ill.

Lydia knew that they were all likely thinking the same thing.

We have lost Dòmhnall. We cannot also lose Eilidh.

Lydia, knowing she was of no use, for the castle women had everything in hand, quietly departed, tak-

ing a last, lingering look at Eilidh as she did so. The
girl remained pale, but with spots of bright red colour
in her cheeks. She had reported a severe pain in her
right side, but the blueness around her lips had eased a
little, or so Lydia told herself.

Returning downstairs, she assisted with clearing up
after the feast, then spent a couple of hours with the
children, entertaining them with games, songs, and stories. Mairead, perhaps feeling uneasy at the grief and
worry in the atmosphere, clung to Lydia much more
than she was used to and even told another child, who
had come to Lydia for a hug, 'No! She is *my* Lydia!'

Lydia smoothed over this, settling both children before distracting them all with a new story. Soon afterwards, their mothers and older sisters arrived to fetch
them for, they said, the men had returned and families
were dispersing to their own rooms and cottages. Lydia
engaged in all the goodbyes with smiles and warmth
and got more than a few embraces from contented children.

Afterwards, she organised some food for Mairead
from the kitchens, then put the child to bed, for the day
had run away from them all and it was now evening.
Following the huge feast earlier, there would be no evening dinner and Lydia was unsure whether she should
even go back downstairs. Standing outside the door to
Mairead's bedchamber, she hesitated. She longed to see
Alasdair again and to revel in the secret knowledge that
she loved him. Equally, it terrified her to think that he
might somehow read her feelings in her eyes or through
her unwitting signs. She shuddered. That would not do!

Besides, she had slept little during the wake—indeed

her last full night's sleep had been last Saturday, before the ill-fated boat trip. And today, the day of Dòmhnall's funeral and Eilidh's collapse, felt like the longest day she had ever lived. Her mind made up, she turned away from the staircase and made for her own bedchamber. Solitude was best this evening.

Alasdair cradled his whisky without drinking it, having had, he knew, quite enough of the spirit for one day. At each lift in the funeral procession there had been whisky, and after the interment they had retired to the croft house of Donaidh and Maggie, where neighbours had laid out bread, cheese and salmon, with yet more whisky to wash it down. Alasdair had done his duty, naturally, but he now felt exhausted. Iain, who had done sterling work in organising some of the practical details around the funeral, had fallen asleep in the facing chair—the combination of the fire, the whisky and the silence too much for him. Of Lydia, there was no sign.

She has probably retired early.

She would be just as fatigued as everyone else, he knew, for he had seen her working with the rest, taking her place among them as though she were truly a woman of the islands. Squirming at this, he reminded himself not to be taken in by appearances. Lydia was a good woman, but she could not be expected to truly adapt to the harshness of life here. And no-one should require her to do it. Lydia was not Hester, but she was also not an islander born and bred.

He thought about this. Life was harsh, yes, but worth it, for surely this place was as near to Paradise as anyone might find on this earth? A lad like Dòmhnall, had he

lived in Lancashire or Lothian, might have fallen prey
to a farming accident, or been killed by brigands, or
even lost his life in a carriage accident, as Hester had.
Instead, Dòmhnall's life had been taken by the sea. And
now possibly Eilidh's life, too. Alasdair had returned
to the castle to hear the doctor was with her and that
worthy gentleman had afterwards confessed to Alasdair that the girl could die.

'Her lungs are inflamed, I am sorry to say.' He had
shaken his head sorrowfully. 'Hippocrates held that
such an inflammation often leads to death on the sev-
enth day, so we must wait and see how she fares.'

*Another death, and as ever I am powerless to pre-
vent it.*

He and Lydia had found Dòmhnall's body six years
to the day since Hester perished. His wife, young and
healthy at the time, had perished in order to escape from
him. From him, from Ardmore and from island life. A
life cut short. A life unlived.

He had visited her grave once, in Edinburgh, regret
and sorrow almost crushing him as he stood there, recalling her vivacity, her strong spirit. Gone, like Dòmhnall. Her family had refused to meet him, clearly
believing him to be responsible for her death. Which,
naturally, he was.

Am I cursed?

Hester, Mairead's affliction, Dòmhnall, and now Eilidh. The common factor was him.

Eilidh will die.

How he knew this, he could not say. *Be logical, man.
Curses are not real.* Yet the hopelessness he felt about
Eilidh's survival was implacable. He called to mind the

doctor's sad expression, the tone in his voice as he had spoken of Eilidh. The man's attitude suggested a miracle would be needed for her to survive, and Alasdair no longer believed in miracles. Death should wait for the old, not take the young. Yet death would do what it willed. Despite his people's crushing faith in him, just now Alasdair knew himself for a fraud.

Again, his rational mind reasserted itself. He could not reasonably hold himself to blame for every tragedy. Dòmhnall, Eilidh and the others had had a boating accident. Hester had made her own choices. He had been young. He squirmed uncomfortably.

I excuse myself, and belittle everyone in doing so.

It occurred to him to wonder if perhaps there was a darker reason why Lydia had not wished to join him tonight. Yes, everyone was weary, but he had behaved badly towards her, had he not, when he had kissed her on the night of the accident? Should he apologise, or would that leave things even more uncomfortable?

I am not rational tonight. I am overcome by dark thoughts, and grief and guilt.

Engulfed by brooding melancholy, he sipped his whisky and allowed his mind to return to Lydia.

She had matched his hunger, or so he had thought. For him it had been the first kiss since coldness had come between him and Hester, a lifetime ago. In that moment though, in the half darkness of the Great Hall, all he had thought of was Lydia. Lydia of the golden hair, eyes as blue as summer seas and a body as divine as that of Venus. Lydia the serene. Lydia the quick-minded. Lydia the compassionate.

Lydia, who had thought to ensure her passage back

to London was confirmed. Lydia, who had left every family she had worked with. Lydia, who was not of island stock. Should he ask her how she liked life in the islands? He shook his head, recognising that, even should she say she was enamoured of island life, he would struggle to believe her, for Hester had soured him.

The second occasion when he had been foolish had been earlier today. Quite forgetting himself, he had flirted with her and teased her as though they were sixteen-year-olds dancing at a gathering. Oh, at the time it had been nothing short of exhilarating, fencing with her, giving her looks that revealed his fancy for her and wondering if she would respond in kind. He frowned. At the time he had thought she hungered for him, too— at least a little. But now, all he could remember clearly was that she had seemed nervous at his actions.

Damnation!

She, a lady in his household, to be respected and protected, might not, after all, have enjoyed his advances, indirect as they were. He was her laird—nay, her employer, but both were positions of power. He had had no reason to consider this before, because he had not made any advances towards her before. He had been raised well by his father to understand the power contained within his role and to use it only in ways that were of benefit to others. Self-sacrifice, his own *papa-idh* had often said, was at the heart of the Laird's work. He would be the first man into battle, the first to enter the burning farmhouse, the first to jump into the sea after a drowning child. The last to think of himself.

Yet what of me? What of my needs?

Loneliness and frustration rose in him like bile and

he shook off the unworthy thoughts in disgust. Raising his glass, he drank. Time to retire.

Normality—or at least what passed for normality—resumed the next day. Dòmhnall was spoken about with great affection and deliberate frequency, and his family would continue to receive support from visitors and neighbours, Lydia was informed. Eilidh remained severely unwell and, Lydia discovered, a list was being created of Ardmore women willing to take a turn in caring for her.

Leaving Mairead in the care of Sadie, one of the maids, Lydia went searching for the housekeeper, who was in her own room writing up her accounts.

'*Madainn mhath*, Mrs MacLeod. I wish to help care for Eilidh.' Her words were uttered baldly, without any artifice.

Will she allow it? Am I seen as the stranger still?

Reminding herself that she had been treated with only kindness, she held her breath, awaiting the woman's reply.

The housekeeper raised an eyebrow and set down her pen. 'Oh, you do, do you? And when do you propose doing this? For you are with Mairead most of the day, with the Laird in the evenings and you need your sleep at night.'

'I—' Lydia was slightly taken aback. 'I had not thought about that. But she is my friend and I need to do *something* to assist her.' She frowned. 'I could suspend my lessons with the other children for a while. I could get up early. I could do one night every week. I could do without my evenings with Iain and the Laird.' Pointedly, she mentioned Iain first, as she felt uncomfortable with Mrs MacLeod's hint that she spent evenings 'with the Laird'. She did not: she spent her evenings with the Laird and sometimes his steward, and had done so ever since her arrival. 'I also used to spend a half-hour or an hour with Eilidh most evenings, either before dinner or later, before retiring. I am teaching her French.' She felt tears sting her eyes at the notion that her French lessons with Eilidh might not resume.

Mrs MacLeod paused, looking at her closely, then nodded. 'Very well. I shall add you to the schedule—though *not* in the evenings, for—' Clearly stopping herself from finishing her sentence, she stepped to the dresser, fetching a paper which, Lydia saw, had a series of times and days with names against them. 'Eilidh's own mother, aunts and sister have the lion's share, but Maggie has asked me to include her and I shall now add you.' She pondered for a moment. 'You may sit with her from four until five each afternoon. That way Eilidh's family can have dinner together every day, even if it is a little early, and Maggie can cook for her own clan. I believe it will be good for Eilidh to have someone different as she recuperates.'

'You think she will recover, then?'

The housekeeper shrugged. 'I know not. "May we be preserved from lawyers and from doctors", they say, and it is certainly true that when one or other of those worthy gentlemen are called for, someone has troubles to bear. But I do know that Eilidh will be offered every comfort and all the attention we can give her. Now then—' her tone turned brisk '—she is to be encouraged to drink as much fresh water as she will take and wine, too, if she will accept it. My tisane made from hyssop and oil of mint is efficacious in clearing phlegm, so we are encouraging her to cough as much of the pestilence out of her as she can. And finally, when her breathing is poor, she may rest on her stomach, for it seems to ease her a little. Apart from that, she needs only the common comforts—her chamber pot, a sponge wash when she has exhausted herself with sweats, and fresh nightgowns and sheets every day or so.'

'Yes, Mrs MacLeod. And thank you.'

The older woman smiled grimly. 'Let us hope and pray that the girl keeps fighting for her life. Her lowness of spirits is just as great a threat as any inflammation of the lungs. She must *want* to live.'

Hurrying back to the schoolroom with the housekeeper's words ringing in her ears, Lydia's newfound insight into her own heart allowed her some understanding of how Eilidh might be feeling.

If anything were to happen to Alasdair...

Her heart clenched in sudden fear. The very notion left a sick feeling in her stomach and an ache in her chest.

Love makes us vulnerable. She remembered her thoughts on the day of the funeral. Love and loss—two parts of the same whole. Briefly, she recalled her former life with the Barnstable twins. She had felt affection for them, yes, but had recovered relatively quickly to the loss of contact with them. Here, she was surrounded by people she had come to care for deeply—the Laird and Mairead most of all. Her governess armour could be pierced from many directions now. Yet she knew deep within her that it was worth it. Love was worth the pain of loss. Once more, she allowed herself to briefly imagine Alasdair dying. Once more, the entire world felt as though it were rocking. She paused, steadied herself, then continued on.

Passing through her bedchamber, she opened the schoolroom door. 'Apologies, Sadie!' She stopped.

'Good morning, Lydia. I let Sadie return to her duties.' The Laird, having risen at her entrance, eyed her closely. 'Is something amiss?'

She felt herself flush.

Only that I had you dead and buried, and myself in mourning for you. Only that I love you.

'Oh, no, nothing at all!' She glanced at the clock. 'You are very early today.'

'Well, I have not seen much of my daughter this week, because of the wake. And as I am sure she has missed numerous lessons, I decided to join you both, rather than take her out of school for another day.' He looked *beautiful*, she noted idly, her gaze skimming over his kilt and jacket towards his handsome face.

'She will not fall behind, I assure you!' she declared earnestly. Was there criticism in his comment?

He waved his hand. 'I do not doubt it, for she is prodigiously clever. Are you not, *mo nighean*?'

'I am,' Mairead replied simply, and Lydia suppressed a smile. Was this truly the same child who had been so lacking in confidence just a few months ago?

'Now then,' she said to the child in a brisk tone, 'have you finished the arithmetic I set for you when Sadie came?'

'Almost, Lydia. I have but one more sum to complete.' She bent her dark head to her work and a wave of affection coursed through Lydia. Glancing at the Laird, she saw a similar softening in his eyes and they shared an understanding half-smile.

'Good. Next we may all speak French together.' Perhaps she would be less flustered if the lesson was a three-way conversation, rather than her having to perform as teacher under his devastating gaze.

This proved to be the case and over the next half-hour she settled a little, although her heart continued to pound in a most inconvenient manner at his nearness.

She glanced out of the window. 'As we have another sunny day, I had planned for us to go outside, for I do not believe Mairead has had enough fresh air this week.'

'Then I shall accompany you!' he declared promptly, 'for I have frequently wished to discover what you do on your sojourns out!'

Mairead frowned, glancing at Lydia. *Will she tell him?* Waiting for a moment to discover if the child meant to share her secret, Lydia then responded into the brief silence, 'Of course! I have agreed to sit with Eilidh later, so we cannot go far.'

'The courtyard?' asked Mairead hopefully. 'It has been an age since we counted the chickens!'

And they never worked on Mairead's exercises in the courtyard. *Very well, child.* 'The courtyard it is!' Lydia moved to lift her, but Alasdair intervened, gathering Mairead up into his strong arms and kissing the child's cheek. The sight made Lydia's heart quite turn over.

She accompanied them through the castle, down the grand staircase and out through the Great Hall, enjoying a sense of companionship with them both. Stepping outside, they all blinked in the strong sunshine. The courtyard seemed to have trapped the sun's heat, for the air hit them in a wave of unusual warmth. Unfortunately, it also reeked with the aroma of animal dung and Lydia immediately fumbled for a handkerchief to bring to her nose.

'The odour offends you, Lydia?' Alasdair's eyes danced with amusement. 'Occasionally I forget that you are a fine London lady and unused to our way of life.'

For some reason this made her clench her teeth briefly. 'Not at all, sir.' Her tone was cool. 'I am a simple governess and my parents were not of the gentry. My father was a lawyer, but his income was modest. I was well raised with a good education, yes, but my blood is of country stock.' Why was she reminding him of her lowly birth? Or was she reminding herself?

'No need to be in high dudgeon with me, Miss Farnham!' he retorted, still laughing at her, 'for I know full well when I am in the suds with you. You do not even need to call me "sir" in such moments, for your demeanour quite gives you away.' His smile faded, replaced by something serious, intent and frighteningly wonderful. 'I have made quite a study of you and believe I am now adept at reading your moods.'

She flushed. *He makes a study of me?* Flustered, and knowing not what to say, she took refuge in aloofness. 'I apologise. A good servant should be unreadable and I consider it a failure on my part that you can divine my humours. I shall endeavour to be less transparent in future, s—' She bit off the *sir* that she had been about to utter, which seemed to restore him to amusement.

'Ah, Lydia, Lydia,' he declared, when he had finished laughing. 'Has it not occurred to you that it is not your behaviour which is so revealing, but rather my discernment in reading it? That this is my achievement rather than your failure? Hmmm?' He sent her a sideways glance. 'And you are not a "servant" in the usual sense.'

This mollified her a little. She sniffed. 'We are spending too much time standing here discussing nothing when I should be continuing with your daughter's lessons! Mairead, I suggest we sit on the bench outside that cottage, for the chickens are at the other side today.'

Without awaiting Alasdair's agreement, she picked her way across the courtyard to the bench she had seen, half listening to ensure he had followed her. Placing Mairead between them, he sat on the sun-drenched side of the bench, stretching his long legs out before him. Lydia, determined not to allow his presence to divert her further, played the usual games with Mairead, but could not shake her continuous awareness of him. His head was turned towards her and his daughter, but she did not dare to check if his gaze was directed towards her, or Mairead. His presence was enough, though, to deeply unsettle her and she was finding it difficult to remember how to behave in a usual manner.

She stopped, listening. Above the cacophony of farm animals and seabirds, a new sound had been added. It came from outside the walls and sounded remarkably like a brawl. There were shouts and exclamations, as well as a peculiar thudding sound. Her gaze swivelled to Alasdair, her heart now pounding with alarm. He was looking at her.

'What is it? What is amiss?'

He grinned. 'Come with me.' Picking up his daughter, he strode towards the arched gateway that led out of the castle courtyard to the countryside beyond. Skipping to keep up, Lydia tried to take reassurance from his relaxed demeanour and from the fact that he was carrying his vulnerable child towards whatever the commotion was.

Outside, on the long flat field lately occupied by some of the Laird's terrifying long-haired cows, a space had been cleared and a group of twelve or fifteen men and youths were engaged in what seemed to Lydia to be a massed battle. All had dispensed with their jackets and ganseys and were fighting bare-chested, or in their shirts. At first, she could discern very little save movement and intent and what seemed to be bludgeons being carried by the miscreants. Why on earth had Alasdair brought his daughter here? Surely the violence could easily spill over and the child could be injured—even accidentally? Lydia's palms were damp with sudden fear and her stomach twisted.

It then occurred to her that, in the short moments she had been observing, she had seen no blows actually land, although the weapons were being swung with alarming intent. She had seen no knives, swords or pistols, which was somewhat reassuring. Strangely, all the sticks had a curve at the end—a crookedness which marked them as being something other than random branches.

But there are no trees nearby! Where did they—?

Abruptly, the entire group of combatants dived across to her left, as if following a common prey. Her hand went to her mouth.

Is this some barbaric form of hunting? Is there some

poor creature beneath their feet being bludgeoned to death?

She gazed intently at the action. The men were not using the curved sticks to attack one another after all, but were swinging at—

'A ball! I see a ball there!' A small brown sphere, which looked to have been formed from dark wood or leather, was being battered about the field by the men, using the curved sticks. Now that she understood, her hand had moved to her chest, where she tried to tell her foolish heart to settle itself. 'Is this a game of some description?'

Alasdair was gazing at her, and she just knew he had been watching her the whole time. 'Aye. It's *camanachd.* Shinty, if you prefer. The sticks are called camans.'

'But what on earth are they trying to achieve?'

He laughed. 'It must be hard to divine for one who has not seen it before. One group must get the ball to this end of the field and through the space marked by the two jackets on the ground, while the other must get it to the other end and through the space there.'

She nodded, only now noticing the four jackets, strategically placed at each end of the field. As she watched, someone's stick shattered and he ran towards them, picking up a new caman from a pile to their left that Lydia had quite failed to notice. His body was slick with sweat and he was out of breath, but he was grinning.

'Come on then, Alasdair, shake yourself. We are a man down!'

'If I must,' the Laird replied, a slow grin growing on his own face. Handing Mairead to Lydia, he divested himself of his jacket and loosened the laces at the front of his shirt. Picking up a caman, he trotted lightly to the fray and was soon lost in a melee of sticks, tartan and limbs.

Well!

Just when she believed this place had nothing more to teach her, along came another surprise. Hefting Mairead more securely on to her hip, Lydia made her way to the pile of camans, where they both sat on the sweet, dry grass. Lydia, fascinated, rummaged through the sticks. All were the same shape, but they had been fashioned out of a range of materials. A couple were formed from precious wood, which would probably have been imported. *Ash*, Lydia guessed. *Or beech.* The majority had been painstakingly crafted from what looked like inter-woven strands of seaweed, fashioned into thick dried staves. One was formed from stiffened canvas sailcloth that had been tightly rolled, then twisted and strapped into the model of a workable caman. Her gaze returned to the action and she could not resist watching Alasdair as he ran and swung, twisted and bent. He was shout-ing orders in Gaelic to his own side and exhorting one man to move away from the melee, in readiness for the ball to appear. Sure enough, another of Alasdair's corps managed to get a good hit along the ground, sending the ball in the right direction. Too late the other side realised what was occurring and tried in vain to reach the player. He sent the ball between the jackets, then wheeled around triumphantly to the cheers and accla-mation of his comrades.

At this stage a few more shirts were discarded and Lydia watched with helpless hunger as Alasdair re-vealed his well-formed shape. Clad only in his boots, stockings, and kilt, and brandishing his caman, he was the very epitome of male beauty. Even the sight of his exposed knees made her feel weak.

Surely, Lydia mused, her eyes devouring his fine form, *the great sculptors could have wished for no better subject?*

Alasdair knew she was watching. He felt it in every moment of the *camanachd*. Once again, he realised he was no better than a youngling, for today he was playing with a heart and commitment that he had not felt for a very long time. He recalled, in his younger days, loving *camanachd* with a passion, but then his father had died and the Lairdship, marriage and fatherhood had reduced his ability to truly engage with it. Today, seeing the ancient game through Lydia's eyes, he hoped she would get a sense of the skill, effort and accuracy required. He was also relishing the opportunity to go shirtless in front of her and hoped it might inspire her in a different way entirely. If only he were closer, he might be able to read her expression. He had genuinely become a student of all things Lydia and, in his more confident moments, could swear that she was developing warmer feelings for him. He could not be certain and he was not yet sure enough of his own path to know what he wanted for the best. Today, though, was not the time for excess thought. Today was sunshine and *camanachd*, and the bittersweet joy of being alive.

Chapter Thirteen

'Men are nothing more than boys with beards and so I shall always say!' It was Mrs MacLeod. Looking about, Lydia saw that a number of the castle staff had come out to watch the sporting. 'We shall get no work done now for the next hour or more!' Despite her words, she sat herself down beside Lydia and Mairead as if she had every intention of staying.

'I had no idea there was such a thing as shinty! Indeed, I have never seen anything like it!'

Mrs MacLeod narrowed her eyes. 'Aye, well. It used to be part of warrior training, for it builds muscle and skill, and the ability to work together.' She nodded towards the field, where Alasdair's side had just succeeded again in putting the ball between the jackets. 'And a good leader. The ability to give orders under pressure and to listen to comrades who may see something you cannot…all of these things are much more than the *camanachd* itself.'

'So do they play all year round? How come I have not seen this before?'

'Most of the *camanachd* games happen in winter

and spring, for there is too much work to be done at this time of year for everyone to be distracted so. But we do have one summer game and so the boys feel the need to prepare. In a couple of weeks on July seventeenth, we shall celebrate the Feast of Saint Alexis the Beggar, and we are to play against Angus and his house. They will come to us this year, for we take it in turn. Every tinker and travelling merchant will come, too. It is not just the game, you see. Our folk will spend the best part of a day clearing the space and raising tents, and afterwards there is always a bit of a gathering outside in the field.' She frowned. 'We need it this year, Lord knows. Aye, and we shall miss Wee Dòmhnall all the more, for his size and strength was very handy for the shinty.'

'I can imagine!' Indeed, Lydia could easily picture Dòmhnall amid the melee and Eilidh sitting watching, along with the rest. 'How is Eilidh now?'

The housekeeper shrugged. 'Much the same. Are you still intending to sit with her at four?'

'Of course! I just hope I may be of some help to her.'

Sitting with Eilidh proved to be challenging in unexpected ways. Not because the girl was demanding. Rather because she was clearly very ill. During Lydia's hour with her, Eilidh slept fitfully, but did not seem to be resting. Instead she tossed and turned feverishly and refused all of the drinks Lydia tried to tempt her with. Lydia was relieved when Eilidh's mother arrived to take over, but was determined to continue to play her part.

Over the next few days Eilidh remained dangerously ill. A week after she had collapsed, they all feared the

worst and the priest was brought in to anoint her. But
some time during that long night Eilidh's fever broke,
and by morning word spread through the castle that she
was sleeping in a natural way. By four o'clock when
Lydia arrived, Eilidh was sitting up, eating soup, and
smiling weakly at Maggie's efforts to cheer her. Lydia
had to pause in the doorway and lean against the frame,
so great was her relief. Her tone, however, was light
as she continued to Eilidh's bedside, saying, 'Well, I
am glad you have decided to get better! Mrs MacLeod
was very cross with me when you would not drink her
tisanes!'

Eilidh made a face. 'They tasted horrible! This soup
is better, but I have had enough now. Oh, Lydia, I cannot tell you how wonderful it is to be sitting up and able
to speak and think!'

'I can only imagine!' Lydia hugged her gently, feeling how thin she had become. Still, the light in her eyes
was very much the old Eilidh.

'Eilidh, you have hardly eaten anything,' Maggie
protested. 'Please, try a little more.'

Eilidh refused and Maggie set the bowl down, sighing. 'You will need to eat to get your strength back, my
girl. Why, your dresses will all be too loose on you! You
would not wish that, would you?'

Eilidh shrugged, then sent a sly glance Lydia's way.
'That would make them just like yours, Lydia!'

'Ouch!' Lydia glanced down. 'I suppose it is a fair
comment, though.' She grinned at Eilidh. 'You have
never liked my too-big dresses.'

'I shall make a bargain with you,' the girl offered,
her eyes bright with glee. 'If I promise to eat well, will

you allow me to take in all your dresses when I am recovered?'

Lydia did not hesitate. Delighted at Eilidh's transformation from lingering at death's door to seemingly regaining some of her former vivacity, she agreed, only afterwards worrying a little about the unwanted attentions that fashionable dresses might lead to. And what of *wanted* attentions? She could not forget that, on the one occasion when she had worn a dress tailored to her form, Alasdair had danced with her. And no one had bothered her. The place had held plenty of men, young and old, yet no one had importuned her. Perhaps, then, it would not be unreasonable to have dresses that fitted correctly?

Eilidh's progress after that was not always straightforward and there were days when she was cross, or weak, but little by little, she began to regain her strength. She and Lydia enjoyed their hour together every afternoon and had even begun trying a little French again. Eilidh sometimes got out of bed, but would tire quickly and sleep for a long time after any physical exertion. Then one day, just a few days before the *camanachd* game and the gathering afterwards, Maggie approached Lydia to ask if she could stay with Eilidh for the full afternoon, as she and the other women of her family were called to her niece, who was giving birth. Lydia assured her she would gladly cover, and took Mairead with her.

Eilidh was delighted to see the child, who hugged her tightly. They chatted together for a little while, Mairead perched on the side of Eilidh's bed, then the child turned to Lydia, her expression solemn.

'Lydia, you know our secret for Papaidh?' Lydia, startled, could only nod. 'Well, I should like to tell Eilidh.'

'If you are certain?'

Mairead nodded and turned back to Eilidh, who was looking from one to the other, mystified.

'Eilidh,' Mairead said, all determined practicality, 'when I was four I was very sick and I was in bed for a long time, just like you.'

Eilidh swallowed, then nodded. 'Yes, you were. We are both lucky to have another chance at life, I think.'

Mairead was only half listening, seemingly entirely focused on what she had planned to say. 'When I was sick in bed I forgot how to use my legs and they changed from girl legs into baby legs.' The child was entirely focused on Eilidh and it warmed Lydia's heart to see how earnestly Mairead was telling her tale.

She has thought much about this.

Eilidh laughed lightly. 'Well, I understand *that* now, for each time I try to walk I am weak as a cat afterwards!'

'You must try though, Eilidh, because if you practise hard your legs will get strong again. Lydia will help you, because Lydia knows *everything.*'

'I would not say I know *everything*, Mairead!'

'Well, it is true you do not know how to tell a bull from a cow, which is unfortunate, and you did not know any of our words at first, but you are learning very fast. You are *very* clever,' she added, in much the same tone that Lydia often used with her. 'Now, can you put me on the floor here?'

'You mistook a bull for a cow?' Eilidh's eyes were dancing. 'That must have led to an interesting encounter. I do hope you were not trying to milk the bull at the time!'

'Oh, hush now!' Lydia picked Mairead up and deposited her gently on the carpet at the side of Eilidh's bed. 'Just watch.'

Eilidh did and her hand flew to her mouth as Mairead manoeuvred herself into the right position, then raised herself on to her knees, all the while gripping the side of Eilidh's bed. 'Oh, my Lord! Mairead!'

The child ignored her, focusing all her efforts on raising herself on to first one foot, then the other. Rising, she stood tall and proud at the side of Eilidh's bed, gripping the counterpane, and finally allowed a broad smile to spread across her face. 'Look, Eilidh, I am standing like a proper girl!'

'You are! Oh, Mairead, you—you *angel*!' She hugged the child tightly and Lydia was unsurprised to see that tears were flowing down Eilidh's cheeks. 'I saw that you were eating more,' Eilidh declared, 'and that you have a healthy colour in your cheeks, but I never anticipated this!'

'So you see, Eilidh, you must eat your dinners, go outside and practise—' Mairead's little face was filled with earnest sincerity '—and then you will be well again.'

After making use of her own handkerchief, Lydia swallowed, hoping that her voice would not waver. 'Now, Mairead, can you show Eilidh how you can walk sideways?'

Mairead did so, carefully side-stepping all the way to the bottom of the bed and back, while using the bed for balance. 'Wonderful!' Lydia and Eilidh both clapped in delight, and Lydia picked Mairead up and hugged her.

'Now, Mairead, shall we show Eilidh the last thing—the thing we have been working on at the sandbanks?'

Mairead nodded and Lydia knelt to the floor, holding both the child's hands. First she let go of one, then the other. Mairead stood firm, without even needing to hold her hands out as she had when they had first attempted this. She had been working hard on her balance and was now able to stand well for quite an extended time. When she tried to take a step though, she often panicked, or lost her balance just at the thought of it.

'Would you like to try a step?' Lydia asked gently.

With a brief glance in Eilidh's direction, Mairead nodded firmly.

Lydia shuffled backwards until she was just out of reach, then held out her arms. 'Come on then.'

Mairead's arms flew out wide as she lifted her right foot, placing it a few inches in front of the other. She almost managed to steady herself, before losing balance and sinking down to the carpet with a firm bump. 'Ow!' she exclaimed. 'Your floor is much harder than the sand, Eilidh!'

Lydia hardly heard her. 'You nearly *walked*, Mairead! By yourself! You *nearly took a step!*'

'I know!' Mairead shrugged. 'I knew I could. I think I shall be walking very soon.'

'In that case,' Lydia said gently, 'I think it is time to show your *papaidh*. He will not wish to miss your first steps.'

'Do you think so?'

Lydia nodded. 'I have heard a very wise saying since I came to the Islands: "It is no secret when three know it." I think we must be fair to your *papaidh* and tell him very soon.'

'Today?'

Lydia considered this. 'Perhaps we should invite him to accompany us to the sandbanks tomorrow? You can practise more easily there.'

It was all agreed, and Lydia waited until the next morning before seeking out the Laird to invite him. She found him in his parlour with Iain, engaged in reviewing accounts. 'Oh! I do not mean to intrude…'

'Something ails Mairead?' He was frowning, so she made haste to reassure him.

'Not at all! But…' she took a breath '…we—that is to say, *Mairead* has asked if you could accompany us to the sandbanks today?'

He grinned. 'Mairead, eh? She is demanding, my daughter.'

'Only occasionally. I still prefer to describe her as strong-willed. She knows her own mind.'

'If she is so strong-willed at six, I dread to think what she may be like at sixteen!' He glanced out of the window. 'This fair weather will likely end later. The castle weather-watchers tell me there will be rain tonight.' He glanced at Iain. 'What say you? Perhaps another hour of this now, then we can continue tomorrow?'

'Of course! Away and enjoy yersels!'

The Laird turned back to Lydia, and she felt the usual thrill when he looked at her. 'I shall accompany you both, but not to the sandbanks. With no spring tide today they will not be exposed.'

'Dash it all!' Lydia could not help the expletive.

'Apologies for my colourful language. I had thought I was getting better at learning the tides.'

He grinned. 'Never worry. I have a better notion.'

'Oh, but—'

'Ask Mrs MacLeod to pack a picnic for us.' He rubbed his hands together. 'Perhaps this is exactly what I need today—a break from my responsibilities before the gathering.'

A little over an hour later they left Ardmore, Alasdair promising to Mrs MacLeod that they would be back by nightfall. *Nightfall!* That was hours and hours away. Lydia's heart sang at the knowledge that she would spend the rest of the day in the company of the two people who were dearest to her in all the world. Alasdair was carrying Mairead and commenting lightly on how sturdy she was getting. Lydia hid a smile.

You will discover later just how sturdy!

Mrs MacLeod had tied the picnic food up in a tartan blanket for, she had declared, Lydia would doubtless soon tire of an awkward basket. She had showed Lydia how to tie the bundle to her, in the way of the islanders, and Lydia was quite enjoying the sensation of being like them, even for a day.

Perhaps, she mused, *I might imagine that this bundle I am carrying is my baby, mine and Alasdair's, and we are out for a family excursion.*

The notion sent her heart soaring and she had to have a stern word with herself for being so fanciful—particularly since Alasdair had not shown any sign of wishing to repeat that thunderous kiss. Still, being in his company already meant that today was special.

He led them across the moors eastwards and north and they all chatted idly and easily as they traversed the countryside. The summer greening was now complete and the brown landscapes were now interspersed with swathes of grassy hills hiding birds and small animals, some of whom objected strongly to the passage of the Laird, his daughter and her governess.

As a governess, nothing like this had ever happened to Lydia before. Indeed, the very notion of striding out with her charge and a man into a wilderness such as this was simply preposterous. There were simply no London parallels that Lydia could even imagine. She attempted to picture Alasdair or Angus or indeed any of the men in Lady Barnstable's drawing room and failed entirely.

'You are smiling about something.' The Laird was eyeing her closely. 'Can you share your secret?'

'I was just thinking how unlike London this all is.' She gestured vaguely.

He frowned. 'I have been to Glasgow and to Edinburgh, but never as far as London. Angus and I may need to go there, if our attempts to purchase the land through letters and agents come to naught.' He glanced at her. 'I cannot conceive of a city so large.'

'It is large indeed and swallows up new villages each few years.'

'You must miss it.'

She shook her head. 'Not at all.'

He raised a sceptical eyebrow. 'Not even the ices at—*Gunter's*, I believe?'

She laughed. 'Not even that. I believe myself to be adaptable, as a governess must, but this place is invading my soul.' She considered her own words, which revealed a truth she had not herself before considered. 'The people are wonderful and the wildness of the landscape enthralling.'

And you. You are enthralling.

'Then you do not intend to leave any time soon?' His tone was mild, but she knew she must be careful in her answer.

'I am truly content here at present and I have no plans to leave.' Unspoken but ever-present within her was the knowledge that he might marry again and she did not think her heart could survive seeing him with a wife. Yet neither could she imagine wrenching herself away from him, from Mairead, from the island community, from the place. She swallowed. 'I hope that you are content with my work and do not plan to dismiss me?'

Asking the question was almost a habit, as she no longer harboured any serious concerns that he was unhappy with her teaching. Yet she had been dismissed so many times before, and so arbitrarily, that she could never feel fully at ease. He was different to her other employers. She knew it. Knew he was of the islanders, who valued loyalty and honour, and who did not behave irrationally with regard to such matters.

They value women here—and not as possessions or ornaments.

Yet she could also not forget that she was the outsider, the Sassenach.

'You are a gifted teacher, Lydia. Is she not, *mo nighean*?'

'She is the bestest!' the child confirmed as her father switched her to the other hip. Lydia winked at her and Mairead giggled with glee.

'What is this?' He looked from one to the other, mystified.

'You will have to wait and see, Papaidh. When we get to the sand you will find out.'

'Very well.' He clearly had no idea what was in store. Lydia hugged the knowledge to herself. While she had a slight concern that he might be angry with her for working on Mairead's walking without informing him, she hoped that his pride in his daughter would be stronger.

They were continuing eastwards and at a certain point he paused, pointing. 'Rossinish,' he declared, before leading them forward. 'Here the Prince landed in a storm after Culloden and from here he departed for Skye, some months later.' As they walked, he told the story for Mairead, who had clearly heard it before. Nevertheless, the child asked excited questions and seemed genuinely interested. Lydia, too, learned more details of the Bonnie Prince's sojourn in Benbecula, how Clanranald had helped and concealed him, and how Flora MacDonald and Neil MacEachan from South Uist had helped him escape, in a daring plan devised by Captain Crawford. Like Lydia, Mairead found it astonishing that the Prince had dressed as a woman in order to evade the English soldiers.

They paused for their picnic on the moors of Rossinish and it seemed to Lydia that they were the only people in the entire world. In every direction, there was no sign of human presence—no roads, no buildings, no tilled fields. This was nature, entirely untamed. The green and brown landscape melded into blue and white sky on every side, while the heavens above were the highest and largest Lydia had ever seen.

We are so small and unimportant. And yet...

She glanced at Mairead who was munching content-edly, a rosy colour in her cheeks and her legs stretched out immobile before her.

What we do with our lives has profound meaning.

By mid-afternoon they reached their destination—a beautiful beach, in the very bay where Bonnie Prince Charlie had left for Skye. The sand was so white it was blindingly beautiful and the sea was a deep, clear blue, with a turquoise hue near the shore. It was perfect.

Alasdair was trying to tell Mairead a little more of the tale of the Bonnie Prince, but the child had lost all interest, merely urging her *papaidh* to 'put me down'.

He did so and Lydia crouched down beside Mairead to remove her slippers and stockings. 'All is well,' she murmured, and Mairead nodded tightly. Lydia could sense her anxiety, but knew not how to alleviate it. Kneeling with Mairead, she simply waited.

'Papaidh.'

'Yes, my love?' Despite the enormity of the moment, and knowing what Mairead was about to do, Lydia still felt a surge of emotion at his words. He had spoken to his daughter, of course, but *oh!* How might it be to be loved by such a man?

'I—' Unusually, Mairead was lost for words, it seemed. 'I shall just show you.'

Chapter Fourteen

Alasdair was in heaven. When he had awoken this morning, in the knowledge that a day of poring over accounts was planned, little could he have imagined that he would instead be enjoying unfettered time on Rossinish with Mairead. And with Lydia. Despite himself, he knew that his fascination with the governess was, if anything, deepening. He had tried his best to not submit to spending so much daily time with her that it would lead to gossip, and today was his reward. It was perfectly reasonable, he had told himself, for him to attend his daughter's lessons for a hour each day, and entirely reasonable for Lydia to dine with himself and Iain in the evenings. Why, they had decided to do so even before Lydia's arrival, for any governess deserved such respect. At that point he and Iain had still expected a stiff, middle-aged dame.

Instead, there had been a golden-haired beauty with an intelligent gaze and a habit of self-restraint. Used to the more open nature of his compatriots, Alasdair had struggled at first to understand who she was. With time, though, had come comprehension. He had not been jesting when he had told her, on the day of the shinty, that he could read her moods. In truth, reading her moods and attempting to divine her thoughts was his current favourite diversion. She was not completely transparent to him. Not yet, at least. But he could generally tell when she was contented, or anxious, or cross. He knew when she was worrying about something and when she disapproved of something he had said or done. He suppressed a chuckle, setting Mairead down on the soft sand in Rossinish bay. As Lydia bent to attend to the child, he gazed hungrily at them both.

My Mairead! My Lydia!

He caught the sense of his own thoughts and checked. Lydia was not his. She was an employee—and a good one, at that. She was clearly devoted to his daughter. And while he had occasionally wondered if she had warmer feelings towards him, he had yet to identify any definitive proof.

Yes, they had shared a passionate kiss—his heart skipped a beat at the memory—and she had chosen to come with him to find Dòmhnall and Eilidh—something for which he remained profoundly grateful. Yet he could not take it to mean she had a partiality for him. Indeed, she was warm towards everyone she encountered and was universally liked and respected. And he, having avoided women for years, now had no idea how to divine if a woman might like him in a *particular* way. Oh, his foolish heart *believed* she did. But proof there was none. And besides, his logical mind continued to attempt to dissuade him from falling for a beauty once again. He found himself frequently arbitrating inner arguments and had even caught himself muttering aloud on occasion.

He sighed inwardly. He had noted carefully her response to his question earlier, which had been decidedly guarded. *No plans to leave.* She had chosen her words carefully and they gave him no assurances whatsoever.

And if she had instead vowed to stay forever, would he have believed her? Hope and fear warred within him. *Probably not.* His experience with Hester had burned deep. Rationality had little to do with the matter.

'All is well,' she was murmuring to the child and he wondered at it. Why would Mairead need reassurance? Observing their two heads so close together, Mairead so dark and Lydia so fair, he was taken unawares by a wave of emotion that shuddered through him. It left him with a thudding heart, a confused mind, and a gut curling with an unknown feeling of warmth, happiness, and something else he could not quite name. Lydia had knelt down on the soft sand beside Mairead, the warm southerly breeze teasing her golden hair, and suddenly his throat was tight with words that could not be uttered.

'Papaidh.'

His gaze swivelled to his daughter. 'Yes, my love?' His voice was husky with emotion.

'I shall just show you.' He watched, puzzled, as Mairead, a look of intense concentration on her little face, swung her legs around and beneath her. Something about it made the hairs at the back of his neck stand to attention. Since her illness Mairead had always been able to move her legs a little, but he could not recall a movement so notable, so co-ordinated, so...purposeful.

While his mind was catching up, Mairead was continuing to act, raising herself on to her knees and taking both of Lydia's hands.

'Careful!' He could not help the exclamation, for years of needing to protect his vulnerable child from falls was embedded within him. Instinctively, he bent towards his child, aiming to catch her, to pick her up and to keep her safe.

'No! No, Papaidh!' Mairead's tone was sharp, so he paused, dropping down beside them. 'Just watch me.'

'I have her,' Lydia murmured, her tone calm.

Very well.

His heart pounding with fear, nevertheless he decided to trust Lydia. 'I am watching, *mo nighean.*'

His jaw dropped as his daughter, her expression still tight with concentration, raised herself up on one leg, then the other. 'Mairead!' he gasped, unable to comprehend what he was seeing.

'Ready?' Lydia's voice was soft. Mairead nodded and Lydia let go of one of Mairead's hands, then the second.

Time seemed to stop and all of Alasdair's senses seemed sharpened somehow. There was still the salty scent of sea and seaweed, the sounds of crashing waves, celebratory gulls and the thud of his own heart. The soft sand felt warm and solid beneath him, yet the world was spinning away into the heavens. His mouth was dry, his palms damp, and there was a decided weakness in his skeleton, as though bone had momentarily softened in shock. His eyes were telling him impossible things. There, in front of him, framed by blue sky, dark blue sea and white, white sand, was Mairead, his weak and sickly daughter. And she was standing by herself, an anxious smile on her face and rosy colour in her cheeks.

His eyes locked with hers and in an instant he understood how much this moment meant to his child.

'Mairead! *Mo nighean*, you are standing by yourself!' His words were stupid, obvious, almost meaningless in the moment. And yet, as his ears heard them and his brain understood them, it somehow reinforced that this was no dream. It was actually happening. 'How?'

'I practised and I ate more, and I went outside. A lot. Ooh—' As she watched, she lost her balance and sat down hard. 'Again!'

Lydia had already offered both hands and, as Mairead once again swung her legs beneath her, then carefully rose, Alasdair allowed himself to accept that the miracle before him was real. This child, again standing tall and proud before him, this girl with bare white feet and sturdy little legs, was his Mairead.

And the woman kneeling close to her, murmuring words of reassurance and holding her little hands, the woman with golden hair, was the angel who had wrought the miracle.

'Lydia.'

She turned to look at him and he was unsurprised to see tears on her face. Belatedly, he realised that he, too, was crying and he reached for his handkerchief. 'How did you do this? How?'

She smiled mistily through her tears. 'Mairead did it herself. I have honestly never known a child so determined.'

'Strong-willed,' he murmured and she nodded, laugh-crying.

'And now my legs are strong-willed, too, Papaidh. I practised all the time and Lydia taught me.' Mairead went on, talking about baby legs and girl legs, and how Lydia had helped her meticulously follow the stages a baby would go through before learning to walk.

'But this is astonishing! I wonder at the expensive doctors who could do nothing for you, yet this governess—' he inclined his head towards Lydia '—this *angel*, has helped you stand when no-one else could.'

'I cannot walk yet, Papaidh.' Mairead's tone was serene. 'But I shall.'

'I do not doubt it.' Unable to contain himself any longer, he enveloped his daughter in a tight hug, noticing how unusual it was to hug a standing Mairead. How tall she seemed! 'You are a wonder!'

'Yes, I am. And so is Lydia.'

'You are entirely correct.' Keeping his left arm around the child, he reached for Lydia with his right. She entered his embrace as if it were the most natural thing in the world, and they stayed like that for a long blissful moment, while the waves splashed and the sun warmed them and the understanding began to sink in that a true miracle was occurring, right here on Rossinish.

As he reluctantly released them, Mairead lost her balance again and so he was able to pass over the compelling urge he had had to kiss Lydia. If he had turned his head just a fraction her lips would have been just there and he might have…

He shook himself, focusing instead on his daughter, and Lydia's role in teaching her. Although he had naturally noted his daughter's increased appetite and how she was gradually losing the pale listlessness that had held her back for so long, he had not allowed himself to even comment on it, for fear she would return to sickliness and tiredness.

They told him of how hard Mairead had been working in secret, how dearly she had wanted to surprise him, how Lydia had insisted they share the secret today. 'She said you would want to see my first steps, so I plan to do them today.'

'Oh, you do?' He raised an eyebrow at this, but Mairead remained composed. Yet they stayed and Mairead practised, and Alasdair and Lydia encouraged her. By the time the afternoon's warmth was beginning to cool, Mairead had managed twice to take a single step, losing her balance as she tried to move her other foot. They clapped, cheered and hugged her, then sat facing one another as Mairead attempted to launch herself from her *papaidh* to Lydia, from Lydia to her *papaidh*. This proved to be a more useful arrangement, and within the hour, Mairead took three clear unaided steps before collapsing into her father's arms.

'I did it, Papaidh! I told you that I would!'

'You certainly did.' Above Mairead's head Alasdair and Lydia smiled at each other and Alasdair felt as though his heart had never been more full.

A sudden gust of cool westerly air brought him back to reality. The sky was darkening as heavy clouds moved in, obscuring the July sun's slow descent towards sunset. 'Lord! They said there would be rain, but I have lost all track of time.' He smiled at his daughter. 'You must be exhausted, *mo nighean*. You have achieved quite enough for one day. Time to go back to the castle.'

'Do not tell anyone!' Mairead was frowning. 'Only

Eilidh knows. I want to surprise everyone once I can walk better.'

Understanding from their conversations all afternoon that the 'secret' element was a great part of how Mairead was able to incite herself to keep practising, he agreed. Besides, there was something special in the thought of keeping the miracle just to themselves for now. He did not mind Eilidh knowing—*heaven knows Eilidh needs something good in her life right now*—but truly, this miracle now belonged to the three of them. Mairead, himself and Lydia.

Lydia.

The hairs on the back of his neck were standing to attention again now.

She is the mother that Mairead never had. And a hundred times better than her own mother would ever have been.

The sense of guilt at speaking, even silently, ill of the dead was fleeting. What was much more apparent was his utter confidence that he was right about this.

'Alasdair?' Lydia was looking at him, puzzled.

'Apologies, I was wool-gathering. What did you say?'

'I just wondered if there was a quicker way back home.'

Home.

He grimaced. 'I'm afraid not. I did not need to bring us here via a scenic diversion because, as you have seen, it is all scenic. Never fear, we shall go quickly.'

Inwardly, he was not so confident and, sure enough, before they were even halfway across Rossinish the rain began, large raindrops turning quickly from spits and spots to a full spate. By the time they had reached the strait they were all drenched. Wet weather did not bother him, but he could feel Mairead shivering with cold and did not dare think about how miserable Lydia must be. Worse, the darkening sky made it hard to spot holes and obstacles underfoot and the likelihood of Lydia twisting an ankle or losing her footing was increasing. Had Mairead fought back from sickliness only to catch a chill because he had failed her as a father? Knowing that it would likely rain all night and calculating that they had at least another hour to walk to get to Ardmore, he made a decision. Instead of turning southwards, he led Lydia in a northerly direction where he knew they could find shelter.

Ten minutes later, he saw it in the distance. 'Look there,' he pointed. 'We can take shelter in the *àirigh*.'

'What is an *àirigh*?' Lydia managed.

Idly, he noted that even when she was freezing cold and soaked to the skin, she still managed to look beautiful.

'It is a sheiling—a shelter to be used in inclement weather.'

'You people think of everything.'

Was there criticism in her statement? He could not pause to consider, because Mairead was now softly whimpering. Mairead, who almost never cried. Lord, what a fool he had been! Caught up in the idyll of Mairead and Lydia, and the beach and the miracle, he had let go of his basic responsibilities to keep his family safe. His *people*. Mairead was family, Lydia was not, he reminded himself. Still, he was responsible for keeping them both safe.

He trudged on, keeping the sheiling in sight. The reason why Mairead had become ill in the first place was that she had had a severe inflammation of the lungs. If it happened again, he could never forgive himself. One step, then another. Trudge forever.

Perhaps this is a punishment. I should not have dared to allow myself to develop feelings for a woman.

Trudge. Ignore the ache in his arm from carrying Mairead. Ignore the wet. Ignore the cold. Keep walking.

Mairead cried again and guilt flamed again within him. 'Hush now, *mo nighean*. We shall soon be inside.'

Thankfully, just a few moments later, they reached the sheiling. It was a low, stone-built structure, with a turf roof and a simple chimney. With a hand that was a little clumsy from the cold, he managed to lift the latch and they stepped inside.

Instantly, there was relief. The roof had held and the little hut was watertight. The rain drummed down outside, a distant thrumming, and slanted down on the two tiny windows. Glancing about, Alasdair was relieved to see candles and a flint box on the only shelf and a small settle beside the fireplace. They would not have to sit on the grimy floor.

Good.

Setting Mairead down carefully in the centre of the settle, Alasdair was unsurprised to note that Lydia immediately began to tend to the child. Ignoring her own needs, she began removing some of Mairead's wet clothing, at the same time untying the bundle that she had loyally carried all the way.

She should have dumped it, for the weight probably added to her discomfort.

He had no energy for speech, however, and so he wordlessly turned away to find the flint. There was a large pile of dried twigs and neatly stacked peat in the corner and he managed to start a fire in the fireplace with little difficulty. Lighting a single candle against the advancing darkness, he noticed immediately that the candlelight created an entirely new sense of intimacy in the sheiling.

Avoiding Lydia's eye, he stripped off his own jacket, boots and stockings, placing them to the left of the fireplace. He knew from experience that the hut would be warm in no time and that their clothes could be dry in a matter of hours. Mairead was now in her shift and Alasdair was relieved to see that large parts of it were dry, with wet patches along the shoulders and where her back had been exposed as he had carried her. Similarly, his own shirt was dry down one side, where carrying Mairead had protected him.

Lydia had had no such protection. He glanced at her, worried to see how pale she was. He looked closer. 'Ach, you are shivering, Sassenach! Can I do anything to assist you?'

She shook her head. 'I am sure the fire will dry my gown. My main concern is for Mairead.' Her teeth were audibly chattering as she spread Mairead's clothes out before the fire.

'Come, I shall pull the settle closer to the fire—' He did so, Mairead gripping the arm of the settle as it moved. 'Now, come and sit where it is warm.'

She turned away, bending to her bundle. 'First, let me do this.' Untying it with some difficulty—*her hands must be as clumsy as mine just now*—she handed him a hunk of bread and some cheese, the remains of their picnic earlier.

'You kept this? I had thought you left it for the birds. You are a treasure, Lydia!' She smiled wanly as he cut it with the small knife he always carried and he was glad to see that both she and Mairead ate hungrily.

Always a good sign when a person wants food.

He chewed his own portion slowly, savouring every morsel. Afterwards he picked up the blanket that had formed Lydia's bundle, hanging one corner on a nail in the wall, and tying the other around one of the roof struts. Almost immediately steam began to rise from the wet parts of the thick woollen cloth as heat from the fire reached it. Lydia had sat beside Mairead on the settle and Alasdair decided to take one last look outside before joining them. Cautiously, he lifted the latch and glanced outside. It was still pouring and almost dark. Somewhere south of here, in the castle, Mrs MacLeod and Iain would even now be worrying that they had not arrived. Hopefully they would have the sense not to send out a search party. Unlike the tragedy where Dòmhnall was lost, the castle folk knew that he and Lydia had not been planning to take to the sea today.

Stepping outside, and heedless of his bare feet, he set his flask upright in the ground, hoping to gather even a small amount of rainwater, for they had drunk the last of the water just now. After relieving himself around the side of the sheiling, he hurried back inside, tending to the fire while Lydia took Mairead outside briefly.

A half hour later, Lydia was still shivering. There was no way he could allow her to sit in damp clothes all night. 'Lydia, I suggest you remove your footwear, for we shall have a long march in the morning and your boots need to be thoroughly dry.'

She considered this for a moment, then nodded. 'Very well. This entire situation is highly unusual and I must be sensible. Besides, my feet are like two blocks of ice.'

'We cannot have anyone catching a chill,' he added gruffly. This reminded him to look closely at his daughter, now perched once again on the settle alongside Lydia. She had begun to warm up nicely and her little face was flushed. 'Well, *mo nighean*, how are you?'

'I am cold, Papaidh. And I should like to go to bed.' She looked about her. 'Where are we to sleep?'

'Did you know,' he offered, leaning close and dropping his voice to a conspiratorial murmur, 'that Bonnie Prince Charlie is said to have slept in this very sheiling the night before he left the islands?'

'Really?' She looked around, wide-eyed. 'So this is where he put on the woman's clothes?'

He laughed. 'I expect so. Now, if this sheiling was good enough for the Bonnie Prince, it will certainly do for us, will it not?'

'Yes, but where am I to *sleep*?' Her tone was exasperated and he could tell that the long march in the rain had taken its toll. Still, at least she did not seem unwell.

'You can sleep on my lap to start with and then, once everything is dry, we shall make you a nest on the floor before the fire.'

'Like a bird's nest?'

'Yes, but made of soft clothing and this blanket.'

'I think I should like to be a bird for one night.' She

eyed him sideways. 'If I practise very hard with Lydia, might I be able to fly one day?'

'Lord, no—and you must not even attempt it!' He extracted a promise from her in this regard, then glanced ruefully at Lydia. She matched his expression, then bent to her boots again. She seemed to be having trouble removing them.

Bending to assist, he discovered that the laces were hopelessly tangled, the knots tightened by hours of rain and tramping through wet grass. He tutted, knowing he could not simply cut through them, for she would need the laces on the morrow. 'This is going to try my patience,' he muttered, then dropped fully on to his knees to begin working on the stubborn knots. Above him, Mairead shuffled sideways to cuddle into Lydia, who began telling the child stories in a soft, low voice.

Finally, one of the boots was untied, and he gently slid it off Lydia's foot, frowning as he felt how cold she was. Quite without thinking about it, he rubbed her slim foot vigorously, as he would have done for any islander in a similar plight.

But Lydia is not an islander.

She was a beautiful young woman who haunted his thoughts and about whom he had had regular imaginings in the dark of night. Her voice had faltered, but he did not dare look up. Resisting the urge to kiss her slender white foot, or to explore her shapely ankle with his fingers, he moved his attention to the other boot. Just as he felt the knot begin to loosen, she stopped talking and he glanced up.

Mairead was fast asleep in the circle of Lydia's right arm and Lydia—Lydia was looking at him in the semi-darkness, her expression inscrutable. There was a peculiar intensity about her gaze, though, and he knew not what it meant. He swallowed. 'She is asleep.'

Lydia nodded. 'The poor child is exhausted.'

'I have no doubt you are equally exhausted. There!' He slid the second boot off, but this time resisted the urge to rub her foot. Setting her boots before the fire, he straightened, stretching to relieve the aches in his back and shoulders. Mairead was no longer a light baby, easily carried for extended periods. With his own eyes he had seen the muscle on her little legs and knew that the miracle had been months in the making. 'Thank you,' he murmured.

'For what?' Lydia seemed genuinely puzzled.

'For helping her to walk again.'

She shook her head. 'Mairead did all of the work. Really, she is the most determined child!'

'Yes, and now she believes she might fly!'

Lydia laughed softly. 'It is wonderful that her belief in her own abilities has been so transformed. When I first met her she had fully accepted her fate. She saw herself as weak and sickly.'

'As had we all.' He indicated the space beside her and she shuffled herself and Mairead along the settle to make space for him. It was a tight squeeze and he was conscious of his right side being pressed up against Lydia's left. After a moment, the coldness of her damp gown permeated his consciousness and he tutted.

'Lydia, you are still soaked, and freezing!'

She shrugged. 'We both know I cannot undress here. I can survive this, you know. I am no wilting lily.'

'No, you are not. You are more like a proud orchid,

standing tall and strong in the machair amid the wind and rain.'

Tall, strong and beautiful.

A flush spread across her cheek. 'I shall have to keep an eye out for Mairead trying to fly. Despite her promise to you just now, I would not be surprised if she secretly means to pursue the notion!'

Allowing her to change the topic, he responded in kind and for the next hour they spoke quietly of everything and nothing. In later years he would remember this time clearly—the flickering candlelight, the scent of the peat fire, the sleeping child, the sound of rain on the windows and the easy, natural connection between himself and Lydia. There was a comfort and intimacy about the moment that, he knew, he would never sense in the same way again. It had been a day for miracles and part of him was vaguely aware that this moment was unique, special and wonderful.

I must not fall asleep, he told himself, *for then morning will come, and this perfect night will have ended.*

Gradually their talk ceased into a companionable silence. He created the nest for Mairead and gently laid her down, where she stretched out in relief without waking up. After building up the fire, he rearranged the boots a little, ensuring the other side would benefit from the fire's warmth. Returning to the settle, he wrapped his right arm around Lydia and she rested her head in the hollow of his shoulder as if it belonged there. Before long, her breathing told him she was asleep.

Glancing down without disturbing her, he felt his heart warm at the sight of her golden head resting so naturally on his chest. Daringly, he lifted his other hand

and stroked her soft hair, just once. *Lydia!* Unable to stop himself, he kissed her golden hair gently, then leaned his head back, closing his eyes. She nuzzled into him and he held his breath. A moment later sleep fully overcame her again and her body sagged against his. As the fire crackled and the rain began to ease, he kept vigil over Mairead and Lydia, and knew that to do so was the greatest privilege of his life.

Chapter Fifteen

Lydia was lost in a delicious dream. Vaguely, she knew she had been cold and wet and horribly uncomfortable. Somewhere still there were irritations—she was thirsty, her stays were digging into her, parts of her clothing were now warm-damp rather than cold-damp, but at a deeper level she was wonderfully comfortable. Consciousness came slowly and, with it, confusion.

Where am I?

She was resting in someone's warm embrace, her head comfortably leaning on to the hollow of his shoulder.

Alasdair!

Rather than panic and move instantly away from him, she decided to savour the moment first. The rise and fall of his warm chest. The feeling of security and safety. The delicious scent of him, mixed with smouldering turf.

Yesterday had been one of the most wonderful days of her life. Being there when Mairead had shared her secret had been an honour, and her heart felt as though it were smiling at the memory. Then, the challenges of the long walk in the rain, feeling uncomfortable and cold…it had been worth it, for it had led to this place. This sheiling, this *àirigh*. This shelter. Cocooned with Alasdair and Mairead, Lydia had never been happier. She went through the memories, trying to fix them in her mind so they would never fade. His dark head bent to her shoelaces. His hands on her foot. His arm around her. And now, this.

Her head rested comfortably on his solid chest and in her sleep she had curled into him, her right arm bent and her hand lying resting on his soft linen shirt. Cautiously, she opened her eyes, careful not to move a muscle. Dawn light had crept into their haven, its glow lending an ethereal air of unreality to the scene.

As long as I live, I shall never forget this.

On the floor, Mairead stirred, then stirred again. 'Is it morning?' she murmured.

Lydia straightened, feeling bereft as Alasdair took his arm from about her.

'It is, *mo nighean*.' He stretched, then stood, bending to add twigs to the embers. 'How did you enjoy sleeping in a nest?'

Mairead was frowning. 'I think I prefer to be a girl and not a bird, Papaidh. My bed is softer than this.' Pushing herself up into a sitting position, she paused. 'Did I really walk yesterday?'

Alasdair, grinning, glanced at Lydia. The smile they shared was for Mairead, and thankfully smoothed over any awkwardness that might have ensued from any acknowledgement that Lydia had cuddled into him all night long. Still, her heart was pounding just at the sight of him, never mind the memories of how intimate their sleeping posture had been.

He bent to pick up his child, throwing her up a little and catching her, while she shrieked in delight. 'You did!' he declared. 'You are a wonder!'

'Again!' Mairead demanded and he obliged, before depositing her on the settle.

Lydia had discovered, to her horror, that her hair was half up, half down. There was nothing for it but to re-move all the pins and try to re-do it as best she could, without a hairbrush or a mirror. She began removing pins as she located them, placing them in a bundle on the settle between her and Mairead.

'Papaidh,' Mairead's tone was thoughtful. 'When I was little you used to throw me up in the air like that, but you have not done it for a long time. Why?'

His eyes widened, then he sobered. 'I think,' he said slowly, 'I was afraid you were too delicate for such things. That I might hurt you.'

She scoffed at this. 'How silly, Papaidh! Only my legs and arms were delicate and none of me is deli-cate now.'

'I am chastised!' His gaze wandered to Lydia and seemed to linger on her unpinned locks.

She flushed. 'Apologies, but I must do this.'

'Lord, no apologies are needed! I am simply unused to seeing… That is to say, not since… Pardon me, I shall leave you now.' Briskly, he dressed, added turf to the fire, then went outside without another word, leaving Lydia in a state of some mortification.

By the time he returned Lydia had finished re-pinning her hair, had donned her boots and dressed

Mairead, and was now folding the blanket that had formed the main part of Mairead's nest. They had also both relieved themselves outside, although Lydia had seen no sign of Alasdair when they were out. Lydia's clothing was now almost dry, although uncomfortable, and her thirst was by now acute.

'The rain has gone,' he declared, 'so we may set off as soon as you are ready.' He held out his flask. 'I filled it at the freshwater loch on Rarinish to the north of here.' Once Mairead was done, Lydia drank the water. It was quite the most delicious liquid she had ever imbibed—pure and clear and islandish.

As they walked southwards towards Ardmore they sang together, Lydia joining in as best she could with some of the songs. It was clearly very early, but as they marched through damp heather, crisp bracken and green sod, the sun slowly rose higher, bringing to life beauty and wonder in all directions.

In strong contrast, Lydia's wet-and-redried boots were chafing viciously at her heels. After a time she found herself striking the earth with her toes rather than heels and a little later her attention had become so focused on her own agony that she was struggling to continue singing.

'Oh!' She could not help the exclamation as her right foot trod on an unexpected stone. The boot leather scraped against her torn skin like a grater and she stopped, feeling as though she could not take one more step.

'What is it? Lydia, what ails you?' Alasdair's face held genuine concern.

Helplessly, she shrugged. 'My boots.' Wiping the

back of her hand across her face, she dashed away the tears that had finally spilled out. 'I am sorry for being so weak. I have been trying to persist, but I cannot—I cannot do so any longer.' Pain, tiredness and frustration at her own weakness welled up, further fuelling her distress. 'I am not normally such a watering-pot, I assure you.'

He exclaimed, then asked her to untie the wool blanket that had served them so well. She spread it on the damp heather and he placed Mairead gently down, then bid Lydia sit beside her. Gently, he undid her boots as he had done the night before, his jaw tightening as he inspected her torn heels.

'Foolish girl! Why did you not say something?'

She bit her lip. 'I thought I could manage.'

'Clearly, you could not.' He thought for a moment. 'Very well. You have, I believe, two choices. You may walk barefoot, or I can try to fashion some sort of bandage?'

'Barefoot?' She flushed at the very notion. 'That would be shocking! I cannot… What are you doing?'

He had untucked his shirt and, as she watched in dawning horror, he tore a strip from the bottom. Sliding his hands to the halfway point, he tore it in two, then bent to wrap her heels in the soft fabric, tying each bandage at the ankle.

His good shirt!

Briefly, it occurred to her to wonder how any of her previous employers might have responded. There would have been irritation for any delay and chastisement for her not having foreseen and prevented this eventuality. Some might have been sympathetic, Lydia supposed, at least initially. None, she was certain, would destroy an expensive item of clothing for the benefit of a servant. Especially when she could easily have torn her own petticoat.

'There! Now I shall put your boots back on.' He did so, slowly and carefully, and she winced as her foot slipped into place. 'Try that.'

She stood, wiggled her feet a little, and pronounced herself satisfied. In truth, the pain was still there, though muted. This time, she vowed, she would make it all the way to Ardmore without any complaint.

She did so, but it was quite a challenge. As the grey walls of the castle came into view, she began counting her steps. Surely she would make it to the gate in a hundred paces? Forty-seven, forty-eight...

He was looking at her, she could *feel* it, but she refused to return his gaze. Fifty-three, fifty-four... Shouts went up as they were spotted and by the time they reached the courtyard Mrs MacLeod was there to greet them.

'Well, and how is everybody?' Her gaze raked them all, then returned to Lydia. 'What ails you, Lydia?'

'Bad boots!' the Laird ground out and Lydia's grimace to Mrs MacLeod contained both apology and pleading.

'Ach, the poor girl, and you traipsing her all over the countryside!' She tutted and took Lydia's arm. 'Come with me, m'dear, and we shall get you sorted.' As they entered the Great Hall she began firing orders at passing servants. Food for the Laird and Miss Mairead. Hot water and food to Miss Farnham's chamber. Someone to fetch her box of salves.

In the fuss and flurry, Lydia missed the opportunity to speak to Alasdair. Well, what would she have said anyway?

Thank you? I am sorry? I shall pay for your shirt?

None would have even begun to reflect the confused cacophony of thoughts and feelings screaming inside her. So instead she allowed Mrs MacLeod to take her upstairs, tend to her feet and help her undress. Sensing that Lydia was utterly exhausted, Mrs MacLeod bade her lie down and rest. Within minutes of the housekeeper's departure, she was sleeping soundly.

Damnation!

Alasdair had barely been home an hour and already he knew that he had gravely erred. Everywhere he went, he was getting knowing looks and subtle teasing from the castle staff. Everyone, naturally, now knew that they had had to seek shelter in the sheiling and that they had remained there together until morning. They also would know that nothing untoward had occurred between him and Lydia. His honour as laird, and the presence of the child, made it certain. Yet, such intelligence did not prevent the speculative looks and pointed comments. The castle folk understood that there was a connection between himself and Lydia and were showing their approval.

Closing the door to his parlour in a deliberately controlled manner, Alasdair paced the floor, raking his hands through his hair. At moments like this one, he almost wished he were a hermit, or lived in a community where he was not well known. Anonymity and privacy were denied him and today, he could wish all of his well-meaning friends and colleagues to perdition.

To be fair, he acknowledged, the same speculation occurred no matter who the subject was. Seeing new attachments form was one of the joys of living so tightly bound. Had he not, in this very room, discussed Dòmhnall and Eilidh with Iain and made plans for Dòmhnall's future? Had he not, along with the rest, enjoyed noting the young couple dancing together, the looks between them, the mortification when they were each teased about each other?

He sighed. That story had ended in tragedy, but Alasdair knew well enough how the Ardmore community operated. Occasionally an unsuitable match had to be managed and the Ardmore folk did so subtly, preventing the pair from spending as much time together, throwing more suitable partners in the couple's path, and letting it be known in a thousand tiny ways that the pairing was not to be approved. Oh, the islanders could be both artful and shrewd when needed. Two fiery characters showing signs of destructive fighting even when courting were gently encouraged to each seek a more suitable partner and often did.

More commonly, when the community approved of the pairing, they made no attempt to hide such approval, encouraging the couple with hints and smiles, looks and teasing. Shockingly, today Alasdair had realised that they saw him and the governess as a pair and were making no attempt to hide it. And this despite all his attempts to be careful with Lydia's reputation!

Only his most senior aides—Iain and Mrs MacLeod—

had maintained any sense of subtlety and decorum. Mrs MacLeod had roundly scolded him for his carelessness and lack of foresight in not returning home before the rain and had informed him that poor Miss Farnham was sore, uncomfortable and exhausted, her heels in shreds and her clothing still a little damp from yesterday's soaking. He had almost welcomed her reprimand, which he fully deserved, and which contrasted sharply with the arch looks and knowing grins he was receiving elsewhere.

Mairead had fared better than Lydia, tucking into a hearty meal with enthusiasm before being carried off to visit Eilidh, who was apparently hoping to come downstairs on the morrow. Alasdair himself had bathed and dressed in fresh clean clothing. Before throwing his ruined shirt into the basket in his chamber for soiled linen, he had held it in his hands for a moment, gently rubbing his thumb along the torn end and remembering the feel of Lydia's dainty feet in his hands.

Lydia.

Apart from his brief foray this morning to fill the water flask, this was the first time he had been alone since the momentous events of yesterday and last night. Mairead had walked! Lydia, the ever-patient miracle worker, had toiled diligently to encourage and support his child. She had also been the one to envision the very possibility that his sickly child could be healed.

Quietly, Lydia had told him more of Master John Pickering, who had been paralysed from the waist down after breaking his back. The boy's legs had not worked at all from the moment of his fall from a horse, whereas Mairead's, Lydia had reported calmly, had just needed strengthening again. Lydia also swore by the benefits

of fresh air and sunlight, and by encouraging Mairead
to rebuild her appetite again. How had she seen and understood something so simple, yet so powerful, when
such wisdom had evaded all of the expensive doctors?

Lost in thought, Alasdair stared unseeingly out of
the castle window, reliving the momentous happenings
on Rossinish beach. How incredible it seemed yet that
Mairead had stood and walked. The child had trusted
Lydia and Lydia had not let her down.

Reflecting on the sense of connection between Lydia
and Mairead, he *knew*—believed fervently—that they
loved each other, and yet had Lydia not loved John Pickering before she had left him? That riddle was yet to be
solved. Despite the evidence to the contrary, he would
swear that Lydia was loving, warm-hearted and true.
So why had she left the children she had loved?

His heart beating a thunderous tattoo, he moved on to
the intimacy of their time in the sheiling. He, Mairead
and Lydia. A family. Her head on his shoulder. His arm
curled about her. If they had been truly alone he would
not have been able to resist kissing her again…

No! It would not do. He was in a position of power,
of responsibility. Of all people, he had to be more careful than most about importuning a maiden. This being
Scotland, the Hebrides, Benbecula, people were blunt
and plainspoken most of the time. As laird, he had more
burdens than privileges. His father, along with that of
Angus, had instilled in both young men the understanding that a lass might be unwilling to say no to a laird,
even if she wished to. And so Alasdair had gone to Edinburgh to find a wife—even then choosing badly—
while Angus was as yet unmarried. They were both so

accustomed to avoid behaving in a way that was even
remotely flirtatious that they had trapped themselves
into loneliness.

As understanding dawned within him, the loneli-
ness itself sent an arrow of pain slicing through him.
Six years of isolation. Of duty and companionship, yes.
Friendship, for certain. But he craved more.

It was all to do with Lydia, he knew. She was what
he craved. Before him he saw an entire new life—one
with Lydia by his side, in his bed, mothering another
child alongside Mairead. A child who was hers and
his...

He was being much, much too hasty. Lydia liked
him, he knew. But did she feel anything stronger towards him? She was so reserved that her deeper feelings, unlike the surface irritations that played out across
her beautiful face, were unknown to him. He was her
employer. She was stranded here, five hundred miles
from her true home. Their kiss on the night of the cri-
sis might have been an aberration, a search for comfort in a time of fear. He could make no assumptions.
Yes, she enjoyed his company and he hers, but could
he honestly claim to have proof that she cared for him
in the way he cared for her?

Proof, no. Instinct?

Perhaps.

And now, she would be subject to the same chatter,
gossip and conjecture that he had experienced since
their return. It was kindly meant, he acknowledged.
The castle folk intended no harm. More significantly,
they were right to think Lydia a good choice for him.
She had quietly and gently insinuated her way into their

lives with good humour and grace, showing herself to be hard-working, kind and intelligent. Her mind was good, her judgement sound and her manners beyond reproach. Yes, she, unlike Hester, would make the perfect Lady of Ardmore.

He frowned. Had he not believed exactly the same when he had married Hester? Was he, once again, allowing himself to be led by the heart—or by the desires of his body—rather than by rational, considered judgement?

But, no.

Evidence there was a-plenty that Lydia was different to Hester. Or did he only wish for it to be so?

I struggle with rationality when it comes to Lydia.

There. He had admitted it. His only wish was to ensure her safety, her comfort, and her happiness—and, yes, to have her for his own. Forming a fist, he leaned against the window's edge, knowing himself to be close to being lost. Lost in love, for only the second time in his life. And the first had been a disaster for everyone, including Hester.

No, he determined, pushing away the temptations that made him vulnerable to making poor decisions. *Rationality must prevail.* And from an entirely rational viewpoint, he now knew what he ought to do.

'Good morning, Eilidh! *Madainn mhath*!' Lydia placed Mairead on the courtyard bench beside Eilidh, blinking in the bright sunshine. 'It is good to see you outside again.' She hugged the girl, then Eilidh turned to hug Mairead.

'Well, Mairead,' her tone was conspiratorial, 'have you been practising—you know—the secret thing?'

Mairead beamed at her. 'I have! And I showed Pa-paidh!'

Eilidh lifted a hand to her chest. 'You did?' She looked at Lydia, then back to the child. 'And what did he say?'

'He says I am a wonder. He was very happy. I practised again just now, in Lydia's schoolroom, and I walked again, like I did on the beach.'

'By yourself?'

The child confirmed it and Eilidh hugged her again. They sat on then, enjoying sunlight and conversation. They talked of Dòmhnall, and Eilidh had a little cry. Strangely, a couple of the castle staff waved at them as they passed, but something about their manner struck Lydia as being odd or unusual in some way. She shrugged. They were probably just pleased to see evidence of Eilidh's continued recovery.

Work was beginning on building a temporary pavilion at the end of the shinty field, so after a while they moved outside the walls, to rest on the warm grass and watch the men build a low stage. The gathering and shinty game was to be held in three days' time, and the kitchen staff were also busy preparing for the feast. Here, Lydia was impressed to note how carefully the men were preserving all of the precious wood, which would be reused in multiple ways after the gathering. Almost no trees grew on the island—a fact that Lydia still found astonishing. The people were so resourceful, though—yet more reason to admire this hardy community.

The strange waves and looks had continued and a

few actual winks had been added, which Lydia was finding most disconcerting. Gradually, she realised they were aimed at her rather than Eilidh. She had no clue what they meant by it and so asked the girl about it.

Eilidh's response was a low chuckle. 'You truly do not know?'

'No!' Lydia was mystified. 'Please tell me.'

'Everyone knows that you spent a whole day with the Laird.' She gave Lydia a knowing look. 'And a whole night.'

'What?' Lydia's gut twisted. 'But nothing untoward happened! Mairead was with us! And we had to take shelter from the rain. Mairead was drenched—we all were!' Inwardly, horror was seeping through her. In London, her reputation would have been destroyed by such an occurrence. Here, she had hoped for more understanding.

Eilidh patted her hand. 'You need not worry, Lydia. I am teasing you! Everyone is delighted at such a match. Can you not tell?'

'A match? A *match*? But there is no match! There can be no match!'

They will force him to marry me? No! A thousand times no!

'Why ever not?' Eilidh seemed genuinely puzzled. 'The Laird has been on his own for a long time. Everyone would like him to marry again.'

'Are you talking about my *papaidh*? Might he marry Lydia?' Mairead's little face was alight with joy. 'I should like that very much.'

'No, no! That cannot happen, Mairead.' Lydia's tone was firm. 'This is all a silly misunderstanding.'

'Do you not like him, Lydia?' Eilidh's brow was furrowed. 'I was certain you liked him.'

'I—I like him well enough. I am not saying I *dislike* him.' Briefly, she pictured his blue eyes gazing into hers. 'Not at all. But it is impossible. Surely you can see that such a thing is impossible?'

'Er—no. Why would it be impossible?' Eilidh's eyes widened as an idea occurred to her. 'Do you already have a husband, Lydia?'

'Lord, no! I have never been married.'

'Then what is your reluctance to consider our laird as a possible husband?'

'I am a governess! Can you not see?'

'That changes nothing. We choose our husbands here according to our own preference. I chose Dòmhnall and lost him. Why should you not choose a good man who will make you happy?'

'And what of the Laird? Does he not also have the right to choose?'

Eilidh looked perplexed. 'But that is what we are speaking of!' She shook her head. 'I do not understand you, Lydia.'

'Nor I you.' Silence stretched between them, a tense silence. 'Mairead, it is time for your lessons. We have lingered too long.'

Despite the child's protests, Lydia gathered her up, offering Eilidh a cordial farewell and making for the castle in some haste. She tried to keep her head down, but could not ignore the bright smiles, pointed greetings and knowing looks that were being sent her way. Now that she knew what they signified, her mortification was complete.

Inside the Great Hall she espied Alasdair, conversing with Iain at the far end of the room. Ignoring them both, she made for the staircase, only to almost collide with a young kitchen maid who was passing through.

'Sorry, my lady!' the girl declared unthinkingly, bobbing a curtsy.

My lady!

Lydia could not bear it. She stood stock still, her hand at her mouth, before abruptly wheeling away. As she hastened towards the staircase, she heard Alasdair call the kitchen maid and knew he would quiz the girl about what she had said or done to make the governess scuttle away. Despite Mairead's not inconsiderable weight, Lydia half ran up the wide staircase, aiming to reach the security of her chambers as quickly as she could manage.

Chapter Sixteen

By the time the Laird arrived for his usual hour to observe his daughter's learning, Lydia had managed to achieve a semblance of control. Inwardly though, she was even more concerned now that she had time to consider the situation. The islands, it seemed, were not immune to some of the rules about honour and reputation that prevailed in England's high society. In London, if a young lady spent the night in the company of a gentleman without an adequate chaperon, then he was honour-bound to offer her marriage. If, however, a gentleman was caught in a compromising situation with a low-born *governess*—or, indeed, any other servant—then the governess would be fired and blamed. That was how it went. That was the practice, the form, the standard.

If the Laird's staff thought she was of high birth, like Lady Hester, they might mistakenly think a wedding was expected. But despite her education and manners, Lydia was of common stock and had already made the Laird aware of that fact. With that in mind, surely he would know he was under no obligation towards her?

Given how strong and connected the Ardmore community was, if they expected him to marry her, then he might feel obliged to make her an offer of marriage. Even if she declined, he might still be judged. That, in turn, might lead to ongoing trouble for him. She would hate to see him condemned for something that was, in fact, perfectly reasonable.

She sighed. No matter how the situation unfolded, Lydia's greatest fear now was that this awkwardness would indirectly lead to her having to leave. Somehow, she would have to make people aware that the Laird had done nothing wrong and hope that the whole incident could be put behind them. And in the meantime the Laird needed to understand that she had no expectation of an offer from him.

The thought of him being trapped into marriage gave her pain. She could dream of nothing better than to marry him, but not like this. For a moment, she imagined what it might be like to be his wife. Her heart pounded and her stomach muscles tightened as a wave of bliss rippled through her. Then she allowed herself to imagine a resentful husband. A trapped husband. An unhappy husband. It would not do.

Briskly, she decided to take a sensible approach to the whole matter. Her first task was to make it quite clear by her demeanour that she had no expectation of an offer from him. After that…well, she needed to be brave and speak to him of this. It was vital for her to make it clear to him that she firmly believed he should not be forced to marry a governess simply because they had sheltered from the rain together. Why, the very notion was preposterous!

* * *

And so it was when Alasdair arrived in the school-room, looking devastatingly handsome in Highland dress and with a decidedly questioning air about him, Lydia deliberately gave him a smile that signalled politeness rather than warmth. She filled the hour with a focus on Mairead. There was no French conversation, no invitation to the Laird to assist his child with a task. She ensured that today, he was very much the observer.

At first, he was leaning forward, making comments as usual, and clearly expecting to take a full part in the lesson. Deliberately, she avoided meeting his eye and after a time she sensed him leaning back in the chair. His usual hour was nearly up when she set Mairead a writing task and he immediately took his chance.

'Lydia.' His tone was soft and it sent shivers through her.

'Yes?' She did not dare call him 'sir', although she wished to. Steeling herself to remain unmoved, she met his gaze. His expression was inscrutable and the contrast with the warmth she was used to from him sent a pang of hurt through her. It was irrational, she knew, since she also was behaving differently towards him. It was just...a sense of something *lost* was in the air.

'I think we must speak. Do you agree?'

Mutely, she nodded.

He glanced at the clock, then turned to his child. 'Mairead, Mòrag is coming to see to you for a little time. Can you show her your writing?'

'Yes, Papaidh.' The child bent her head to her work and soon afterwards, Mòrag arrived.

Lydia knew that the time to talk was upon them. He

knew it, too, and had clearly asked Mòrag to attend to Mairead for just this purpose.

Alasdair gestured for her to lead the way out of the schoolroom and Lydia did so, her head held high. Together they walked wordlessly through her bedchamber, through the castle and down the stairs until they reached Alasdair's parlour. Lydia knew she should be using this time to rehearse what she might say, but her mind was too paralysed with apprehension to allow for much logical thought.

Once inside the parlour she turned to face him, but found herself entirely unable to speak.

There was a pause. He seemed to be considering his words. Her heart sank.

'I wish to apologise to you, Lydia.'

Her eyes widened.

For what?

'Why should you apologise? I am not aware that you have done me any harm.'

He grimaced. 'This place…' he gestured vaguely '… is both heaven and hell, I think.' He thought for a moment, then shook his head. 'We islanders are a strange breed. History has taught us to value loyalty, to be suspicious of outsiders and to look after each other in every way possible.'

She swallowed.

Suspicious of outsiders, eh?

'You came to us in good faith and have wrought a miracle with my daughter. Even without knowing this, the Ardmore people have already accepted you. I must say that I believe you have earned such acceptance and that I entirely approve.'

Tears pricked her eyes. Such wonderful words from him—and quite different from what she had expected him to say. 'Thank you,' she said. She took a breath. 'You may be aware, Alasdair—indeed, you cannot *fail* to be aware—that the castle staff have come to some… er…*conclusions* following our need to shelter from the rain and, er…' Her voice tailed away and she could feel herself blushing furiously. Those *conclusions* might be based on an assumption that he had made love to her. The notion was wonderful to consider, even for an instant. His lips on hers, his strong arms around her, she with the freedom to touch and taste, and explore his wild beauty… She coughed, dropped her gaze and squeezed her hands tightly together. She could not bear to look at him, lest he see how much she desired him.

Astonishingly, he chuckled. She looked up, all astonishment.

'You are yet to learn, Sassenach, how to ignore the well-meaning but unwelcome *conclusions* that people may come to in Ardmore. They will move on to tease another victim in a day or two, I assure you!' He eyed her closely. 'I must ask you in all seriousness, though, if you feel your reputation has been tainted in any way.'

She was quick to reassure him. 'Not at all! For they surely must know that nothing happened between us! Mairead was there and…'

He was looking at her in a way that made her pulse quicken and her innards curl with desire. 'I assure you, if I believed your reputation to be in any way compromised, I would make you an offer of marriage this very instant.'

'You…you would?'

'*However,*' he continued inexorably, 'I would much prefer to make an offer of marriage on my own terms, in my own manner and at a time of my choosing.'

'Yes, yes, of course.' Was he speaking generally? He had to be speaking generally. And yet, there was something most *particular* in his gaze.

'And you are entirely correct.' His voice was soft and he took a step towards her. 'Mairead was with us and we were otherwise alone in the sheiling. Nothing could happen…then.' Lifting his hand, he trailed it down her face, then brought his thumb across her lips.

Instantly, her insides kicked as desire flamed into full, aching life. 'Alasdair…' she whispered.

He groaned and closed the space between them. An instant later they were together, arms wrapping tightly around one another and their lips meeting. The aching sense of relief reminded Lydia briefly of sipping the loch water after a thirsty night. This was similar, but *more*. More thirst, more hunger, more aching need. This kiss was necessary, somehow, and she—they— had been deprived of it for much, much too long. Their tongues touched and danced in a sensual delight, her hands were in his hair, and his were busy on her back and—*oh!*—her bottom.

Pausing for breath, they rested their foreheads together, then he began planting tiny kisses on her face. Her closed eyes, her nose, the line of her jaw. She arched into him like a cat and finally he found her lips again. This time the kiss was slow, measured, deliberate.

Alasdair! she was able to think. *Alasdair.* He was truly kissing her. *This is really happening.*

'Lydia,' he murmured against her mouth. 'Beautiful, lovely Lydia.'

They kissed again and again. Ten times. A hundred. Their hands joined the exploration, seeking, searching, enjoying the thrill of touching and being touched. Dimly, some part of Lydia's mind worried about someone coming into the parlour, but she was simply incapable of stopping.

Alasdair, it seemed, was made of sterner stuff. 'Lydia,' he groaned, 'we must stop, while we still can.'

Knowing he was right, she leaned against him, gathering her breath and her faculties. They stayed like that for a long moment, then he slid his hands down her arms and took both her hands.

Leading her to the sofa near the fireplace, he bade her sit and took his place beside her. 'Tell me, are you happy here, Lydia?'

'I—I am, yes. Everyone is so kind and Mairead is wonderful and—yes, I am happy here.'

A shadow flitted across his face. 'I have often wondered why you left the other families that you worked for.'

He paused and she felt herself flush. If she told him the truth, especially after her wanton behaviour just now, might he think she was *fast*? That she had done such things before? That she was somehow contriving to earn a proposal from him? If she was honest about John Pickering's brother and the Honourable—or *dishonourable*—Geoffrey, and the others, the common pattern in her tales was she herself. Especially now, with speculation rife in the castle. Her mind was all disorder and she could not think what to do for the best.

'I would prefer not to speak of it,' was all she could say. 'Not yet, leastways.'

'I see.' There was a silence. 'Whatever it is, you can tell me, you know.'

'I—' She turned, alarmed. There were voices outside the door.

Alasdair jumped to his feet and by the time the door opened he was standing two feet away from the sofa.

'Sir?' It was one of the men. 'You are needed at the pavilion.'

'Very well. I shall be there directly.'

A moment later they were alone again, but the air in the room had changed. 'I shall speak to Mrs MacLeod, ask her to address the teasing. No-one would wish you to feel uncomfortable, Lydia.'

'Thank you.'

There was nothing more to say. He bowed, turned on his heel, and was gone.

The next two days were deliciously strange. In public, Lydia and the Laird were pleasant and self-contained and Lydia drew on all the skills of polite self-concealment she had perfected in the drawing rooms of London. During the after-dinner visit to the Laird's parlour, they would discuss matters of no importance with Iain—who, sadly, was there on both evenings. Lydia was careful to behave in an identical, friendly fashion with both gentlemen.

Twice more, however, she and Alasdair had had the opportunity to kiss and had seized it with enthusiasm. Lydia knew he was as aware of her as she was of him and her heart was singing with the glow of his regard.

They had not had the opportunity for private speech. Indeed, they were much more interested in stolen kisses than in conversation. That, Lydia mused wryly, was wonderful in one sense, but it left her in a continual state of bewilderment. She knew not what to think. He was too honourable to trifle with her, yet she could not dare hope that he felt for her what she felt for him. He desired her, certainly, but she knew enough of men to understand that a man could desire, yet not love. Some women, too, could indulge their desires in *affaires* while their hearts remained untouched.

For her, it was altogether different. Because she had never loved before, she had never felt desire before. Now that she loved Alasdair, she desired him and only him.

She had not seen him yet today. The shinty game was to take place in the afternoon, with dancing afterwards, and Ardmore was in an uproar of excitement. Lydia had succumbed to pleading from Eilidh and Mairead and agreed to change into her special dress later—the blue one she had worn to Calum and Màiri's wedding—but for now, she had donned a serviceable day dress. She had been fitted with new, soft boots at the Laird's request. A prosaic gift, yet she treasured them. Her heart skipped with excitement at each new day. Surely, in the chaos of the gathering, there would be an opportunity for them to share a stolen kiss later?

In the meantime, her work with Mairead continued to bring her joy. The child's walking was progressing dramatically and she was now managing ten or more steps at a time, without losing her balance. 'Heavens!' Eilidh declared, as Mairead demonstrated her increasing skill in the schoolroom. 'If this gathering was even a few weeks later, I expect you would dance at it, Mairead!'

'I think I shall be a good dancer,' Mairead declared, in a prosaic tone. 'Lydia, can you teach me dancing?'

'You forget, Mairead, I am not from the islands and I do not know your dances. Perhaps Eilidh may teach both of us, when she is fully recovered?'

Eilidh agreed to this and, as they went slowly together through the castle and out to the courtyard, Lydia reflected on her own words.

I am not from the islands.

Despite the Laird desiring her and despite his cryptic words when he had *not* made her an honourable offer, Lydia reminded herself not to get carried away with dreaming. He might not even have mentioned the topic of marriage without the subtle force of the staff. Thinking back to a time before the happy delirium of the past days, Lydia reminded herself of her firm belief that he would be happier with someone born and bred in the Hebrides.

She shrugged. Her mind was now in such bewilderment that she truly knew not what she believed. Having reminded herself of her status as a Sassenach—an outsider—Lydia also could not help a flush of pride as she mingled with the castle folk at the side of the shinty field. They rarely spoke English with her now and her Gaelic continued to progress quickly. Thankfully, the Laird had been as good as his word and the knowing looks and winks had ceased.

So it was with a good deal of contentment that Lydia and Mairead took their place among the spectators at the edge of the field. Lydia had brought a blanket—the same one that she had used in the sheiling and which was also now precious to her—and she, Mairead and Eilidh sat together in comfort, the sun warming their backs. They spoke of Dòmhnall with great affection and a number of people, including Maggie, made a point of coming to see Eilidh and to remark that Dòmhnall Mòr would be a huge loss today. Instead of making Eilidh sad, this served to flush her with pride and shared memories, and the bittersweet acknowledgement of loss.

There are lessons here for me.

Dòmhnall Mòr was gone forever, yet, somehow, Eilidh had found the courage to live on without him. It was not easy for the girl, Lydia knew, and she had as many bad days as good ones.

At least I have known what it is to love.

If her heart would be broken, then she would have to survive.

I must enjoy this happiness while I may.

The game went on for what seemed like hours. Lydia had no idea of any rules, or how they would know when it ended, but she was in heaven watching Alasdair play. The men had stripped to the waist within the first half-hour, but Lydia's eyes could rest on no one but the Laird. How fine he looked, how strong and handsome! Her hands now knew the feel of him—his firm back, hard chest, strong arms. She had explored him—through his shirt, it was true—yet the memories made desire kindle within her once again. She smiled inwardly. She seemed to be in a constant state of desire these days.

How perfect this is!

The sun on her back, Mairead and Eilidh by her side,

Alasdair in front of her, and a feeling of warm contentment within.

Then, abruptly, it was done. Cheers went up from the Ardmore folk, while Angus and his men groaned in frustration. Then they all went about the field, slapping and hugging in congratulations and commiserations.

'They did it for Dòmhnall,' Eilidh declared, wiping away a tear, and Lydia put an arm around her. 'The sword of Fergus Liath will return to Ardmore this year.'

'The sword of what?'

'We have a common ancestor called Fergus Liath and when he died it was a matter of contention where his sword should rest. Someone came up with the notion of playing for it each year and that was how this tradition began. Angus took it last year, but our laird has now won it back.' She grinned. 'The alternative was a mass brawl, I suppose.'

Lydia snorted, rising to her feet and picking Mairead up. 'The shinty seems to have many of the hallmarks of a mass brawl, I must say.'

'But the skill! The heart!' Eilidh began folding the blanket.

Lydia laughed. 'That, too.'

Alasdair ran lightly towards them, grinning like a child. 'Well, *mo nighean*, what say you?' He held out his arms and Mairead transferred across to him.

'You were good, Papaidh.' She wrinkled her nose. 'But you smell funny.'

He glanced at Lydia, his eyes dancing. 'I must apologise to all you ladies for...er...smelling funny.' He swung Mairead around until she shrieked with joy, then handed her back to Lydia. 'I must leave you now. I am required to drink whisky and talk nonsense for at least an hour, after which, I assure you, I shall have a bath!'

'See that you do!' said Lydia primly, but she was twinkling at him. Her eyes, naturally, had been devouring him as discreetly as she could manage. The sight of his bare chest, stomach and shoulders, seen so close, was doing wonderful things to her insides. As he walked away she took one last look at his back before turning towards the castle.

Truly, her life had never been better.

Chapter Seventeen

The dress was just as beautiful—and just as tight-fitting—as Lydia remembered. As she smoothed her hands over the cerulean silk, she was conscious that, today, she felt very differently about wearing the gown. Alasdair's regard had changed her views about herself. Now, she not only accepted the fact that she had a reasonable figure and face, she positively welcomed it. Eilidh had already begun taking in one of her plain day dresses and Lydia foresaw that, very soon, she would be accustomed to wearing well-fitting clothes all of the time.

Mairead was also wearing her own best dress—the white muslin trimmed with blue ribbons—and they had both done their hair in a more elaborate style. Lydia had braided the top part of Mairead's hair into a pretty chignon, while leaving the rest flowing over the child's shoulders. At the last, she had added a flower circlet made up of machair orchids, their soft petals bursting with colour—purple and lilac and spotted pink. When Mairead stood before the mirror, she gazed at her reflection, then turned to wrap Lydia in a tight embrace.

'Thank you, Lydia. Thank you, thank you!' She looked up at her. 'Promise you will never go away?'

'Of course I shall never go away!' Lydia declared unthinkingly, before adding, 'That is, I should *hope* to never go away. Sometimes things happen that we do not wish.'

Mairead tilted her head on one side. 'Like Dòmhnall dying? And my mama?'

Lydia's throat tightened. 'Yes. My mother and father both died. They did not wish to.'

'My *papaidh* could be your *papaidh*, if you marry him,' the child offered, somewhat confusingly.

'Oh, hush now, Mairead, that is not going to happen. Are you not happy to have me as your governess?'

'I should much rather have you as my mother!'

Lydia kissed her cheek, then picked her up. 'That is a sweet thing to say and I am grateful. But please do not say such things in company. I am your governess and that is all. Agreed?'

Mairead sighed. 'Very well. But even if I do not say it, I shall *think* it, and no one will stop me.'

Lydia snorted, her heart warmed by Mairead's attachment to her. 'I should like to see anyone so brave as to attempt it!'

They made their way downstairs and outside to the shinty field, where what seemed like hundreds of people were milling about. A group of musicians were playing on the low stage, though no one was dancing as yet. Along the edges of the field, amid the chairs that had been placed there, merchants, tinkers and travelling pedlars had set up their wagons and carts. Some had even pitched pavilions of canvas and sailcloth and were inveigling people to purchase their wares. Lydia, having already succumbed to vanity, bought some ribbons and buttons from one man and some lace from another. If she was to wear nice dresses, they would need suitable trimmings. She also made a gift of some pink satin ribbon to Mairead and bought a simple straw bonnet for Eilidh. The girl seemed delighted when Lydia handed it to her and immediately began planning how she might trim it.

The dancing began a little later and Lydia was pleased to have offers to dance every time. She accepted some, rejected others, and ensured she spent most of her time with Mairead. The Laird had made his reappearance a half-hour ago, his hair damp from his bath, and had greeted Lydia and Mairead briefly before being taken away by some of the shinty players to settle a debate about some aspect of the game. It gladdened Lydia to see him so merry and carefree.

He seems happy, these days.

He had not, so far, danced with anyone.

As the day dimmed towards evening, lanterns were lit on the long poles that had been erected around the area. With the sky goldening towards sunset and the lanterns glowing softly, it gave the entire gathering a magical air. Lydia sat with Eilidh Ruadh for a while, enjoying her company and the sense of friendship that she had always felt with the other young woman.

'Angus means to go to London in the spring,' she said, 'if our attempts to purchase the land near Rueval are unsuccessful.'

Lydia eyed her keenly, struck by her form of words. 'He goes alone?'

Eilidh laughed. 'You are too perceptive, Lydia! He believes Alasdair may not go—' she sent Lydia a sly, knowing gaze '—so he *thinks* he is going alone, but that is not the case.'

Lydia grinned, ignoring Eilidh's teasing look. 'You mean to accompany him.'

'I do and so I shall need you to teach me everything I need to know about London, and the *ton*, beforehand.'

'Of course!' Briefly, Lydia described the parks and Gunter's, and the daring masquerade balls in Vauxhall Gardens. She had attended one, once, in the safe company of one of her employers, and had thoroughly enjoyed it.

Eilidh seemed fascinated. 'Perhaps I may have the opportunity to experience such delights when Angus and I travel there,' she declared with a saucy smile. 'I must know more. I intend to learn as much as I can before I go.' She patted Lydia's arm. 'It can be our project for this winter.'

Lydia agreed with pleasure. How wonderful it was to anticipate that she would still be here then! She could imagine herself saying goodbye to Angus and Eilidh, perhaps receiving letters from her friend, awaiting their return some months later. It gave her a good feeling to look further into the future and still imagine this happy life.

Glancing around, she saw that Mairead was seated with Mrs MacLeod and eating a sweetmeat.

All is well.

When two gentlemen approached to invite Lydia and

Eilidh Ruadh to dance the next reel, Lydia declined, having had a better idea.

She hurried off through the dusk to a particular trader she had noted earlier. He was selling fabrics, threads and gloves, but she had absent-mindedly noticed something else among his wares when she had rummaged through his stall earlier.

'Good evening, miss.' His eyes gleamed as she approached the stall. He had probably assumed he would make no further sales tonight, given that the crowds were now devoting their attention to dancing, talking, eating, and drinking. 'How may I assist you?'

'How much for this?' Lydia asked, pulling what she wanted from underneath a bale of cotton. It was a masquerade half-mask of black satin and would make a perfect gift for Eilidh Ruadh. She had been surprised to see it earlier, for masquerades and masked balls were unknown in the islands.

'Ah, that is a special piece, that came all the way from Lunnain.' He named an outrageous price and she raised a sceptical eyebrow.

'I too, came all the way from London, where such masks are commonplace, I assure you.' She set the mask down. 'It is worth no more than five shillings and that is all I shall pay.'

He moved around the table and came to stand beside her, picking up the mask. 'You are Sassenach, then? And you have attended masked balls in Lunnain?'

She took a step backwards, for he was standing uncomfortably close. Abruptly, all her senses were alert. This part of the field was worryingly quiet and the music and noise down the far end might mask any sounds from this far away.

'It is none of your concern who I am and what I may have done. You may keep the mask. It would be a simple matter for me to fashion one for my friend.'

He grinned, displaying numerous gaps where teeth should be. 'Ah, now, do not be hasty, pretty lady.' He laid a hand on her arm, preventing her from leaving. 'I shall make a bargain with you. You may have the mask for five shillings, if you also give me a kiss!'

Before she could even cry out, he had wrapped his arms around her and was trying to cover her mouth with his. He smelled strongly of whisky and sweat and her stomach heaved. She struggled furiously, managing to turn her head and scream, at the same time shoving him away with both hands. He stumbled into the table, laughing. The entire incident had lasted only a moment.

Lydia was struggling to remain standing. She felt dizzy and weak, and her pulse was tumultuous. She was breathing rapidly and her knees felt as though they could not support her.

I need to get away.

She turned and began walking, yet somehow, her legs refused to hurry.

In an instant, all of the hopes she had built were shattered. Once again, a man had forced his attentions upon her, despite her making her distaste apparent in the clearest possible way.

There is clearly no place on this earth where I can be safe from the worst of men.

With a stifled sob, she stumbled on—away from the pedlar, away from the smell of him and the putrid taste of him, and the dawning realisation that she would likely be forced to leave this place if anyone had seen what had just happened.

'Lydia!'

Eyes wide, she halted, as the inevitability of events settled around her. It was Alasdair, and he had clearly seen what had occurred. He was grey-faced and grim and in his eyes she saw anger and—was that mortification? Well, naturally he would feel awkward about dismissing her, given how well she had done with Mairead, but she understood what must be done—perhaps even better than he, for had she not been in this situation before?

'I saw what happened!' He eyed her closely, seemingly reluctant to touch her. She stood impassively, retreating behind the wall of shamed nothingness that had served her well before. His jaw hardened. 'I shall return instantly,' he murmured and left.

Feeling bewildered, she turned to watch him as he made his way to the pedlar's stall. His expression must have been formidable, for the trader began scrambling backwards, declaring in a wheedling tone, 'I meant no harm, sir. She is no islander and I only wanted a little kiss! Why, *she* came to find *me* and it getting dark! It was her doing, really. I—'

He had run out of time. The Laird floored him with a single punch. 'She is more an islander than you are, *amadan*!'

Lydia's jaw dropped. Her shock was quickly tempered by the realisation that this was the first time one of her assailants had ever had any sort of punishment.

Maybe because he is a pedlar we shall both be blamed and not just me.

Still, it was undeniably satisfying to see the man floored. Her own sudden bloodthirstiness surprised her, though it should not.

The man scrambled to his feet, holding his busted nose. 'Yes, *a thighearna*! I meant no harm, truly.'

'You are never to return to Ardmore. And should I hear of any similar incidents elsewhere, I shall ensure you are banished from the islands altogether!'

With a final sound of disgust, the Laird turned on his heel and began walking back towards Lydia. At the same time, his earlier words began to sink in.

She is more an islander than you are.

Could it be—had he actually taken her side?

He was standing right in front of her. His Adam's apple moved in his throat, but he seemed unable to speak. He lifted a hand, as if to touch her face, then paused, letting it fall.

Lydia remained entirely bewildered. Everything was happening much, much too quickly and her mind was struggling to keep up.

'Lydia!' he said finally, then opened his arms. The expression on his face was one of raw pain. Without conscious thought, reacting only to the pure emotion on his face, she stepped forward, feeling his arms close around her.

Almost instantly, as though walls had collapsed, her whole body began to shake and tremble. Tears soon followed, then gut-wrenching sobs. Dimly she knew that her reaction was not just to tonight's assault, but to all of them. All of the times when she had been distressed and attacked, and helpless and alone. All of the times when there had simply been no one there to offer her a hug of comfort. She had spent her entire adult life alone and isolated. Now, finally, here was someone to hold her. Someone who, astonishingly, had defended her.

After what seemed like an age, her distress began to ease. At some point he had provided her with a clean, soft handkerchief and she leaned back a little, wiping her face and neck and delicately blowing her nose. Afterwards he held her close for another moment, dropping a kiss on her head, then leaned back to look at her.

'Lydia.' His hands were on her back 'I apologise that you had to experience such an ordeal on Ardmore lands. I have failed in my duty to protect you. I assure you, you will never see that unprincipled villain again.'

'You hit him!'

It still seemed as though it might be a dream.

He grimaced. 'I only hit him once, which I may regret. His craven cowardice saved him from a proper drubbing.'

'I did not seek an assignation with him, I promise!'

He laughed at this. 'What a preposterous notion! Of course you did not, *mo leannan*.' He drew her fully back into his embrace. She could already feel her tumultuous pulse slowing as her mind began to understand that she was safe from further harm and that she was not being dismissed from her post.

Mo leannan. My sweetheart. She translated the endearment in her mind, saving it to think about later. 'Yes, even Lady Barnstable would not have blamed me this time, perhaps,' she murmured into his chest.

'Who is Lady Barnstable? And why should she blame you?' He leaned back, and she looked up at him.

Tell him.

'You have asked me before why I left Master Pickering and the Barnstable twins, and the others.' Her face twisted. 'Men do not always behave as they should. Although I have never offered them any encouragement, I have been…importuned on numerous occasions. Afterwards, I was always blamed for their wicked actions and let go.'

'Outrageous!' He had stiffened in anger. 'Why, anyone who knows you can see you are an innocent!'

She eyed him shyly. 'You are the only man I have ever kissed by choice.'

His arms tightened about her. 'I am honoured by you.' He bent his head, pausing an inch away from her lips, seeking permission.

She gave it, joy flooding through her at this further evidence of his regard. The pedlar was forgotten as she arched up to claim her laird.

Alasdair led her to the dancing area, his heart filled with a mix of pride, joy and hope. Somewhere, anger at the pedlar still lingered. With a quick glance, he had ensured the man was gone, driving his wagon away from Ardmore in the fading light. He knew exactly who the man was and would ensure word of his villainous actions was spread among the lairds and captains.

He shook his head, reflecting on how lucky it was that he had seen the incident, Eilidh Ruadh having pointed him in Lydia's direction. He had followed Lydia to the trader's stalls, witnessing the entire episode between her and the miscreant. He frowned briefly. Assumptions about the moral code in profligate London had undoubtedly fuelled the villain's behaviour, though it were no excuse.

The heinous incident had changed everything. Witnessing Lydia being assaulted by that *bleigeard*, comforting her in her distress afterwards...all of it had served to finally force him to let go of his last remaining doubts. His head and his heart were finally at one and Lydia was his love.

As the music began now he took his place opposite his darling, feeling honoured to have the regard of such a woman. Her beauty he had seen from the beginning. Her character had revealed itself slowly, each day, each week, giving him more and more reasons to love her. The knowledge of her ill treatment at the hands of scoundrels—yes, and by her cowardly employers— made his blood boil with rage. Yes, he had failed to protect her from assault here, in the heart of his lands, but at least he had not afterwards blamed her for it. He looked at her now, skipping through the set with a wide smile, and his heart felt fit to burst with love for her. He was done with hiding, done with tormenting himself with self-doubt. He loved Lydia and he cared not who knew it.

They moved through the dance, sharing smiles and glances. All the while his mind was working furiously, thinking and planning. It would soon be time for the formalities...yes, that would work well.

And so, when they came for him at the end of the dance, he bowed to Lydia, kissed her hand and told her that he hoped to be back at her side very soon.

And sooner than you expect, he added inwardly.

Chapter Eighteen

Lydia's heart was full. Already, the incident with the pedlar seemed a long-distant nightmare. Unlike all of the other occasions when men had tried to kiss her, this time Lydia had not been dismissed. Quite the opposite, for the Laird had planted a facer on her assailant that had completely floored the man. Lydia was fiercely glad he had done so. In a small way, Alasdair had made up for all of the occasions when she had had no protector, no strength but her own wits, and no justice.

She harboured no further doubts about his regard for her and had tonight allowed him to see the love shining in her eyes. The dance with him was dream-like, as though she were some other person—one who deserved happiness.

No sooner had the music ended than Iain and two other men came to claim him. It was time to accept the sword of Fergus Liath, they said. As he walked with them towards the stage, Lydia saw him stop and say something to Mrs MacLeod, who was still holding Mairead. Crouching down beside his daughter, he spoke to her for a moment and she replied. He kissed the girl's cheek, then continued on towards the dais.

Hurrying, she made her way towards them. 'Ah, there you are, Lydia.' Mrs MacLeod was all smiles. 'It was good to see you and the Laird dancing together. Now, you need to take Mairead up on to the stage, for she must be present when the sword is accepted.'

Lydia glanced at the stage and frowned. Two chairs were currently being placed at one side. 'Should I leave her there by herself? Surely I should not be in a position of prominence?'

'You may get used to it!' Mrs MacLeod returned cryptically. 'Yes, you will need to sit with the child.'

'But—I am just the governess!'

'Just the governess? Now wheesht, and quit being so foolish, my girl!' She rolled her eyes. 'The sooner things are straightened out around here, the better. Now go!'

Lydia went. Carrying Mairead, and feeling decidedly nervous at the thought of so many eyes on her, she mounted the three steps at the side of the dais and walked directly to the chairs. After settling Mairead, she took the chair beside her, keeping her eyes downcast. Maybe people would ignore her if she did not look at them.

A cheer went up as Alasdair moved to the centre of the stage. Now Lydia did lift her head, enjoying the sight of her beloved Alasdair in full laird duty. His speech was wonderful, congratulating his Ardmore team mates, commiserating with Angus and their players, and speaking with fondness of Dòmhnall Mòr. He then called upon Angus to return the sword of Fergus

Liath, as Ardmore had won the privilege of holding it during the coming year.

Angus mounted the dais, thanked Alasdair for his hospitality and vowed to win the sword back next year. He then unstrapped it from around his waist and handed it to Alasdair. Surprisingly, Lydia noted, it was not some beautiful, jewel-encrusted blade, but a simple unadorned weapon.

Of course it would be.

Another cheer went up as Alasdair held it aloft, then strapped it around his own waist. Iain served them both whisky and they raised their glasses to the crowd, shouting *'Slàinte mhath!'* in unison.

Lydia, sensing the end of ceremonies, could only be grateful that she would soon return to the anonymity of the assembly below. The Laird, however, had other ideas. Gesturing to the crowd to hush, his expression turned serious. 'You will all know,' he said, 'that our dear Mairead was a sickly child and was left weakened by illness more than two years ago.' The hairs on the back of Lydia's neck were standing to attention.

What is this?

He turned to look at his daughter, asking softly, 'Are you ready?'

'Ready, Papaidh,' the child confirmed and Lydia's heart began pounding. This, then, was what he had spoken to Mairead about on his way to the dais.

Deliberately, he walked to the far side of the stage, then waited. Mairead, seemingly suddenly nervous, glanced at Lydia.

'You can do it, darling,' she murmured and Mairead nodded.

Slowly, carefully, the girl stood, to gasps of astonishment from the crowd below. She paused for a moment, seemingly gathering her courage, then stepped
out. Falteringly at first, then with increasing confidence,
she traversed the entire width of the stage, collapsing
into her father's arms at the far side. By that point wild
cheering had broken out and Lydia, looking at the people, saw tear-stained faces incredulous with joy.

'This miracle,' Alasdair continued once the noise
had died down a little, 'was wrought through hard
work, dedication and secret practice. I am proud of my
daughter and immensely grateful to the woman who
has brought this about.' He threw out an arm. 'Miss
Lydia Farnham!'

Every eye turned to her and she paused, blushing,
in the act of drying her eyes. She sat, feeling dread-
fully uncomfortable, yet at the same time wonderfully
pleased, as the Ardmore people and visitors both hailed
her. Pressing both hands to her cheeks, her throat closed
with emotion, she met the Laird's eye. He was, naturally, grinning delightedly. Mairead, suddenly overcome, was hiding her face in his side.

He was not yet done. Hushing the crowd once again,
he quietly bade Mairead sit on the floor, then walked
back to the centre of the stage. Strangely, he then turned
his side to the crowd, facing Lydia instead. The look
in his eyes took her breath away. In it she saw love and
passion, and—was that determination?

'Lydia.' His voice was lower than it had been when
he was addressing the people directly, yet firm enough
that they would still hear him. A hush came over the
crowd. Indeed, it seemed to Lydia as though the entire

world held its breath. 'When first you arrived at Ardmore, I could see that you are a beautiful woman.' He gestured. 'Indeed, we all could. But as the time went on and our friendship deepened, I saw your beautiful heart and your beautiful soul. You have become one of us and have worked hard to earn that acceptance, for we are a proud people, wary of strangers, yet ready to welcome new friends.'

Every word dropped into Lydia's mind as though she were being showered in diamonds, in flowers, in sunshine. Never had she felt anything like this.

'Mairead adores you,' he continued and her gaze flickered to the child, who was smiling happily. 'You are a mother to her in all but name.'

Someone in the crowd had had enough. 'Enough with the pretty speeches, Alasdair. Ask the woman to marry you, for God's sake!' This earned a ripple of kindly laughter, as well as some commands to wheesht from the women.

Alasdair did not even acknowledge the interruption. 'All of these are good reasons to ask you this question, but my true reason is much more simple.' He took a breath. 'I love you, Lydia. Will you be my wife?'

A roar went up from the men. Clearly they all assumed she would accept. Ignoring them—in fact, doing her best to ignore their extremely large audience—Lydia stood and walked towards him, aware that she was trembling. 'You are drunk,' she declared in English. This was not a moment to risk misunderstandings based on her current grasp of Gaelic. She had to be sure of his reasoning.

He grinned. 'I really amn't,' he replied, also in English. 'I promise you.'

She took another step towards him. 'Then you are simply grateful that Mairead is well again.'

'That is true—I am profoundly grateful. But it is not why I want you for my wife.'

'Why then?' Old doubts assailed her, for she did not dare hope. There were many pretty maidens in the assembly below. 'Why me?'

His eyes stayed on hers. 'There is only you, Lydia. I have not felt this way for any woman. Ever.'

Her eyes widened, then she swallowed, knowing she had only one more concern to voice. 'But I am not from here.'

He smiled. 'You are now. Only say yes and you will never have to leave.'

She paused, a million thoughts crashing around her mind. Bidding them all to silence, she allowed her heart to speak. 'Yes. Yes, Alasdair, I shall marry you.'

With a bound he had reached her and his arms were around her, and his lips were on hers. Dimly, she heard the cheering and shouting from the crowd.

By mutual agreement, the kiss was brief. 'We shall continue this later,' he vowed and the heat in his expression made her heart pound with desire. 'Lydia, *mo ghaol.*'

My love! She translated it instantly in her head, and could not prevent a happy smile from breaking through. 'I love you, Alasdair.'

The next few weeks were the happiest of Lydia's life. The banns were read, Eilidh worked on the wedding gown, and all the preparations began for the Laird's wedding. Lydia gradually became accustomed to the congratulations and the heartfelt joy that the Ardmore people expressed. Not one made her feel less worthy because she had been a governess, or because she was Sassenach. In truth, they never had. Mrs MacLeod had already begun instructing her in the duties and responsibilities she would take on as Lady of Ardmore and had assured Lydia not to be nervous, because she would be always there to assist her and keep her right.

Alasdair and Lydia, now betrothed, were given more privacy and time alone together and they made the most of it. Lydia now truly understood how much he loved her and that, strangely, he felt just as lucky to have found her as she had with him. They came preciously close to anticipating their wedding vows on more than one occasion, but agreed together they would prefer to wait until their wedding night which, after all, was fast approaching. To ease his frustration, Alasdair made sure he kept himself busy with other projects. There were some days when he was gone for a long time and Lydia barely saw him. On those days, as well as being with Mairead, she would often take some quiet time for herself, to sit in her chamber or to walk on the moors and wonder at how perfect her life now was.

Finally, the day arrived. On a golden sunny morning in August, the Much Honoured Alexander Mac-Donald, Laird of Ardmore, known as Alasdair, married Miss Lydia Farnham. The bride wore a silk and lace gown fashioned by her personal maid, Eilidh, and the groom wore his ceremonial Highland dress, the sword of Fergus Liath slung by his side. The Laird's daughter, Mairead, walked all the way from the back of the church to the front, attending the bride, and afterwards she danced for the first time in the Great Hall at Ardmore Castle.

At a certain stage in the proceedings, the bride and groom slipped away. Alasdair bade Lydia don her stout new boots and a cloak, and asked her to walk with him outside the courtyard. She did so happily and slipped her hand into his as they passed through the castle gates. They talked as they walked, stopping to kiss occasionally, and reviewed their perfect wedding day. How well it had all gone! How happy Mairead had seemed! How genuine the good wishes of the community—including the Laird's cousins, Angus and Eilidh Ruadh. Alasdair had teased Angus about the fact that he was now twice married, while Angus himself, who was of a similar age, was yet to take a bride. Angus, grimacing ruefully, had promised to give the matter his attention.

Lydia had smiled along with this, feeling secure in Alasdair's love for her. He had been honest with her about his first marriage and she had felt pity for both his younger self and for Hester, who had made each other so unhappy.

After a time it dawned on her that they were still walking and Alasdair seemed to have no intention of returning to the castle. Thoughts of her wedding night uppermost in her mind, she tentatively enquired as to their destination.

'Wait and see,' was all he would say, distracting her with yet another heady kiss.

To their left, the sun was setting, sending gold and

pink and purple tones rippling through the heavens. Spectacular sunsets were not uncommon in the Hebrides, yet Lydia could not help but feel that this one belonged only to them. Above, the sky was paling, the pale blue of day giving way to *dubh-ghorm*—the black-blue coolness of night. Ahead of them—

'It is the sheiling!' she exclaimed, working it out in an instant. 'Are we to sleep on the settle again tonight?'

His grin was answer enough, and by the time Venus the Evening Star had appeared in the western sky, they had reached the sheiling. 'Give me a moment,' he murmured, dropping her hand and striding ahead to the door. She waited, a minute later seeing the glow of candlelight through the tiny windows and hearing the crackle of twigs catching alight in the fireplace. He returned, and wordlessly held the door open for her. She stepped inside—into a wonderland.

The sheiling had been transformed. It was spotlessly clean for a start, the glow of candlelight revealing freshly whitewashed walls and a neatly finished roof. The space was dominated by a large bed dressed with crisp sheets, plump pillows, and warm blankets. The glow of firelight and candlelight also revealed a tiny table and two stools in the other corner, the table set with supper—including a flagon of whisky and two beautiful crystal glasses. There was even a small mirror on the shelf and her very own hairbrush beside it. Alasdair had thought of everything.

'Oh!' Finding words inadequate, Lydia simply turned to Alasdair and embraced him. 'I love you,' she murmured against his lips.

'My love!' he replied, then again in Gaelic, '*Mo ghaol*! Lady of Ardmore, lady of my heart.'

And as the kiss deepened, Lydia knew that she was finally home.

* * * * *

Look out for the next book in Catherine Tinley's
Lairds of the Isles miniseries
coming soon!

And while you're waiting for the next book why not
check out her other miniseries
The Ladies of Ledbury House?

The Earl's Runaway Governess
Rags-to-Riches Wife
Captivating the Cynical Earl
'A Midnight Mistletoe Kiss' *(in Christmas Cinderellas)*